AT THE EASTERN EDGE OF KALAMAZOO COUNTY, AUTUMN woolly bear caterpillars hump across Queer Road to get to the fields and windbreaks of George Harland's rich river valley land. With their bellies full of dandelion greens and native plantains, these orange-and-black-banded woolly bears travel at about four feet per minute, in search of niches where they can spend the winter. Near the oldest barn in Greenland Township, many of them settle in and around a decaying stone foundation overgrown with poison ivy vines. It is land they have occupied for centuries, this tribe of caterpillars, since long before George Harland's great-great-great-grandfather bought it from the federal land office for a dollar and a quarter an acre.

More than a century and a half after that purchase, on October 9, 1999, David Retakker pedaled his rusting BMX bike south along Queer Road, with the Harland property on his right and the sun rising over Whitby's pig farm on his left. David, twelve years old, hungry, and wheezy from asthma, didn't mind the pig stink, but he couldn't understand why all the caterpillars wanted to cross the road. There must be millions of them, David thought, for already hundreds lay flattened or stunned or dead alongside, and more kept coming. He'd seen woolly bears before, but he couldn't remember if it had been spring or fall, and surely they were never as plentiful as this. David steered with one hand; the other he rested on his knee, with the index finger folded in a way that mimicked amputation at the lower knuckle, so he could pretend he had the same injury as George Harland.

Off to David's left, dozens of rust-colored Duroc hogs appeared no bigger than caterpillars as they snuffled in the grass and mud behind long, low whitewashed structures. David imagined them chopped into hams, bacon, and pork steaks, smoked and sizzling for breakfast in cast-iron pans. Beyond the soybean field on his right rose the tall trees surrounding the Harland house and out-buildings, and as David got closer, he made out Rachel Crane, standing in front of her produce tables with her arms crossed and her rifle hanging over her shoulder on a sling. Rachel was seven-teen, only five years older than David, but she was always looking out for him, which was okay. Still, she was staring so intently at the pavement that she didn't seem to notice his approach, and he told himself he might even sneak past. That would be a feat, he thought, to sneak right past her, first thing in the morning.

Rachel's roadside tables were set up in front of George's old two-story house, and just to the side was parked a utility wagon piled with dozens of pumpkins. The tables were heavy with winter squash, tomatoes, a few melons, bushel baskets of striped and spot-ted gourds, and on the ground sat five-gallon buckets of Brussels sprout spears. Hungry as he was, David could turn down Brussels sprouts; and the big, flesh-colored butternut squashes gave him the creeps, made him think of a pile of misshapen mutant bodies with-out eyes or mouths or limbs. Rachel's gardening enterprise didn't much appeal to David, because he wanted to work in fields of corn, oats, and soybeans the way George did. Those grains went into bread and breakfast cereal, food that could fill a person up.

As he got closer, he studied Rachel's black hair and her face, which appeared to glow orange in the light coming from the east. Whenever she was standing somewhere, you got the idea that she'd already been there a long time and it would take a lot to move her. He used to want to be just like Rachel, but a couple years ago she'd swelled dangerously, becoming thick with breasts and hips, and since then he'd tried to keep some distance between them. When she looked up from the road this morning, her dark eyes sent a jolt of electricity through him, and he jerked his handlebars and veered straight at her. Rachel jumped out of the way and David careened into the shallow ditch in front of the stacked cantaloupes. His bike tipped over sideways onto him.

"Are you okay?" Rachel said.

"I'm okay." David stood up and righted his bicycle.

"Well, you sure as hell don't know how to steer."

"I lost my balance."

"Well, then use both hands when you ride."

David checked his index finger, which was still not severed at the knuckle, and rolled his bike backward until he was beside her.

"Damn it," Rachel said, "you just backed up over that woolly bear."

"Huh?"

"What did that woolly bear ever do to you?"

"There's so many I can't help it," David said. "And besides, you kill lots of things."

Rachel threw up her arms and yelled, "What's the hurry? Next year you can all fly across the damn road."

"Huh?"

"I was talking to the woolly bears." Rachel adjusted her rifle

3

strap. "I watched this woolly bear crawl all the way from the other side of the road, and then you came along and smashed it."

David looked down at the pavement to where Rachel pointed out a caterpillar flattened beside a dark smear of guts. To avoid feeling bad about it, David looked up, to the bright ceiling of sycamore leaves, each as big as a person's face, extending across the driveway to the edge of the pasture. David glanced up the driveway, tracing its path to the silos of corrugated tin, the big wooden stock barn, and beyond to the silver and red pole barns where George kept his tractors, balers, and combines. David didn't see George's truck.

Beside the driveway, just beyond the reach of the branches, stood a pony, a donkey, and a long-haired llama, side by side, pushing against the barbed wire in places where they'd already mashed the barbs down with their chests. David considered going over and petting the animals, but then he wondered if his bedroom clock at home might have been slow and if he might already be late. He'd woken up repeatedly during the night worrying about the time. And now George's truck was nowhere around; maybe George was already down there waiting for him.

"You don't know what time it is, do you?"

"Why are you in such a damn hurry?" Rachel said.

David knew Rachel worked hard to put swear words in most every sentence; she'd told him that plain talk, without swearing, was weak and invited argument. And he could see you had to keep in practice with swearing, even when you didn't feel like it.

"I'm helping George put a wagonload of straw in the barn," David said. "Didn't he tell you?"

"Maybe I don't hang on every damn word out of his mouth like some people."

"So how come you married him then?" David's raspy breathing was painful to hear this morning.

"If you don't know by now why I married him," she said, "then it's none of your damn business. You're not out of your medication again, are you?"

As David fumbled with the white plastic tube from his pocket, Rachel looked away and stacked some pumpkin gourds. Her neighbor Milton Taylor had been right about planting these—at a dollar each, the rutabaga-sized pumpkins sold by the dozens—but Rachel found herself annoyed at their smallness this morning. It seemed wrong to raise vegetables that didn't have a chance at growing to normal size. And besides, you couldn't eat them. She'd gutted one and cooked it, just to see, and she found the paltry bit of meat gritty and flavorless.

After David put his inhaler away, Rachel said, "Your ma didn't get any food for breakfast, did she?"

He shrugged.

"No wonder you're running off the road," Rachel said. "Do you want an apple?"

"I guess I'd take an apple."

Rachel went to the far end of her tables and tipped up an empty bushel basket. "The damn deer chewed through my chicken wire. Let me get some apples from the barn."

"I don't want to be late for meeting George."

"Fine, then get the hell out of here."

Neither of them moved or said anything until David shrugged again. Some nights when David slipped out of his house on P Road, he trekked the half-mile shortcut trail over here, and tried to sneak up on Rachel in her garden. He liked to study her from as close as he could, to try to understand why George couldn't live without her, and it was a lot easier to look at her when she wasn't looking back. Sitting in the dark she seemed muscular like Martini the pony, but she could also move as stealthily as Gray Cat. The way she shot practically everything that came into her garden, she was no one to complain about other people killing anything. David would creep as quietly as he could those nights, but a hundred feet away she'd hear his footsteps, his noisy breathing, or his stomach rumbling, and she'd yell, "David, what the hell are you doing out here?" and he'd yell back, "Nothing," and come out of hiding. Then she'd make him sit still while she waited for an animal or whispered a story about the Indian she called Corn Girl or explained how a skunk would roll a woolly bear on the ground until all its bristles came out before eating it. Other people said Rachel didn't talk much, but she made David listen to advice about growing tomatoes and skinning muskrats and saving money in coffee cans to buy land, even though David had no interest in tomatoes or muskrats. He didn't even want to own land; he just wanted to drive tractors and combines and pull hay balers and cultivators across George's hundreds of acres.

"What happened to the window?" David pointed at the broken pane in the lower left corner of the big window facing the road. He wore a long-sleeved T-shirt, but Rachel thought he probably should have a jacket on, too.

Rachel said, "George's stupid-ass nephew threw a pumpkin at the house in the middle of the night."

"How do you know it was Todd?"

"I heard his hooligan voice."

"Are you going to track him down and shoot him?" David figured it must feel great to launch a pumpkin through the air like a missile and to hear the crash that meant you'd struck your target.

"No, I'm not going to shoot him. I don't shoot people."

"You shot at me."

She stared at him. The memory of almost killing David three years ago could still make Rachel stop breathing. "You know that was an accident. I thought you were a coyote." Even in the dark, though, she should have seen those bright eyes, that freckled face. "I can't believe you keep bringing that up."

David said, "Maybe you'll get mad and think Todd's a coyote."

"First of all, I don't shoot coyotes anymore," Rachel said.

"They eat the woodchucks that eat my garden. And anyways, Todd looks more like a giant rat than a coyote."

David shrugged again. Actually he was glad Rachel had tried to shoot him, because she'd been nice to him ever since. She wasn't nice to anybody else as far as David could tell, not even George. Even now, six weeks after she'd married George, Rachel didn't seem to realize how lucky she was that she'd get to live here with George forever.

"Now, why don't you wait one goddamn minute and I'll get you some apples out of the barn."

"I've got to go." David jumped on his bike and pedaled south. This was the first time George had ever asked him to stack hay in the barn, and David needed to do everything right. George's nephew Todd had been working for him over the summer, but he'd become unreliable, not showing up when he said he would, and often doing a lousy job if George wasn't watching him. George'd had a talk with Todd yesterday, which was maybe why that window ended up busted. David stood up on his pedals.

The donkey, the llama, and Martini the spotted pony all stamped their feet and followed the bicycle along the fence line, then returned to the pasture corner to watch Rachel, in anticipation of getting oats.

"Damn stupid kid." Rachel fought the desire to shout something after him about being careful or coming back to eat later. Even though David's mother, Sally, didn't pay George any rent to live in that house over on P Road, she couldn't be bothered to feed her kid. Rachel thought that woman seriously needed her ass kicked.

Some of the people in Greenland Township figured Rachel herself had had it tough growing up. She didn't see it that way. While her own mother might have been eccentric, while she might have lost her mind in the end, she'd at least taught Rachel how to feed herself. Until Margo Crane disappeared three years ago, the woman had wrenched a living out of the local farmland by hunting and trapping, and she'd taught her daughter plenty about getting by. Rachel had lived much of her seventeen years out-of-doors, which was why she knew so much about the wild creatures of this place, for instance that these woolly bear caterpillars were the larvae of the dusty white Isabella moths and that they would not spin cocoons to protect themselves during the winter but would instead curl beneath stacked firewood or patches of bark or decaying wooden rowboats to await the winter. Their bodies were somehow able to endure the freeze, and in spring, they survived the thaw. And only after all that miraculous survival did a woolly bear build its cocoon and begin its transformation.

Crazy hermit mother aside, even just growing up with a face like Rachel's might seem to some like tough luck. Such a face might have been too much for a more self-conscious girl to bear, but Rachel refused to take it as a hardship. Most folks would not say she was ugly, exactly, but nobody would honestly call her pretty; the mystery of her face was that while no individual aspect was freakish, the striking sum of her features demanded a person stop and stare, and then, after dragging his eyes away, look back for confirmation. And despite all that looking, the looker would probably be at a loss to describe the face to anyone later. Technically speaking, Rachel's was a broad face with big cheekbones and a small chin, giving, straight on, the illusion of being round, and although her skin was not pale, the illusion of roundness fed into a suggestion of whiteness, especially in contrast to her long, dark hair, which she remembered to brush about once every three days. As with the bald faces of certain cattle breeds, as with the china-doll visage of the white-breasted nuthatch, when you got close, Rachel's face seemed to spill and stretch over its edges, continuing into her neck and hairline. Her close-set eyes were always a little bloodshot, and though she didn't much like talking, she never hesitated to make the kind of steady eye contact people found disconcerting. Other kids had been confused by her gaze, but Rachel had dropped out of school a year and a half ago, and the only kid she cared anything about now was David.

Rachel watched David's puny figure grow smaller and finally disappear behind roadside walnut trees. She would swear David had scarcely grown in the three years she'd known him. She focused on another woolly bear, a scrappy one, more orange than black, which had ventured out at a good pace from Elaine Shore's asphalt driveway across the road. Rachel told herself that this fast little guy was destined to make it, but when a pickup truck belonging to one of the Whitbys rattled toward her from the north she just had to stop looking. Damn those caterpillars, Rachel thought as she arranged a bushel basket with every variety of gourd showing, damn them for not having a sense of self-preservation. Damn them for their tiny brains, their subservience to nature. Damn their broken bodies strewn about like overripe mulberries. The caterpillars were stupid like a lot of people around here, picking up and leaving without even realizing where they were to start with. Rachel knew exactly where she was, and she planned to stay and occupy George Harland's acres—more land than she could see from any one place on that land—for as long as she lived and breathed. She didn't know about David, but when she died, she intended to be buried right here in this dark, rich soil.

2

A HALF HOUR BEFORE DAVID ARRIVED AT THE FARM STAND, Elaine Shore sat in the breakfast nook of her custom-made prefabricated house across the street, watching. The black-haired girl had been arranging vegetables in the predawn light, pausing occasionally to cross her arms and glare at the pavement. Elaine watched Mr. Harland drive off in his rattling menace of a truck, and as always Elaine kept an eye on the herd of three animals at the fence, hoping they wouldn't get loose and wander over to use her lawn as a toilet again. Her lawn already seemed treacherous this morning, with the grass outside her nook window crawling with orange-and-black caterpillars that might be able to inch their way into her house through crevices the installation crew hadn't sealed two years ago. When she noticed the black-haired girl staring back at her, Elaine lowered her head and studied the *Weekly World News* center spread, a depiction of aliens descending a spaceship ramp in single file. She found the vision of smooth gray alien bodies without hair or sexual organs comforting. Elaine's own short hair needed trimming; she could feel it tingling with growth at her scalp, as well as stretching down onto her face.

From her corner perch, Elaine could also see into the south-facing rooms of the standard-model prefabricated home belonging to the young couple next door. The wife was so petite and pretty that Elaine imagined her sometimes as being a heroine from one of the romances she used to read. So far there was no movement over there, but Elaine kept watch. She looked forward to a time when there would be more than two sets of people to observe. Her lawyer assured her that soon there would be plenty of neighbors, just as soon as George Harland started selling off his farmland.

"That woman is staring over here again," Steve Hoekstra said. He got out of bed and yanked closed the bedroom curtains.

The words pulled Nicole Hoekstra from a dream of driving over her husband's body on the concrete floor of their two-car garage, of then backing up and running over him a second time. In the last month, she'd been entertaining ever more violent thoughts of killing Steve, but this was the first time she'd actually dreamed it. She tried to soothe away the image of his twisted limbs and mashed internal organs by considering the wholesome brilliance of her wedding day, eighteen months ago, a sparkling day to which, surely, no other in her life would ever compare. In the wedding photos, Nicole looked as lovely as a fairy-tale princess, if she had to say so herself. Now she covered her face with blankets and pretended to be asleep, because she didn't like Steve to see her before she'd fixed herself up a bit.

Steve dressed and went to the kitchen where he started coffee. Through the sliding glass door he watched Rachel across the street arranging her yard-long Brussels sprout stalks. She wore a ragged, oversized barn jacket and rolled-up jeans, but even those clothes couldn't disguise her lush shape. Though he hadn't been able to get anywhere near her in the six months he'd lived in the house, Steve always waved hello, always told himself that eventually she'd return the gesture. Women of all ages liked Steve, and he didn't see why Rachel should be any different. He'd been thinking he might buy a pair of binoculars to get a better look at her—he would tell Nicole they were for bird-watching. Steve was glad to see the woolly bears out in full force this morning. Over the last few days he'd found the caterpillars to be a good conversation starter with folks in the township, a few of whom had purchased thousands of dollars' worth of insulated windows from his company. Each time Steve smiled and said to a new woman, "Where the heck are those little fellows going?" he felt as though he were saying it for the first time.

As Steve watched through the sliding glass door, the curly-haired neighbor boy nearly careened into Rachel and then crashed his bike into the ditch beside her. Steve wondered if that was what it took to get her attention.

"I suppose you're going to work this morning." Nicole sat down across the table from Steve wearing a plush bathrobe and a steaming towel, which she'd wrapped around her hair and adjusted in the bathroom mirror to make sure it framed her face attractively.

"Did you take a shower already?" Steve said. "I didn't hear the water."

"I'm preconditioning," Nicole said. She wondered if Steve still believed she was a natural blonde. Way back when her hair was medium brown, the strands had been as soft and fine as spun silk, but bleaching had made her hair brittle, in need of special treatment.

"What's preconditioning?" Steve asked.

"It's an oil treatment you use before your regular shampoo and conditioner."

"So after all that, I guess you use a *post*conditioner."

Nicole used to think her husband charming, but now she wondered which of the six knives in the knife holder above the sink would most easily slice the fabric of his sport shirt and the connective tissue between two of his ribs before penetrating his heart. She said, "Isn't this bedroom cute?" and turned her *Beautiful Home* magazine around and pointed a flowery, ruffled bedroom scene at her husband.

Steve knew that no man could sleep in such a room. He said, "Look next door. Mrs. Shore is still watching us."

"She is such a freak," Nicole said. "She should get a life."

"Speaking of neighbors," Steve said, "I stopped in yesterday to check on a bay window I sold to April May Rathburn right down Queer Road."

"I wish you wouldn't call it that."

"She's the lady who told me people here really call it 'Queer.' She's got to be seventy years old and she calls it 'Queer.'"

"What's wrong with *Q Road*? Just because some kid sprays graffiti on the street signs doesn't mean you go and change the name."

"Anyway, she said the original house next to the barn down there was destroyed by a tornado a long time ago, and nobody has ever rebuilt. Wouldn't that be the perfect place for a new house, right beside an old barn? There's even a creek that runs behind it."

"I never noticed a creek there." Nicole imagined a two-story white house with a wraparound porch rising out of the cornfield, a house as perfect as a wedding cake. She'd seen a plan for such a house in the *Kalamazoo Gazette* two Sundays ago.

"The creek runs under the road, then down to the river."

"Maybe we could put a little arched bridge across it."

"Be nice to have an office in an old barn like that," Steve said. "Maybe if Harland has a bad year he'll be willing to sell us a plot of land there."

The promise of a new house and an arched bridge made Nicole

think that there was hope for her and her husband. Maybe everything would be fine if they could get themselves out of this pre-owned prefab and into a real house built just for them.

In truth she hadn't paid much attention to the barn she drove past every day, and so the barn in her imagination was freshly painted, not rotted around the foundation, and did not lean as a result of 135 years of winds from the north and west.

A half mile to the south, meanwhile, inside the barn under discussion, April May Rathburn was crouching, filling a bushel basket with loose straw. When she felt her lower back muscles stretch too far, she tipped forward onto her knees and remained perfectly still. Shortly she heard a vehicle with a loud exhaust rattle up from the field road and stop. Probably as a result of her awkward position, her right foot began to throb.

"I wouldn't have taken you for a thief," a man's voice said.

April May watched George Harland approach the barn's entrance. "Help me up, will you?" she said.

When George reached out, she used his arm to bring herself up nearly as tall as him—he was just over six feet. He picked up the basket of straw for her. "Are you making Halloween displays already?"

"Christ, I must be getting old," she said. "I guess it's a good thing I didn't try to put in a garden this year."

"You want me to carry this over for you?"

"I'm fine once I stand up." April May accepted the wire handles. "Did Rachel bring out pumpkins yet?"

"She put some out last night," George said. "Are you sure you're okay?"

"I'm fine, really."

"How's your husband?"

"Larry's off for the day visiting his brother."

"Tell him hello when he gets home."

April May said so long, and limped outside and across Queer Road to her house. She sat and rested on her porch steps to watch the cardinals, chickadees, and nuthatches at the feeder Larry had built for her, a detailed miniature version of the barn from which she'd just gotten the straw. She and Larry had never farmed, but in the half century she'd lived in Larry's old family house, she'd seen local farmers go broke and lose their land, and she'd seen others unable to resist the temptation to sell at a good price while they were flush, and she hoped George could hold out, because she couldn't imagine him as anything other than a farmer. His piece-of-shit brother, Johnny, had been a different story altogether.

April May took off her shoe and sock to check whether maybe a bee had stung her, but she saw only her old tornado scars. Perhaps it was the sharp pain in her foot or the dullness of the sky that made the bird feeder and the barn seem so bright this morning. In fact, every object in her field of vision seemed bright and a little blurry around its edges. She massaged her foot and wondered if something was going to happen today. Something good or bad, she didn't care—she'd welcome any excitement.

There have been those days in Greenland Township, as anywhere, that have changed the course of local history, days that have so clearly determined the future that afterward it was hard to believe the future had ever been uncertain, that arrows had ever pointed in other directions. None of the Queer Road neighbors, nor George Harland himself—owner of more than a square mile of the earth's surface, bridegroom of a girl one-third his age—could know whether today would be one of those days. A length of board was missing at the back of the barn, and through that space, George watched three of the cattle in the barnyard stamp their feet and bellow impatiently. The fourth, a white-faced Hereford steer, drank calmly from the creek, against the backdrop of woods separating George's property from the golf course. When it finished drinking, the steer turned and looked up at George in a way that suggested it knew something he didn't.

George fed the cattle by pushing a broken bale of hay through the trapdoor into the lower level of the barn, then walked back outside. Though this was the oldest barn in the township, it still had some of its original ten-inch white-pine planks intact, and the repairs his grandfather had made were holding up almost as well as his own more recent ones. Having the barn built on a low hill kept the upper level dry, less subject to rot, but at the same time made it more vulnerable to lightning strikes and tornadoes. Originally the barn had been roofed with cedar shingles, but when those deteriorated, his grandfather had installed a galvanized tin roof. A few years ago, George and Mike Retakker, David's father, had covered that leaking tin with black asphalt roll roofing and a lot of tar. George would have liked to paint the building red again, but he couldn't make it a priority. Ten years ago, when his first wife left him, George had rebuilt the barn's sliding door, and though he hadn't oiled the hardware since, the door rolled smoothly enough that a child could pull it open and shut. The paint on the door was brighter than on the rest of the barn.

George studied the horizon for a while, then the haze above, but the sky was as cryptic as the mind of that Hereford steer. If the sun burned off the cloud cover, the day would brighten and dry the oat straw nicely in the field, but if the air pressure and clouds got any heavier, rain might well destroy George's two hundred bales' worth of mown straw. He looked north, over the poison-ivy-clad stone foundation of the house built by the son of the man who'd originally bought these acres. Along with the barn's silo and several sheds, the house had been destroyed in the 1934 tornado. The only person other than George's ancestors to live in it before then was a schoolteacher, a young widow named O'Kearsy who stayed not quite two years. George had seen only a faded picture of her, but he believed his grandfather Harold, who told him the woman was as beautiful as the day was long. Though the tornado had struck before George was born, he still occasionally came across chunks of metal, white china, or bits of varnished wood trim that must have scattered that day. George would never father children of his own, according to his doctor, and so he didn't know whether, in a hundred years, anybody would know the history of this place.

Back at the farmhouse, Rachel Crane fed the pigs a corn and soy mix along with some kitchen scraps, then dumped three pounds of oats into the wooden trough for the spotted pony, the llama George's ex-wife had left behind, and the donkey, who was gray with black markings. As she lugged a bushel of Jonathan apples from the barn, she told herself this was a hell of a day to wake up into, with deer chewing through chicken wire to eat your apples and a neighborhood brat smashing a pumpkin into your window.

"Punk son of a bitch," she said, surprising herself by speaking aloud again—she didn't usually talk to herself. She didn't talk much to George either, and she didn't want that to change anytime soon. Once she started to talk, he and everybody else would expect her to keep on talking and answering their stupid questions. Heaviness crept into Rachel's limbs at just the thought of all that talking: a river of words, just like a regular river, could drag a girl down. When the desire to talk didn't go away, she took a deep breath. "Goddamn stupid caterpillars!" she howled, loudly enough that Elaine Shore looked over from across the street. Maybe later, Rachel thought, she'd go into her garden and tell the Brussels sprouts to stand up straight, or else demand the flowers stop blooming and settle down for the winter. Tonight she'd haul the pumpkin wagon inside the barn, the apples too.

As on other mornings, Rachel gathered what flowers she could from around the foundation of the house and from nearby ditches: mums, black-eyed Susans, and stray garden phlox, along with the last of the wild asters. Now that even the late-blooming flowers were in short supply, Rachel added branches with berries and bright leaves. Rachel used to yank flowers from her garden like weeds, but last summer April May Rathburn had suggested she sell bouquets for two bucks each. April May was all right. She smiled a lot and didn't seem to have an agenda beyond offering gardening advice, and never once in three years had she hinted about what she might have seen in the barn the night Rachel's mother disappeared.

After Rachel bundled the flowers randomly with rubber bands, she still felt agitated about the broken window and about David. Damn him for being so ignorant and narrow-minded, the way he crushed woolly bears without even noticing, the way he wouldn't wear a jacket to stay warm or eat so he would grow.

She opened the combination lock on the metal honor box, which was bolted to the table, and found it empty, not surprisingly, since she'd emptied it twenty minutes ago. She slammed it shut and locked it. She folded up the sign that said PUMPKIN GOURDS $1, and put it in her pocket. She took out a blank card and wrote on it with black marker, PUMPKIN GOURDS $1.25.

3

THE WOOLLY BEAR WAS ONE OF THE FEW FURRY NATIVE creatures that Rachel's mother, Margo Crane, had never shot or skinned in her decades on the Kalamazoo River. Margo had managed to scrape out a primitive living for herself and her daughter by trapping and hunting on farmland long after the men of Greenland Township had given up such pursuits. Margo taught her daughter to shoot with accuracy, to identify animal tracks in the mud along the river, and to differentiate among the dens carved out by woodchucks, skunks, and possums. As a child Rachel built her own hollows and mounds alongside cultivated fields; she spent hours tramping barefoot through the woods near their houseboat, the *Glutton*, and in the sandy places near O Road, where crusty seagreen lichens sent up spores that looked like frozen drops of blood.

When Rachel played, it was mostly alone and mostly in the dirt, and when she was nine, instead of making friends, she began to grow plants in a small garden plot she cleared between the woods and the water. First she grew green beans and corn from seeds her teacher handed out in class, and later she put in tomatoes and any other plants the neighbor to the south, Milton Taylor, would give her from his cold-frame greenhouse. She didn't think to plant in rows, so the garden grew in random clumps, and back then it didn't occur to Rachel to worry about who owned the dirt beneath her plants. From a young age, Rachel's love of land dwarfed the importance of school, her clothes, her face and the looks it got. She loved her garden and all the land rising out of the Kalamazoo River, expanses broken by maple and walnut trees or dotted with barns and houses, land stretching and rolling as far as the eye could see, then curving around the planet and eventually coming up again behind her on the other side of the river. She appreciated all that grew above the surface—her tomatoes and peppers, Harland's corn shooting upward and browning for harvest—but she loved just as well the blue clay and silt from which the plants sprang, the sandy creek mud beneath the watercress, the soil itself. What she did not like was asphalt and concrete, and too many buildings clustered together. Fences too tall or difficult to climb seemed cruel. She wanted to be surrounded by farmland, swamps, meadows, and forests, and she wanted to tramp across every patch of solid earth north and east of the Kalamazoo River, on whose bank the *Glutton* was moored.

At a young age, Rachel had pressed her ear against the ground and listened to what she thought was the earth breathing, and sometimes she imagined the land was two giant animals, one north of the river and one south. These were the only animals too big for her mother to kill and skin—they would not get themselves caught in her mother's traps on the riverbank, because their soft curving backbones *were* the two banks of the river, and if her mother fired her .22 rifle into the earth, their dirt bodies would absorb the bullets unharmed. The only danger to the giant land creatures was all the concrete and asphalt being poured; with the foundations of so many more buildings being laid, someday the creatures would no longer be able to breathe through their skin of topsoil. Rachel's mother, Margo, on the other hand, had little interest in the land beyond the river's edge. Furthermore, she told her daughter, any place on a river was as good as any other, so long as people didn't bother her.

By the time Rachel came along, Margo was already well established in Greenland as a local crank and hermit about whom the neighbors knew little, apart from what she had made clear to them, that she preferred to be left alone on the homemade houseboat. The farmers were grateful to her for taking out the woodchucks, raccoons, and deer that otherwise ate their crops, and so they didn't bother her with inquiries. Margo knew herself well enough to seek isolation, and she certainly had not meant to have a child, but during those several passionate days with the stranger who showed up on the riverbank, her mind hadn't focused on consequences, nor on anything else about the man, such as his name or where he lived. Nine months later, Margo's hands were covered with her own blood as she disentangled herself from her baby. Throughout the all-night ordeal, Margo had thought that one of them might not survive, but Margo herself had no intention of dying, and the child was an angry red thing who was not giving up either.

After a few days, Margo had bundled the baby and walked to Greenland Center, then took a taxi to Bronson Methodist Hospital in Kalamazoo to get a birth certificate, Social Security number, inoculations, and the other indignities society forced on human beings. A person would be mistaken to assume that Margo was unable to navigate the society she rejected. She kept her boat registered, paid for a post office box in Greenland, and regularly updated her comprehensive lifetime license for trapping. She knew that if she avoided the formalities involving the baby, there would be inspections and probation periods and yammering social workers. Margo arrived at the hospital dressed in clean, dark clothes, her reddish hair gathered elegantly at the back of her neck. Margo charmed those nurses with a story about being stranded without car or telephone, and gave as her address 2271 Q Road, the address of the big Harland barn, where she got her fresh water from a hand pump. When a nurse seemed wary, Margo noted her name tag. "I'm calling the baby Rachel," Margo said. The nurse Rachel softened.

Though Margo hadn't wanted a child, she never considered giving her daughter up for adoption. She was determined to give nothing to society, and that included the flesh of her flesh.

Mother and daughter lived together on the *Glutton* in relative if unconventional peace until Rachel was fourteen. That was when Johnny Harland, younger brother of George and just out of prison, started coming around. Upon his return, Johnny found himself unable to comprehend the bizarre fact that George, after his divorce, had deeded a triangle of land between the creek, the river, and the Taylor farm to eccentric Margo Crane, while refusing to give him any. This was the first Rachel had heard about any land being owned by her mother, who had always said she didn't care about owning anything; she lived on the river, she'd said, precisely because no man could own the river. Margo scoffed at Johnny's complaints, but he kept showing up, alternately flirting and demanding the deed, behaving just as Margo said the worst of men behaved. Rachel thought Johnny was fascinating, with his lazy gait and the way he smiled and winked at her while arguing with her mother. Margo's threats would have struck fear into most men, but Johnny didn't even flinch the time Margo leveled her rifle at him. Margo was so upset at his lack of response that hours later, when their mild-mannered neighbor Milton Taylor walked by on the path, she pointed the gun at him and said she'd shoot him if he came near the boat again.

When Johnny left empty whiskey bottles on the riverbank, Rachel couldn't resist opening them and sniffing the liquor, which she thought smelled rich the way aged meat and aged manure smelled rich. One September evening, not more than a week after the Milton incident, her mother looked up from skinning a skunk on the picnic table and saw Rachel on the riverbank, tipping a bottle to her mouth. A skunk hide could be worth up to twenty bucks, because few people could skin one the way Margo could, without busting open the scent gland.

Margo stopped cutting and yelled over, "Put that bottle down!"

Rachel drained the last bit of whiskey before dropping the bottle at her feet.

"Are you sure you're a daughter of mine?" Margo said.

"Maybe I'm a daughter of my father," Rachel said, returning to a common theme in their recent arguments, but in a voice more rebellious than she'd used before. "Maybe you should tell me who he is."

"All right. Maybe you deserve to know." Margo made a quick turn with her knife, and the air became poisonous with skunk musk. "Are you listening?"

"You did that on purpose!" Rachel held her nose, but the scent came in through her mouth and eyes.

"Your father wasn't hardly even a man to me," Margo said. "Your father was more like a ghost. He came drifting in here talking about the land of his ancestors. That's all men ever think about is property, whether it's a woman they want or a truck or some land. At first, I told him stay away, but then I became as stupid as any woman ever was."

The combination of the stink and her mother's words made Rachel feel faint, shell-shocked. She squeaked, "But why did he come here?"

"He came to see where his ancestors lived, and he spent four days here on the river, and I started thinking he was better than other men, but I was wrong." Margo resumed skinning as though there were no blinding stench.

Rachel gave up holding her nose. She tried to speak but couldn't.

"He told me he'd found a Potawatomi grave," Margo finally continued. "He said it was the grave of a girl from his tribe, a girl who grew corn. She died not long before the Indians were sent away. So he said."

"Are you saying my father was an Indian?" Rachel wished the moon would pass in front of the sun or the river would dry up or something else huge would happen.

"It's obvious to anybody but a damned fool that your father was an Indian—just look at you."

Rachel wiped at her eyes. "Why did he care about a girl who grew corn?"

"That's the kind of crap the man spouted," Margo said. "He told me this girl didn't want to get married, so she threw herself out of a tree and the river washed her ashore. He said the girl was the sister of an ancestor of his."

"And she killed herself?"

"Who knows? The man was drunk half the time I knew him. He dropped his empty whiskey bottle the same way you just did and he claimed he could feel the body of that girl beneath the soil. As if a man could feel anything," Margo said. "If men could feel anything at all, they wouldn't all want to own women."

"Not all men want to own women. What about Milton?" Rachel's thoughts were all scrambled, but she wanted to argue somehow against her mother. "Why did you have to go and threaten Milton?"

"You watch out for Milton," Margo said.

"He gives me clothes from the church box," Rachel said, "and plants, and he doesn't want anything."

"That kind of man doesn't want a woman for himself. But you watch out—he'll hand every woman he can get over to Jesus. Milton's a damned pimp for Jesus."

"Where did he go when he left? My father."

"He had a train ticket back to his wife, to I-don't-know-where."

"He was married?"

"I didn't care then." Margo clutched the knife more tightly. "And I don't care now."

"Where was the grave of the girl?"

Margo didn't look up.

"What was my father's name, at least?" Rachel looked at her mother's face and imagined she could see through her skin to the blood flowing beneath.

Margo spat out, "I thought I could raise a girl to be something on her own, but you act no better than a creature clawing its way up the riverbank to get caught in somebody's trap. And now you can't live without a damned father." The birds had stopped chirping, either because of Margo's anger or the stench. The bloody knife was pointed toward Rachel.

Rachel turned and ran barefoot away from her mother, up the creekside path, gulping fresh air. Before reaching the road she splashed through the creek, then slipped into the lower part of George Harland's barn where it was cool and smelled of dusty mold, a comforting dry land scent. She sat alone for a long time, until the sun was setting. She knew from experience that the foulness of skunk would remain at the boat for days. The knowledge of her father felt like some kind of wound inflicted on her. How could words, the simple truth, cut through you like the bitterest cold or the fastest river current?

As long as Rachel had known the big Harland barn, it had been empty of animals, except the occasional stray cat, but on this evening she found six dark hens. The barn's lower level seemed to Rachel a dumb place to put chickens, since they could likely escape under the rotted bottom edge of the siding, or else raccoons or foxes could squeeze in and grab them. Rachel sat up on the higher wooden rail of the central stall and watched the chickens cluck, fuss, and settle in the fading light. She had often climbed through the trapdoor and slept in the barn's upper level in order to get away from her mother's snoring and to escape the slapping, slurping river sounds. She figured the Kalamazoo River was nothing more than a swirling, muddy, factory-poisoned starting place. To make any sense of the world, a person had to first drag herself up onto dry land. And furthermore, Rachel told herself this evening, her mother was crazy.

Rachel heard lazy footsteps approaching the barn, and she knew it was Johnny. Normally Rachel would have hidden, but she thought listening to Johnny might make her laugh, might make her feel less raw. With each approaching footstep, though, she imagined some new ravaged thing: the burned smell of river fog, the carcass of venison now hanging on the *Glutton*, trap jaws snapping shut in the distance, an Indian girl's body washed up along the river. If Rachel'd had her mother's rifle, she might have aimed it at the door of the barn just to see how Johnny would respond to finding himself in her sights. A few paces away from the barn, the footsteps stopped, and Rachel heard the sound of piss on dirt for what had to be minutes. She envisioned the stream of urine flowing toward the creek, which then flowed down into the river beside the *Glutton*. The door opened and Johnny dropped a burning cigarette in the threshold and crushed it with his shoe, and did not even bother to close the door behind him, despite the chickens being able to get out. When he noticed there was somebody sitting on the fence rail, he stopped and squinted into the dimness, and then grinned when he apparently recognized the somebody as Rachel. He kicked a rust-colored chicken out of his way, and amidst squawks, he walked around the pen and came up behind Rachel. He slid both arms around her.

Rachel stiffened against his arms, intending to pull away and jump down, but the sensation of another human body holding her was rich. Her mother hadn't ever done that, and the boys at school had grabbed other girls, not her. Nobody had told Rachel that an embrace was going to feel as nice as resting in cool woods on a hot day. Rachel had watched those other girls at school twist away from boys, and now she understood that their protests were false at each turn. Johnny's arms encircled her with such certainty that it seemed having another person hold your body was the most natural thing in the world.

"What're you doing out here in my barn, girl?" he whispered. His breath was smoky and alcoholic. Usually after Rachel picked up his bottles near the riverbank and smelled the whiskey, she tightened the caps and tossed them into the water to watch them float downstream; she sometimes thought about putting messages in them, but there wasn't anything she wanted to say. Johnny, up close like this, had another smell too, the sharp musk scent of a trapped animal. She imagined her mother down by the boat, gutting some new dead thing as the sun set, gutting and gutting and gutting.

"Were you waiting for me?" Johnny said into her neck. "Is that why you're in my barn? Or were you going to steal my new chickens?" Rachel reached out and held the wooden rail on either side, in case Johnny suddenly let go of her.

"This isn't your barn," she said. "It's your brother's."

"So the little creature can talk, after all," he said. "But I guess your ma wouldn't never have taught you to be nice to a man." Johnny pressed his bristly cheek against her shoulder, and the whiskers poked through her flannel shirt. Johnny said, "This barn and everything else will be mine sooner or later when George gives himself a heart attack from working so much. For now I just want that piece of land my brother give your ma."

"That land is ours." Rachel had meant her words to be hostile toward Johnny, but instead, her voice came out soft, and even the word *ours* seemed to forge a connection between her and Johnny.

"I can't figure why my brother would give your ma that land. If you looked a little more like George I'd know why, but you sure as heck aren't his."

His comments swam through her undigested, and Rachel felt

herself being swept into a quicksand of bodies embracing and words that didn't matter. Rachel wished Johnny would cover her whole back with himself, and her front too, and yet she was scared and even felt a little sick. She didn't want Johnny to leave or let go of her, but she wanted time to slow way down so each second was large enough to move around in, while she figured out what was happening. This was not cows jumping onto each other's backs with their sharp hooves at the Taylor farm, and it was not tomcats yowling outside April May's house while her girl cats purred on the windowsills. And yet it *was* like those events, and like carp leaping on each other in the overflow marsh on the other side of O Road. Rachel stretched her bare toe toward the ground, but found herself too high up to touch.

"There's something about your face," Johnny said, "that could drive a man crazy." He moved his whiskered cheek to her other shoulder and kissed her neck.

Rachel said nothing, only breathed deeply in her attempt to slow time and to fight this new sort of nausea. Her body seemed to be growing softer, the pores of her skin seemed to be opening, and the sharp smell of animal was now coming partly from her.

"I'm guessing you haven't been spoiled by other men yet. I'm guessing I could still teach you something."

"Go to hell," Rachel whispered. She liked the feel of saying "hell." She also liked the sensation of her own long hair brushing her neck and shoulders. Rachel knew her mother would be so mad, madder than ever before, if she knew what was happening.

"Do you know this is the oldest barn in Greenland?" Johnny whispered and slid his warm hands beneath her flannel shirt.

Rachel felt she might vomit, but her skin rose in bumps to meet his hands.

"My great-great-grandfather built this barn," Johnny said, "chopped down his own trees to make the lumber. Where the guy got the energy for that shit, I don't know. I guess he stayed sober like George, the damn dull, penny-pinching son of a bitch. Me, now, I can relax and be generous."

Rachel was thinking of saying "What do you got to be generous with?" but she was no longer sure what Johnny did or didn't have. She was considering that a person's body was something to know the way a stretch of woods or a sandy place was something to know.

When Johnny slid his arms out from around her, she felt bare. He stepped through and around the rail, and Rachel grabbed his arm to pull him toward her on the other side. Johnny laughed and unbuttoned Rachel's shirt. He unwrapped her shoulders to reveal the hint of breasts. She didn't help him undress her, but neither did she resist. Johnny rubbed his whiskers against her flat chest, and when he kissed her mouth, Rachel did not kiss him in return, did not even know how, but just kept concentrating on slowing time, on lengthening all those seconds in which she might become accustomed to his smell. He yanked off his cowboy boots, tossed one, then the other, into the straw. A chicken squawked and flew up.

"Maybe I should wait for you to get a little older." Johnny dragged his pants off. "But I'm the sort of guy who might not be around here long."

Rachel gasped as he laid his warm body on hers on the barn floor, gasped not because the man was too heavy but because he was moving too fast. She had the sense that weight and speed were somehow the same thing, that even a small woman could lie with a giant, just so long as he moved slowly. Despite his experience with dozens of young girls, Johnny didn't understand the way a girl needed the adventure to progress more slowly. For Johnny, such girls were like the illegal swimming holes he used to sneak into as a teenager—even as he was undressing and diving in, his mind was set on getting away without being caught.

Johnny was not as muscular as Rachel, and when she felt his ribs slice against her chest she placed her hands on his sides to protect herself. Rachel never closed her eyes and neither did Johnny.

He stared into her face, while the brief stab of pain she felt inside dissolved into a kind of easy weightlessness. Johnny's hair fell forward, his face relaxed, and some drool on his lip gave the impression of melting. When Rachel screamed "No!" she was not expressing pain, and she was not afraid of what was happening to his face, nor was she alarmed at the cool sensation of a blob of chicken shit that had soaked through the straw beneath her. She screamed because the footsteps approaching were those of her mother, now standing in the doorway with the .22. There would be hell to pay, Rachel knew. As Johnny moaned, "Oh God, girl," the air exploded. Feathers flew up, and Johnny's body slammed hard onto hers as though another man had jumped onto his back.

"You animal!" Margo yelled.

Rachel tried to pull away, but her mother fired three more times and Rachel felt a bullet drive her shoulder into the barn floor. Her lungs emptied beneath Johnny's weight, and she had to fight for the strength to push him off her. Johnny's body was lifeless, and a chicken lay dead beside him. Rachel smelled skunk and looked up at her mother, then back at Johnny and the dead chicken. She couldn't grab hold of what had just happened. She could only wonder what the hell that chicken had been doing so close.

4

ON THE MORNING OF OCTOBER 9, 1999, GEORGE WALKED down behind the oldest barn in the township, and around the little pasture adjoining the building's lower level, to where a set of bedsprings was tied into the woven wire fence. He grabbed hold and shook the rusty metal bedsprings and found the repair stronger than the rest of the fence, the way scar tissue from a wound was usually tougher than the skin around it. The white-faced steer looked up from the hay pile on the barn's dirt floor to see what the rattling was about. When the cattle had busted down the fence a few days ago, George wasn't around, so Rachel, resourceful girl that she was, dragged some bedsprings over from the O Road dump and patched the fence herself. Thirty years ago, when George inherited his grandfather's farm, it was orderly barnyards, freshly painted buildings, neat woodpiles, and taut fences. Today it was quick, cheap repairs and never mind cosmetics. Now that you could hardly buy a cup of coffee with the money you got for a bushel of corn, George knew he had to give up those old ideas about mowed lawns and perfect fences. The bedsprings were an announcement to the world that farming was no longer a sensible way of making a living, and George couldn't help but also see them as an admission that he himself was no longer a respectable man.

George's father had never liked farming, which is how George inherited one of the largest tracts of land in the county at the age of twenty-two. Neither George's father (now living in Florida) nor Johnny should have been surprised at Old Harold's decision, since five generations of tradition held that the land should be kept whole rather than being split among heirs. Johnny had claimed he wanted to be George's partner, but he was bone lazy, often in jail, and George had seen neither hide nor hair of him since an argument they'd had three years ago September. In the last few years, George had been entertaining a hope that his nephew Todd—actually his ex-wife's nephew—might have an inclination toward farming. That was seeming less likely, though, especially after the broken window this morning. The long and short of George's life in Greenland Township was that he continually repaired his aging farm equipment, that between planting and harvesting he owed hundreds of thousands of dollars to the bank, and that until two and a half years ago, he'd farmed with the mindlessness of a woolly bear crawling toward hibernation. Two and a half years ago he'd come across Rachel Crane standing in a field near the river, dangling her .22.

A few minutes before eight o'clock, George walked up the incline to his truck, to wait for David Retakker. He noticed that April May was still sitting on her front steps across the street. For her part, April May noticed David the neighbor boy approaching on his bicycle. Her back had loosened up fine, but the pain in her foot had gotten worse. This was not the usual ache; she must have clunked against something in the barn without realizing, must have hit the exact spot where sixty-five years ago a nail had gone into the bottom of her foot and come out the top.

Harold Harland had been some sort of cousin to April May's mother, and when April May was a little girl, the old man often reminded her she was special for being born half in one month and half in the next. Hurting her foot so dramatically the day of the big tornado made her special too, Harold said. The day of the 1934 tornado was the same day that April May's beloved elementary teacher Mrs. O'Kearsy failed to show up at school, and even the little girls of Greenland knew she would not be back. When the tornado began to roar outside, April May crouched under her desk as she'd been instructed, and in her cramped position she considered that Mrs. O'Kearsy might be causing the storm because the townspeople had sent her away. When part of the schoolhouse roof was torn off and a patch of green sky became visible, April May thought maybe the storm was caused by her own anger about losing her favorite person in the world. When the winds died, the man who'd been filling in as teacher finally let the students go. April May ran outside to find the schoolhouse chimney toppled, and soon she discovered that nearly every building in Greenland Center was damaged. April May did not go straight home, but ran through the streets, alongside downed power wires and mangled fences and outbuildings torn off their foundations and left slumping in the road. She spun through the chaos as though she were a tornado herself. She couldn't bear to pick her way carefully around the debris after that monstrous coiled wind had sprung open her whole neighborhood. After hours of running, jumping, and climbing trees to look at the wreckage, April May had stepped on a nail stuck to some cabinet trim. She came onto the finishing nail at precisely the wrong angle, stepping straight down so the nail's tip went all the way through and protruded near her middle toes. When she yanked it out from the bottom, the amount of blood astounded her. She limped home, then waited four drowsy hours with her foot elevated before the doctor arrived to give her the injection. She fell asleep the moment the needle pricked her skin, and didn't rouse until the following morning.

This gray morning sixty-five years later, the pain in her foot seemed as fresh as the day of the tornado, and April May thought maybe she was being woken up once and for all. Just then David Retakker reached the driveway leading to the barn, and April May watched him stop and hide himself and his bike behind a clutch of bright red sumac.

David peered through the branches and tried to catch his breath before approaching the barn. George seemed eight feet tall to him, and though George did not wear cowboy boots—he wore tan steel-toed work boots—David thought he looked the way a cowboy ought to look, tall and straight as a fence post. George did not wear a cowboy hat, but he rested so easily against his truck that he reminded David of the Marlboro man on the poster his dad had hung in the hallway before he left. David had changed bedrooms recently so he could sleep in what had been George's room growing up.

David's dad, Mike, used to work for George, before he moved to Indiana four months ago to live with a woman who had three other kids. The one time David had visited his dad down there, neither of them had known what to do. Mike took him out to a breakfast of pancakes and eggs and bacon, and they stayed there at the restaurant a long time, Mike leaning back into the corner of the booth, sucking at one cigarette after another and blowing out smoke. Mike asked David: How was sixth grade? Was it any different than fifth? and David shrugged and stifled a cough. David waited until after they'd finished eating, then used his breather in the bathroom; otherwise Mike would have said, "You still having to use that old puffer?" or, worse, "I guess I shouldn't be smoking around you."

David glanced across the road at April May's house and noticed she was sitting on her steps watching him. He straightened his shoulders and tried to pretend he hadn't been hiding. When she waved, he waved back, then threw his leg over his bike and rode up the driveway toward George.

"Eight o'clock on the dot. Right on time," George said, without any reference to watch or clock. "You're the most on-time kid I know."

David was so happy at George's compliment that any words he might have used to express himself would have embarrassed him. David was grateful it was Saturday and he didn't have to be at school, glad the leaves on the maples at either end of the barn were blazing orange, and ecstatic that he would be helping George. He didn't mind that the sky was dreary this morning, or that he was still out of breath. Or that he hadn't eaten a meal since his free school lunch the day before. The lunch had been chili, a stick of cheese, a square of corn bread with butter and a pear half in syrup.

"As soon as you catch your breath, you climb up top," George said. "I'll throw the bales to you."

David nodded yes again and again until he reminded himself to stop. He tried not to smile too much, but when George jostled his shoulder with a callused hand, David almost lost his balance with smiling.

George looked away from David, figuring it was best to let the kid collect himself. George wasn't accustomed to this sort of wholesale admiration. Rachel didn't admire him that way, which was fine with him. Yesterday, Rachel had come into the house and stood by the back door with her arms crossed, watching him. Watching him was something she had started doing in just the last few weeks. Her gaze was so intense that it seemed to George wise to avoid meeting it too often. George had been paying bills, and he'd muttered something about David's mother, Sally. Until four months ago, the free rent on George's other house was part of Mike's pay as the hired man, but when Mike went away, he left

Sally and David here to be George's responsibility, the way people from the city of Kalamazoo drove out to the country and tossed their unwanted kittens and puppies out of the car near a barn, hoping someone else would take care of them. Since George wasn't getting a farmhand, he ought to be getting rent for that house. George felt softhearted about David, but he also saw that living out here with his ma wasn't doing the boy any good. Maybe if they were in town, Sally'd get a job and get some structure in her life, and maybe then she'd take better care of her son.

"Do you want me to kick the sorry bitch out?" Rachel had said.

"No." George's heart jumped at realizing Rachel might just go over there and tell Sally to leave. "Not yet." He wanted her gone, but if something bad happened to David as a result of sending them away, George might end up bound to Sally by regret, and he wasn't ready to take that chance. Anyway, George had listened to his grandfather's stories long enough that he couldn't feel right about passing judgment on Sally. Morality, Old Harold said, was a more complicated business than it might seem on the surface, and sending people away was about the worst thing you could do.

Inside the barn, David scrambled to the top of the wagonload of straw by grabbing hold of the ends of bales. He stood unsteadily atop the wagon, and when he was sure George was watching, he jumped over the five-foot gulf between the loaded wagon and rest of the stacked bales, where he landed on his knees and hands. David crawled to the edge and looked down, terrified and grinning, his chest heaving. David, you scare me, George thought. George climbed the hay wagon slowly and expertly, but he remembered how it was to be a boy, to feel the need to take chances.

"Are you ready?" George said.

"Ready."

George threw the first bale from the wagon past David, right into place so David had only to push it an inch or so with his knees. Immediately upon asking David to help him yesterday,

George had remembered David's breathing trouble, but the boy had seemed so happy to be asked that George couldn't take the invitation back. George would do as much of the work as possible himself.

"Ready again?" George threw the next bale.

David pushed it into place and stepped aside to await another, and another.

"Okay, that was four," George said. "Will you help me out by counting the bales as you stack?"

David nodded.

"That would be a big help. Here's five."

"Five," David said.

"The beans will be ready to harvest on Friday," George said. "That means I've got a lot of work to do before then."

"I can help."

"I think I've got that knotter fixed, but the power take-off clutch on the Case needs some work before I can bale the rest of the straw."

"I can drive the tractor anytime you want me to."

"This afternoon I'll fill the oat bin, put the rest of the oats into the silo outside the stock barn." George was thinking aloud. There was too much to do, but that was always how it was, and George figured that a person could only work all day long, and he couldn't work any more than that. Starting next Friday, and continuing through the next two months, every day from six in the morning until midnight, George would be in the field taking in soybeans and then corn. He'd drive the combine, but he needed somebody to haul the wagons south to the elevator in Climax Township as fast as he filled them. Nobody'd answered the ad he'd posted at the grocery, and he didn't know how he'd pay a person anyway—maybe with a couple of his cows. Rachel hadn't offered to help, and even if she wanted to help, she didn't have a driver's license.

As he took bale number nine from George, David said, "Would you ever want to go to Southern California?"

"Oh, I don't know," George said. "It's hard to take time off to travel."

"I mean to live." David's mother had said that David absolutely couldn't tell George or Rachel she was intending to move them to California, where David's half brother, Jim, and his wife lived. David barely knew Jim, who was eighteen years older and had a different dad.

"Must be a nice place." George threw bale number ten. "An awful lot of people leave here for there."

"Are there farms in California?"

"Oh, I think they grow a lot of grapes. Lots of fruits and vegetables. Avocados."

"I mean regular farms like yours." David adjusted the tenth bale.

"There's not enough fresh water. Maybe in parts of Northern California."

"Well, I don't ever want to live out there," David said. He didn't know if there were woolly bears or eighty-foot-tall walnut trees or anything else nice in California. He didn't know how much another place on the planet could differ from this place, and he wished he wasn't going to have to find out. David knew his mother would make them leave without warning. One day, maybe even today, she'd say the word, and they would pack a few bags and head west.

George wasn't considering anything as exotic as travel plans. As he picked up the eleventh bale by the strings and tossed it into place, he worried mostly about getting the grain to Climax. For more than a decade, George had felt he was working under the shadow of a monster perched on the western horizon, a monster that was not a creature but a point in time, a day somewhere in the future, when he would have to sell off pieces of his land to pay taxes or else lose it in one fell swoop, and he knew that all his hard work served only to push that day a little further off. As Milton Taylor always said, the farmers would soon be gone from this river valley the way the Indians were already gone. When George's ancestors arrived in this spot, there had apparently lived what the settlers called the Horseshoe Clan of the Potawatomi, a group who erected their wigwams around a central fire in a three-quarters circle precisely on the site of this barn. Old Harold said the barn's construction had buried any evidence of a three-quarters circle, or a fire pit, or a civilization, but George figured that plenty of relics were buried around here, if only a person had the time and inclination to dig.

Old Harold had become a kind of neighborhood authority on the Potawatomi, and he used to speak with regret about sending those Indians away, as though he himself had witnessed the 1840 exodus. Though the event occurred a half century before the old man was even born, he seemed to feel he had something to do with forcing those folks out of this paradise into a hostile land across the Mississippi. Harold said that so many Indians died along the way that the westbound trail itself became a graveyard nine hundred miles long. As Harold got older and maybe even a little senile, he told two stories over and over again: the Potawatomi being sent away by the U.S. government, and the widowed schoolteacher Mary O'Kearsy being sent away—fired and evicted—for loving one of Harold's hired men, name of Enkstra. The story of the tornado that destroyed the house and rerouted the creek became part of the schoolteacher story. Harold said he was responsible for the eviction of Mary O'Kearsy, and the tornado's veering up north onto his property had been a kind of punishment for his self-righteousness, he said, a kick in the rear.

George figured that in the old days, when farming made sense, a farm could survive the kind of devastation wrought by tornadoes and floods and complicated heartaches, but now farming was a precarious business, and even a small disaster could take George's whole enterprise, his whole life, down with it.

"Ready?" George said, grasping the strings on bale number twelve.

David said, "Ready."

5

ACROSS THE STREET FROM RACHEL'S FARM STAND, STEVE Hoekstra sat at his kitchen table, paging through a windows industry magazine and listening to his wife, Nicole, shower. Nine o'clock was about the earliest a man dared knock on a stranger's door, and Steve liked to start his day, even a Saturday, by reminding himself of prices, mechanical information, and heat loss statistics, and about new products in which he might be able to interest folks. He sometimes offered gutter systems, hot water heaters, even lawn furniture, but those items generally turned out to be ways of making conversation. No matter what came on the market at what price, he mostly sold vinyl siding, vinyl replacement windows, storm doors, and the occasional hollow-core insulated metal door. He loved being able to make houses look better and be more energy efficient, and he was glad to be doing so in his own neighborhood. People loved their houses at least as much as they loved their spouses, which seemed natural to Steve—after all, you didn't get to remodel the person you married.

As George and David stacked the first dozen bales to the south, Steve listened to warm water rain upon his wife and thought of her trim, pretty body enveloped in steam. He could just walk into that bathroom and touch her, but he liked the thought of her alone, touching herself, washing herself unmolested. This house was really more hers than his, and it didn't surprise Steve, for women usually occupied houses more substantially than men; that was why women were more inclined to want vinyl replacement windows and storm doors. When he heard the shower water shut off, Steve collected his materials and slipped out. Before getting into his car he looked around for Rachel, but she'd disappeared. As George threw the fifteenth bale to David in the barn to the south, Steve backed out of his driveway. He paused in the road to search for Rachel once more, and when he didn't see her, he headed north.

Steve's company had a high turnover rate for salesmen, because most people didn't like the business of traveling door-to-door. Steve himself liked nothing better than stepping out of a cool October morning into a woman's house, inside of which warmth emanated from furniture and kitchen cabinets. He loved his own perfectly proportioned wife—who must be toweling herself off about now—but he didn't think he could live without also going into other women's houses. Not that he had sex with those women, for that happened rarely, only once in the year and a half since he'd been married. His lone infidelity had occurred a month ago, and he'd felt bad about it. Really he liked just being near different women, smelling their perfume and lotion mixed with the scent of potpourri or plug-in deodorizers and Crock-Pot cooking, even the adhesive smell of new construction or a crafts project. Most of the longtime women residents of Greenland Township worked odd hours, on their farms or gardens, or at the greenhouses in season, or part-time as school lunch ladies, so you didn't know when you'd catch them at home, but Saturday morning was a good bet. The population of Greenland was growing, especially in the new housing developments, but those new people didn't need windows or siding.

If a woman were home alone and invited Steve in, he'd always sit in the chair which he figured to be the husband's chair. By sitting there he assumed the authority of the man of the house, and the woman took him more seriously, listened intently while he talked about insulation and resale value. As he spoke, he imagined the women giving the same pitch to their husbands later in the evening, retelling Steve's tales of fuel savings, even exaggerating the importance of safety lock windows with easy removal for cleaning. Single women were no different; though there was no tangible man, there was an ideal man they dreamed of, who would come home someday and sit in the chair Steve chose. (Or in some cases there might be an ideal *woman,* and Steve was not afraid to stand in for *her,* either.) A single woman sometimes made her decision then and there, after he'd walked through the house, followed her into halls, bedrooms, a warm cluttered bathroom, which might still be humid from a morning shower, with shampoos and conditioners askew on the shower shelves, still coated with water droplets. If he gave a woman an estimate and she made the decision on the spot, he'd have a crew chief on the phone in ten minutes, and by the end of the day that crew chief would have stopped out, met the woman, and confirmed the price, date, and time of installation.

Steve didn't abandon a woman after she'd signed the papers or even after the crew had installed the windows. He'd stop by a few weeks later, ring the doorbell, and get himself invited in. He'd tell a woman her windows looked great. "Everything go all right?" he'd ask, and the woman would assure him that the men who installed the windows were nice fellows who didn't leave a mess. He'd ask that right off: "They didn't leave a mess, did they?" In fact, plenty of women would follow the men around and clean up after them before they even had a chance to clean up after themselves.

For the most part, Steve preferred dealing with women over

forty or fifty, women who wore little or no makeup, women whose houses were not too clean. Such women usually had an easier way about them, weren't anxious or excessive the way young women could be, the way his Nicole sometimes was. Steve's first sale in the neighborhood had been that big window for April May Rathburn. He hadn't given her a hard sell, but had seen her out feeding the birds and merely stopped by to say he was a new neighbor, and when she asked what line he was in, he couldn't deny he sold windows. April May brought out a few chocolate chip cookies, saying she'd expected her grandchildren but they'd gotten sick, and Steve said that, sick or not, those kids were fools for missing such delicious cookies. April May had insisted he take another and invited him inside.

When Steve had been inspecting the plate glass picture window she wanted to replace, he noticed that April May was a strong woman. Though she must have been seventy, her long arms were muscular and veined. Together they decided that a bay window would work well exactly where she wanted it. Steve made her the best deal he could—he worked for a straight 40 percent above installation and materials cost, and the pleasure he got from giving his neighbor a good deal outweighed the pleasure he would have gotten from a bit more money. Steve felt there was something cocoonlike about April May, as though she were going to burst open and emerge as a much younger woman, or else she might wither suddenly from a cancer that nobody knew was growing inside her.

6

AFTER JOHNNY HARLAND WAS SHOT AND SECRETLY BURIED, the skunk stench of Margo's second-to-last kill hung in the air around the *Glutton* for a week. During this time Rachel kept her distance from the empty boat, except to get salve for her torn hands and for the wound near her armpit. She regretted pushing so hard about her father, and she didn't know what to do with the information she'd extracted at such a high price. When Milton offered her a job helping with his garden in those first few days, Rachel was grateful for the distraction as much as for the money; and from Milton she learned about another neighborhood tragedy. Beef prices had been falling steadily for the last few years, Milton said, and his family had no longer been able to compete with the big western feed lots. Milton's parents had found themselves unable to pay summer taxes in July, and rather than going further into debt, they'd decided to sell.

Rachel didn't tell Milton that July was also when Johnny started coming around; or that July was when her mother began skinning possums, even though nobody wanted a possum skin—when the skin man came up the river he wouldn't pay her even a quarter for them. Now Rachel learned that just as Margo's decline culminated in her shooting Johnny, the Taylor family's problems resulted in their butchering most of their remaining cattle and selling the bulk of their property to a company that would put in a golf course.

And just as Rachel found herself alone with a ramshackle boat (really an old camping trailer riveted to an iron hull), the Taylors' youngest and most peculiar son, Milton, aged thirty, was left with three acres on the corner where Queer Road crossed the Kalamazoo River. The river curved to border the land on the south and west, and the property included his family's vegetable garden and their oldest cow barn. Milton's parents had originally planned to move just a few miles down the road so his mother could continue to garden, but they changed their minds and moved to Florida instead, to a town not far from George Harland's parents. It was as though, once losing their grip on the land, they were spun off by centrifugal force toward the edge of the continent.

Rachel wasn't sure what she'd learned from her mother's decline, but observing the transfer of the Taylors' land taught her that a person could buy somebody else's property and suddenly hundreds of acres of grazing land became a golf course. Rachel had lost not only her mother this autumn, but also the morel mushrooms near the Taylors' dead elms, and the Black Angus and red Hereford cattle munching only a few hundred yards from the *Glutton*. Still, she could not help but be impressed with the power wielded by a human being who owned a parcel of the planet and could alter that parcel at will, or else will it to stay the same. A person who owned land could make sure she would always have a place, no matter what stupid, brutal thing her mother or anybody else might do. In October, the golf course people would show up with earthmoving equipment. They would kill the old native grass with chemicals in order to plant hybrid tropical grass; within a few months they would replace the decaying Taylor farmhouse with a pole barn–style clubhouse and convert the remaining three solid outbuildings to utility sheds, which they'd paint red and white like toy barns.

Milton had always been more religious than the rest of his family, and from the time he was young he had found his strength and solace in Jesus Christ. As a boy, Milton used to watch his family's cattle move slowly across the field, and he considered that those beasts might be Christians too, without their even knowing it. He admired the way they brushed against each other easily and the way they clustered together at dusk like a congregation, mooing gently as they stamped their feet and swished their tails. His parents' decision to sell the farm saddened him and, though he was a grown man, that sense of loss gradually overwhelmed him, became unbearable. A few weeks after his parents left town for good, there was a full harvest moon, and sometimes the roundness and tug of a full moon are too powerful for those who've become detached from the planet, and Milton just kind of let go.

It was the very same night Margo shot Johnny, in fact, that Milton experienced Jesus coming to his bed in the form of a body of light, both vaporous and solid, and Jesus entered him through every opening, even the pores in his skin, so that Milton's whole body of flesh glowed the way Jesus' heart glowed in the pages of Bible study books. A half mile to the north, meanwhile, Rachel dug into the floor of the Harland barn with a round-end shovel. As Rachel's hands blistered and as those blisters broke open, Milton experienced the soothing caress of His holiness and an embrace from both within and without his own body. A feeling of acceptance flowed all through Milton, assuring him that Jesus loved him even when his thoughts were reprehensible, and Milton in turn loved wholeheartedly every soul in his community, Christian or no, the quiet farmers and the troubled teenagers alike. Bathed in the soothing light of His touch, Milton knew his own mission in this life: to bring the people of Greenland together as their community changed, to discourage folks from going away as his parents and so many others had done. Milton wept and prayed his thanks to Jesus and His love for hours, until the sun rose.

Milton emerged from his night of holy bliss feeling cleansed and redeemed, filled with joy at knowing he would create a place where bodies and souls could mingle in the name of Jesus. He opened his Bible that morning to the following passage:

> Honour the Lord with thy substance, and with the firstfruits of all thine increase: So shall thy barns be filled with plenty, and thy presses shall burst out with new wine.
>
> —PROVERBS 3:9–10

From the farm's sale, Milton's parents had left him enough money to build a modest house, but after that night he decided instead he would spend the money remodeling the barn into a church center for evening activities such as Bible discussions and staged dramas, worship of all kinds. He contacted the church officials immediately, but to his surprise the Greenland Methodists resisted any association with such a venture. Though Milton assisted in teaching at the Bible school, the church officials had always held back from embracing Milton fully; they worried that his enthusiasm flowed too easily, that there was something altogether too expansive and expressive about him. Before a new despair could begin to settle into his heart, however, Milton miraculously (praise Jesus!) came upon a new and better option. With the help of several gentlemen from the church, who preferred to remain anonymous, Milton got a line on a liquor license, and he began transforming the barn into the Barn Grill. Milton's vision of the establishment included a small vinyl Bible beside the napkin holder on each table, to serve as a reference for such discussions as he hoped would take place. He would also copy and frame some appropriate verses, starting with the Old Testament favorite: "Eat, Drink, and Be Merry." Of course the jukebox would offer hymns and spirituals, along with a few country-western tunes. He camped out on a mattress in the loft and began the remodeling, certain in his heart that folks would joyfully drink in His spirit alongside the wine and beer Milton would place before them.

Though the barn's foundation turned out to be solid on its footings, there would be a lot of work involved in bringing an old barn into health department compliance, starting with plumbing, sewer, and electric, and moving on to ceiling, floor, and walls. Folks told him he'd be wise to level the structure and rebuild from scratch, but he had a strong attachment to the building and to its historical value as the second-oldest barn in the township, and besides, the proverb specifically said *barns*. He probably should have chosen to ignore the garden his parents had abandoned when they left for Florida, but he couldn't bear to let God's bounty rot in the field, and so he hired Rachel to help him.

Milton had plenty of work to do, but he often paused to watch Rachel tend his garden in much the same way he used to watch the Angus and Hereford cattle graze, and she quickly became an integral part of his landscape. Rachel, he knew, would be his greatest challenge, and the need to save her soul swelled so large in him that at times he wanted to dance around her and shout up to Heaven for God to please help him show her the Way. Milton was grateful that when he watched Rachel, or even when he considered Rachel in the abstract, his thoughts and desires were entirely pure, focused only on her salvation.

"Aren't you mad as hell at your parents for selling all that land?" Rachel asked one afternoon. She looked out over the old grazing field, now dotted by landscapers' trucks and men in coveralls raking away cow flops. So far the local frosts had missed Milton's garden, and Rachel was filling a bushel basket with the season's last tomatoes, most of which Milton would give away at church.

Milton reached down to take out some lamb's quarter and yanked out an acorn squash plant along with it. He stared down at the dark, undeveloped fruits dangling from it, as though uncertain what crime he had just committed.

"Three acres isn't shit, Milton." Rachel stepped across the row between them. She took the prickly stalk out of Milton's hand and replaced it in the soil, though she didn't think there was much hope in any case of the squash ripening. "How can you stand losing all that land?"

"All the farmers are going to lose their land," Milton said. "The time for farmers has come and gone."

"You sound like you want the farmers to fail."

"When they sell their extra land for houses, our community will grow. That's God's plan, and there's no sense resisting the change. But I'm not going to forget the past—that's why I'm putting together the farm museum."

Rachel was sick of hearing about the farm museum, which would start with a mule plow, a hand thresher, and a rusted-up mower, all of which he planned to sandblast and repaint with bright colors for display in and around the barn. She said, "Well, if I was in with God the way you are, I'd be asking God to *get* me some damn land." She formed a little hill around the torn-up squash plant and pressed it down with her bare foot. She wondered if the plan cooked up by Milton's god included Margo, Johnny, and herself, or if some people were just plain outside His circle of interest.

"Will you come to church with me this Sunday?" Milton said.

Rachel shook her head. "My mom doesn't want me to go to church."

"How is your ma? I ain't seen her lately."

"She's fine, but you know how she hates Jesus."

"What on earth does your ma have against the Word of the Lord?"

Rachel couldn't believe that Milton hadn't noticed Margo missing more than two weeks. Apparently he was focused on his own absent parents.

"My mother says Jesus is just another damn man who wants to boss women."

Milton's face deflated. "You don't feel that way about Jesus, do you?"

"Hey, I don't even know Him."

"Do you want me to try to talk to your ma? I don't think I've seen her since she threatened to shoot me awhile back."

"Hell no," Rachel said. "Promise me you won't try to talk to her."

"You don't have a regular father you can turn to, but God is the Father of us all." Milton felt desperately sorry for a girl without God or a father, with only a crazy, recluse mother. A rush of compassion reinflated and softened him. He had half a mind to go talk to Margo, but he didn't want to risk getting shot, and there wasn't much chance she'd listen anyhow. She was a woman who resisted change of any kind, living as though it were 1896 instead of 1996, so it was no wonder she was getting crazier. He mumbled a prayer instead, tried to light up a path between God and the girl, a holy landing strip on which Jesus could fly into her life. Milton looked up at the sky. "Every day I pray that Jesus will come into your life, Rachel. Jesus will save your soul from the fires of hell." Milton's voice always took on a shaky, hopeful excitement when he talked this way. His arms waved around, without his seeming to notice them. "He will touch your soul and suddenly you won't even want to swear anymore."

Rachel wiped her hands on her pants, and reached down and cuffed her pant leg. The jeans were from the church box and were both too long and too tight. At fourteen she was as tall as she would ever be, but she was starting to become hippy. She said, "Swearing makes people know I damn well mean what I say."

"I'm just saying you should keep your mind open, Rachel, in case Jesus comes to you. Don't resist Him, just let His spirit enter you."

The spirit of Jesus, or even the living Jesus, with His deep, compassionate eyes and smooth brow, with His sweetly scented body draped in soft robes, wouldn't have lured Rachel. She might have become interested in Adam, naked and made of mud, subject to earthly temptations, but Milton knew only the one official way into the Christian church. Rachel figured she'd already left herself open when a man came to her one night, and she had let him enter her, and no good whatsoever had come of that.

In her time living alone on the *Glutton* that fall, Rachel killed only as much as she needed to eat, and she boiled the meat for hours, days sometimes, to tenderize it and to kill parasites, as her mother had taught her. For the most part she avoided contact with anyone other than Milton and the people she had to see at school. She didn't let herself think about the night with Johnny and her mother in the barn, but she knew those details were swimming around the island of her conscious mind, and she dreaded lying down at night for fear of what might come to her in the unguarded moments between waking and sleeping. On the season's last warm nights she slept on straw in the upper level of the Harland barn, but usually she burned a kerosene lamp in the boat, where she cleaned her mother's rifle and read library books about gardening and wild plants and animals and the Potawatomi, whose name she found out meant "people of the fire." Rachel read that these local Indians sometimes sent their kids into the woods alone to gather what wisdom they could. Rachel felt that in her time alone she was learning plenty, and not just about plants and animals.

She was learning that loneliness could deepen with every passing day, even when you thought it couldn't get worse. Rachel wished she had tolerated the skunk fumes longer to learn more, her father's name, at least, and anything else about her ancestor who grew corn here. Rachel learned from books that the Potawatomi came down from the north four hundred years ago and took this land from the Miami tribe. Good for them, Rachel thought; they must have really loved this place if they went to the trouble of driving other people away. She also learned that the children within a clan were considered brothers and sisters and could not marry, and so when a girl married, she went to live with a new clan. That suggested to Rachel something about Corn Girl. It might not have been the prospect of marriage to a man that made her kill herself, as Margo had suggested. It made more sense to Rachel that Corn Girl would have killed herself to keep from having to leave the place she loved. She had no idea what evidence her father'd had for his claim of discovering the girl's grave, so when Rachel wandered on her own, she searched for anything at all—a depressed spot in the earth, a big stone curiously placed. People now buried their dead high on hills, but back then the Potawatomi put folks into the lower, more fertile land near the river, and instead of securing them in houselike coffins, the Potawatomi wrapped bodies in what, in the drawings in library books, resembled collapsed wigwams of skins and grass mats. Rachel dreamed repeatedly that she herself was lying on the bare ground, surrounded by mounds rising up around her as though they were rows of the dead, lying end to end, not buried but merely stretched out with a little dirt piled onto them, dangerously easy to uncover.

Though Rachel sometimes fantasized about going to Milton or April May or even George Harland and telling what had happened, she needed only to remind herself that it would mean confessing she was living alone, and since living alone was illegal for a fourteen-year-old, she had to keep her mouth shut. The authorities would probably send her away to an orphanage in Kalamazoo if they found out. Losing her mother was bad enough—losing her place here would be the end of everything. So that nobody became suspicious, five days a week Rachel went south of the river to school, where she kept quiet and ignored kids who teased her about her worn-out clothes. She honestly didn't give a damn what they thought, but she resented their calling attention to her.

In those first months without her mother, Rachel settled on a focus for her new life alone: to earn as much money as she could in order to buy land from George Harland when he would have to sell, as Milton insisted he and all the other farmers eventually would. With the money Milton paid her, Rachel first went to the township office and paid the overdue taxes on her mother's wedge of property, explaining to the clerk that her mother had sent her on the errand.

A few times that autumn, Rachel tried speaking prayers to Milton's god, begging to be allowed to stay where she was, but she didn't feel right asking a favor of somebody she couldn't even imagine. She spoke aloud to Corn Girl more often, figuring a girl buried in the ground nearby might understand her better than a man living in the sky. Sometimes as she washed her clothes in a tub of creek water she'd heated on the woodstove, she told Corn Girl that really she was fine alone. She said aloud that she wouldn't know what to do with a father even if he showed up and introduced himself. On rare occasions Rachel felt so lonesome and agitated that she used her pocketknife to dig at the bullet lodged near her armpit. Though it was not buried deeply, it was at an impossible angle, and her efforts only resulted in new wounds that she had to bandage and salve. In general Rachel tried to take care of herself, and in her hours alone she was making up her mind about the world, concluding that not only was land the most important thing, but that everything else—school, buildings, people—meant nothing.

There came to be one exception, however. Rachel was carrying the .22 one sleepless night when, close to the river's edge, she sensed a coyote. She caught the glint of teeth and a fawn-colored coat, and she lifted her rifle, aimed, and shot into raspberry brambles. When David Retakker, a sandy-haired, freckled kid in a tan sweatshirt with a Higgins Dairy logo, slowly stood, Rachel let the gun fall slack against her arm. Johnny had been dead on the barn floor, and now, two months later, here was this scrawny kid standing straight up in her line of fire, clearly alive, eyes sparkling with fear. She'd seen David wandering the neighborhood, knew his father worked for George Harland, but she'd never cared about him any more than she cared about any other idiot kid. When he stood unharmed, however, Rachel knew he was some kind of miracle. This little boy, only chest high to her, had come back to life in a way that Johnny had refused to do. She walked David home to P Road and told him he ought to be more goddamn careful, that he shouldn't be out so goddamn late, and that he should wear brighter goddamn colors for safety and a jacket, too, on such a cold night.

Three days later when she saw David squatting, eating something from his hand and throwing bits of whatever it was into a mud puddle, Rachel's whole body flashed with heat at the memory of almost shooting him.

"Hey, you," she finally said. "I hope to hell you're being careful."

David stood as though rising again from the dead and wiped his hands on his jeans, letting pale nuggets fall around his feet.

"You're eating raw soybeans?"

David shrugged. "They were left after the combine went through."

"I've never been hungry enough to eat raw soybeans," Rachel said. "Follow me. We'll go eat something better."

Rachel jogged toward Queer Road, stopping repeatedly to allow David to catch up. He was panting when they got there.

"What the hell's the matter with your breathing?" When he only shrugged again, she said, "Fine, don't tell me."

She squatted down, and he squatted in imitation beside her. She picked up a walnut that had been run over by enough cars that the tough green husk was worn off. She placed it on the edge of the road and cracked it open with a fist-sized rock. "And don't smash your damn fingers when you do this." She handed him both halves of the walnut, and was impressed when he pulled out a pocket-knife.

"I'm going to be a farmer," David told her, as he dug specks of walnut meat from the shell. "I'm going to grow hundreds of acres of food."

"Don't bite down hard or you might break your teeth on a piece of shell." Rachel decided that the only way such a small, wheezy, hungry kid was going to survive out here long enough to become a farmer was with her help. Rachel threw a couple dozen more walnuts into the road so that cars could run over them and they could eat them another time.

In the months following, she taught David things her mother and Milton had taught her, such as never to drink water from the river, not even if you boiled it for twenty minutes. She taught him about borrowing tools from the Harland shed, making him promise to always return them to the exact positions he'd found them in, so George wouldn't start locking the toolshed. She often petted and talked to the Harland animals in the pasture, and when she found a blood-swollen tick on the spotted pony's neck—a tick as big and hard as a kernel of corn—she showed it to David and made him promise to check himself for ticks before going to bed. She didn't bring David to the *Glutton,* for fear he'd notice her mother was missing, but she told him without hesitation that the Potawatomi had loved this place, and that the Corn Girl used to cut her hair and bury strands of it with her plants and then talk to the plants until they were big enough to grow on their own. Rachel herself invented the stories about Corn Girl, but once she told the stories to David, she never doubted the truth of them.

Throughout the ensuing winter, Rachel worked whenever Milton would hire her and she sought out David every day. The coldest nights kept her inside the boat, though, and made her feel more alone than she thought she could bear, especially when she awoke from her dreams of the dead lying under dirt. And there was another dream, one that occurred just as she fell asleep sometimes, a dream in which her mother stood silently before her: Margo started out solid, but gradually she grew translucent, and finally invisible. In a variation, Margo would break up like oil on water and flow away downstream. Rachel had long known the river divided the world into halves, but she was coming to realize that her mother had been her center point on the river, and a landscape without a center was an uncertain place, even if you'd known it all your life. Daytime, on her own, she continued her search for Indian graves, as though the dead could give her some new insight. It was the following spring, on such a search, that she came face-to-face with George Harland. She was standing in a field near the river, feeling so alone and heavy that when George's tractor approached, she didn't run away.

7

ON THE MORNING OF OCTOBER 9, 1999, DAVID RETAKKER'S
mother lit a menthol cigarette and emptied the pint of bourbon into
her coffee in the kitchen of George's other house. Sally had tried a
few times recently to quit smoking—namely when she'd run out of
cigarettes. At Mike's insistent nagging, she'd also tried to quit
drinking once about three years ago, but she didn't intend to try
that again. She felt bad for David not having a father around, but
she was relieved Mike was gone, because she'd grown tired of fight-
ing with him. Now that she was rid of Mike, she was ready to be
out of this place, away from this whole damned climate. She was
ready for California and sunshine and year-round warmth.

As her son accepted the seventeenth bale of straw in the barn on
Queer Road, Sally knotted the belt of her flannel robe, carried her
cup out into the backyard and sat in a lawn chair beside a rickety
picnic table. She'd have preferred to live on Queer Road because
she could more easily walk or hitch down to the Barn Grill, but

when she got out of this place, she'd be moving a lot farther away than Queer Road. And when she got out of this town, she'd be drinking in bars that didn't have pictures of the Lord Jesus staring down at you from the walls.

Sally had heard David get up this morning and leave to go help George do something or other. Sally didn't know George very well, despite living for more than a decade in a house he owned, nor did she understand why George was letting her stay there rent-free now. She half expected him to come wandering in some night with a bottle. She'd never seen him drunk, but all men had to get drunk once in a while. She'd seen him have a beer or two at the Barn Grill plenty often. A few times he'd even bought her a beer and joked with her about some new piece of Jesus artwork Milton had picked up, like the picture with the red lightbulb behind it to make the Lord's heart appear pinkish beneath his white robe. George had also taken her to the store several times when she'd asked. Though she didn't particularly desire George, she didn't desire him any less than she desired anyone else, and if he came in smelling of alcohol and talking sweet to her, she wouldn't refuse him. In the last few months, however, George hadn't even come by to suggest Sally pay the light bill.

Sally tried to look at the bright maples, but settled her gaze instead on the cluster of tall brown walnut trees. People didn't understand how hard it was having a twelve-year-old son at her age. She'd been through all this before with the first two boys, and she'd only just finished raising them when David came along. Of course David couldn't have been a nicer kid, and of the three boys, David was the only one who resembled her. The older boys looked like their father, stocky with broad shoulders and meaty fists. David looked nothing like his father, but was fine-featured and pale with freckles like Sally's. He had her long, big-knuckled fingers. The first time Sally had a boy, she was still a teenager and stupid in love. Back then she'd been full of energy, but it was just too hard to have a son when you were fifty and you'd been through it all before.

Sally shivered and wrapped herself more tightly in her bathrobe; the air was cooler than she had originally thought. Sally hadn't liked the farmhouse where she grew up, and she'd never wanted to live in this one. Farmhouses were too drafty, too much to care for, and they stank of the past in their creaking, splintery pine floorboards and their shabby wallpaper. In farmhouses like this one, men had bossed their wives and children, had demanded hard work and compliance. In such houses, women had prepared meals to fill rough-hewn tables, and they'd sweated over stoves, boiling jars and lids to preserve food in seasons of bounty, canning hundreds of quarts of tomatoes, the acids of which scrubbed their hands raw. In lean years when crops were destroyed by animals or weather, the farm women processed fish and cabbage, even dandelion greens in a pinch, anything to fill all those empty men. Sally had watched her own mother toil and from a young age promised herself she would not have such a slavish relationship to husbands and sons, nor to land and weather.

California would put an end to her connection with farm life, once and for all. As soon as Sally's oldest son wrote and invited her to visit, as he surely would any day, Sally would pack a few bags and be California bound. She'd say good-bye to Milton at the Barn Grill (he'd give her one for the road, and maybe one of the other fellows playing darts would send a beer her way for old time's sake). Then she'd hitch a ride to Kalamazoo, and hop a bus to Los Angeles, where she'd sit by the ocean every day, let the sun burn away the Michigan dust and mold from her skin.

Along with David, of course.

8

WHEN GEORGE FIRST CAME FACE-TO-FACE WITH RACHEL near the river two and a half years ago, he didn't know she'd been living alone on the *Glutton* for more than seven months. From a distance he saw her standing on clods of dirt in a field he happened to be disking. Even as he got close, he didn't recognize her right away as Margo's daughter, because Margo was a fairly tall, slender woman, with reddish-brown hair flowing in a way that gave a man the sense he was seeing her through clear water. When George had last noticed Rachel working in Milton's garden, she had seemed a smallish girl with her hair pushed under a bandanna. The person standing before him in his field was thickly built, sturdy on her bare feet, with heavy, straight hair hanging alongside a round face. George stopped the Case tractor beside her and let it idle. He took off his ear protectors and opened the door, and Rachel yelled up to him, asking if he'd ever come across any "goddamn human bones" down here.

The question startled George, even frightened him for a moment, and he flashed on a vision of his brother, Johnny—missing more than seven months—as a skeleton with all his flesh withered away. But the girl before him seemed familiar, as though he'd spent time with her and was accustomed to her. Maybe he had some unconscious knowledge that she had spied on him as he chopped wood, that she had borrowed tools from his sheds and had been at least as much a part of this place as the donkey, llama, or pony. When the clump upon which Rachel balanced herself crumbled into loose dirt, she climbed onto two smaller clumps. It was too cold to be barefoot, George thought. He switched the tractor key off, and when the machine went silent, the barn swallows who'd been following him to dive at bugs flew off toward their nests in the old barn. The girl stood as solidly as something growing from the soil, as though, in the minute she'd been standing in her new spot, she'd already sent down roots.

She said something about *goddamn bones* again.

"What's that?" George was glad for an excuse to get down out of the tractor and look more closely at her. Had he really not seen this girl in years? Seeing that face was like waking up from a long sleep, like the day starting over. He expected something else surprising to happen, say, for Johnny to come walking along the river, grinning about his clever departure last fall or maybe over some new debauchery.

Rachel took a breath before speaking, giving the impression that speaking took a great deal of energy. "Do old bones work their way up through the damn soil or what?" Her new clumps of dirt collapsed, and she stepped onto another clod, as though she intended to break up soil all day.

George couldn't tell from her face whether she was serious or, for that matter, why the bones and soil were *damned*. He said, "I don't know."

"My mother told me there's a damn Indian grave somewhere

around here." Her voice gave the impression of being rusty from disuse, requiring the force of curses to get the sentences out at all.

"Go ahead and look," George said, though she hadn't asked his permission. "How's your ma? I haven't seen her in a while."

"She's fine." Rachel crossed her arms.

George didn't know what to do with his hands, so he lifted one foot and rested his boot on the tractor wheel tread, put both hands around that knee, and thought of something he hadn't considered in ages. "I don't know about graves," George said, "but there's Indian gardens beside my house."

The girl stared at his knee, and he felt self-conscious about the way his right hand looked mangled, for its scars and butchered index finger.

"What the hell's Indian gardens?" she asked.

He unclasped his hands from his knee. Her gaze was making him feel uneasy, so he focused beyond her, around her, at land he owned. Until now George figured his worst crimes had been inaction and maybe excessive pride about this farm. Even in dealing with Johnny, George had not been cruel. Despite George's refusal to deed Johnny property outright, George had offered him a place to live when he got out of jail, and George would not have denied his brother anything, if only Johnny had hung around and worked a little instead of taking off again. George now felt tugged by a rare urge to stand close to this girl—as close as possible, to touch her even. Politeness and patience, however, kept him where he was, a few yards away. He knew he could easily calculate her age, but he didn't. Perhaps if she'd been a complete stranger, the attraction he felt toward her would have made sense, but he must have seen her from a distance at least once a week for her entire life.

George said, "The Indians had a strange kind of garden. You'll have to come see sometime. I'm George."

"I know who you are. Owner of all this damn land."

Another man might have been bothered by her tone, but George was so accustomed to the unpredictable and sometimes violent forces he encountered in nature that he didn't take the anger personally. He was thinking he could stand there all day puzzling over her face, but she looked back at him with a burning gaze that made him start to feel like an intruder on his own farm, made the hair stand up on his neck. George said so long and climbed up into the Case tractor. He went back to work in such a way that he didn't stir up dirt around her. He liked the idea of her digging into the ground where he could watch her, but by the time he turned around at the end of the row, she was walking away in the direction of the *Glutton*. The rifle swung so easily over her shoulder that George imagined the metal of the barrel might be soft like human flesh. As the girl moved farther away, he felt himself unraveling, as though she had caught the end of the ribbon of his gut on her bare foot and was uncoiling him as she walked. She disappeared behind the walnut trees near the creek.

After that day, every time he turned his tractor around at the end of a row, he hoped to see the girl searching for her graves, and at night he tried to remember the contours of her face. He'd been fine living alone for years, but now he began to feel all broken up. Of course he'd missed his ex-wife, Carla, who'd shared his home and life for eighteen years, and he'd long missed his father and mother, who'd moved to Florida more than two decades ago, and Johnny, who made things lively, if problematic, whenever he was around. His best friend, Tom Parks, had moved to Texas years ago, but until George saw that girl, his loneliness had been tempered and calm, constant and bearable. For years George had been like one of those clay-heavy fields lying frozen in winter; this girl showing up in front of him was like a big spring rain whose waters were too heavy to soak in. When Milton opened the Barn Grill that summer, George went often in hopes of seeing Rachel working in the garden out back.

"Poor girl," Milton said, when he saw George watching her through the new insulated vinyl windows he'd installed.

"Why poor girl?" George was thinking about ordering a third draft beer.

"Oh, having that crazy mother and all." Milton walked away from George and straightened the dartboard, at the center of which he'd affixed a tiny cartoon Satan. "Margo hasn't ever threatened to shoot you, has she?"

"Actually she did, once," George said. "Lately, though, I'd have to say, she hasn't been much of a threat to anybody, including the woodchucks that are eating my soybeans. I wanted to tell her there was a nest over on P Road, but I haven't seen her."

Milton said, "And that poor girl doesn't believe in Jesus Christ, Our Savior. I'm not giving up on her, though. I don't want a girl like her burning in hell."

George nodded. Way out in the garden, the girl turned toward the Barn Grill and crossed her arms. George stepped back from the window and looked beside him at the plastic-framed icon in which Jesus sat at the Last Supper; as George tilted his head, a 3-D prismatic effect made Jesus ascend toward heaven. Milton seemed to have gained all the Christianity George had lost over his lifetime— maybe there was only a certain amount of religion to be spread around in a community. George thought Milton's newest acquisition, a wooden crucifix above the cash register, gave a surprisingly muscular interpretation of Jesus.

After serving drafts to a couple of guys in John Deere caps, Milton returned to stand beside George and gestured to the two-foot-high crucifix.

"Nice piece, eh?"

George nodded.

"Got it from a Polish fellow up north, a wood-carver," Milton said. "Say, George, I know it ain't none of my business, but I always wondered. I hope you don't mind my asking, but why'd you give that girl's ma a perfectly good acre of your land?" Milton gestured toward Rachel. "You made Johnny mad enough to leave town."

"Wasn't a full acre, more like three quarters."

Outside, Rachel squatted and resumed weeding.

"Well, why anyways?"

"I guess when you think about a woman like Margo, it reminds you that you're going to die someday," George said. Way back when George surprised Margo and encountered the business end of her rifle, Carla was threatening to leave him, and Johnny was in jail and asking for money George didn't have, and his father in Florida was saying that before George went any deeper into debt he should sell the land and split the money among everyone in the family. Having a woman like Margo pointing a rifle into his face somehow put it all in perspective—his head cleared instantly. When Margo realized who he was, she'd apologized and acted civilized.

"You mean you thought she might kill you?" Milton said

"I guess I thought she deserved something for keeping the wildlife from eating my crops."

Milton said, "Why do you think a woman like her would turn her daughter against Jesus? A woman has a right to forsake her own soul, but why her daughter's soul, too?"

George said, "I couldn't farm that piece of land, anyways. I'd have to build a bridge to get my equipment over the creek. That's why I'd always left it as woods." There was another reason he'd given Margo the land, one he didn't want to admit to Milton. George had figured the breakup of his farm was imminent and fast approaching, and he'd wanted to get the first cut behind him. Then somehow his sacrifice of less than an acre had paid off—it was as though he'd butchered a calf for one of those old gods. Things had picked up somewhat since then; six years ago, George had even bought the Parkses' land across Queer Road, though maybe he'd paid too much per acre.

Whenever George dragged his irrigation machinery with the tractor that summer after seeing Rachel, or trekked out to problem spots in his fields or drove the half mile between his house and his oldest barn, he watched for the girl. Whenever he searched the horizon, it was in hopes that she would step from behind bushes or rise out of the ground. Even a glimpse of her would suffice, he told himself. George thought this desire didn't belong in his life, but was of some other world where men savored desire as pleasurable in itself, apart from its object. For George, such desire seemed foreign, a remnant of a past civilization or of a decadent future dreamed up by idle men who spent their days not in fields of grain but in tiled bathhouses, oiling their bodies and taking massages. The unseemliness of his thoughts gave him the idea that he owed the girl an apology.

Rather than disappearing or becoming routine, his desire continued to grow, shift and absorb him, sometimes striking with such intensity that it blurred his vision, such as when a deer lifted its head in the distance or when he noticed something bright floating in the river. After months of grappling with this hunger, he felt that there was no patience left in him, no kindness, no sleep or sense, and after a weeklong stretch without any rest whatsoever, he took to roaming at night, as he hadn't done since he was a kid.

One night in September, George walked across the plank bridge over the creek, to within a few yards of the dark *Glutton*. He listened to the slurping sounds of night, the splash of water creatures hunting and returning to nests to feed and protect their young. He followed the creek upstream. As he neared his big barn, he tried to cross the creek by balancing on rocks the way he used to, but he lost his footing and sloshed in water the rest of the way, pausing in the deepest part to let the cold current run over the tops of his work boots. He knew there should be a moon three quarters full—it must have been at an angle behind trees or hills. Soon he would begin harvesting, working late into the night, but that would be in the combine with lights and noise. Now he heard only creeping, swishing, and rustling in the grasses and trees. Standing at the edge of the field beside the creek, George thought he felt the ache of the soybeans to be harvested, the sound of the earth hushing and soothing the plants, as though this land were some native creature he didn't really own. He worried that, as a farmer, he was becoming useless and dull: he hadn't noticed a rust fungus affecting over an acre of beans until Mike Retakker had pointed it out to him last month. With Mike's help he could go through the routine of harvest, but if anything went wrong, if he had to make an important decision or a fast, tricky repair to the combine, he didn't think he could be trusted. When the moon finally appeared, the stones of the foundation of the old house shone like grave markers. He turned away from them and approached his old barn. The sliding door he'd rebuilt rolled open with a sound like a sigh. Alfalfa, sweet and dusty, masked the manure smell from the lower level, where George kept the beef cattle a farmer had traded him for some hay. Over the course of the summer, he and Mike had more than halfway filled this upper level with hay and straw, and he hoped they'd get the rest in soon. George sat on a bale of alfalfa and looked into what should have been empty darkness, but instead he saw a glimmer of light reflected in the eyes of Rachel Crane. He identified her shape crouching on the hay-strewn floor by the silhouette of her rifle, which she slowly let drop.

"I'm sorry," he said, and fell forward onto his knees. He wasn't sure which apology this was—the one for disturbing her or for desiring her. "I'm sorry," he repeated, and moved closer. When she laid her gun in the straw, he reached toward her face, but with no more hope of touching it than of touching the moon's far side.

"Christ," he said, at the shock of his fingers meeting her warm cheek.

"Johnny?" Rachel's voice sounded shaky.

George moved closer and cupped her face but didn't dare look into those eyes. Her breathing was quiet, as though she were controlling it to track an animal. She reached up and touched his mangled hand, studied the stump of his index finger with her own fingers.

"What the hell do you want?" she said, but she didn't pull away.

George ran his hand over her hair, which was cool and coarse. He meant to say something about her being beautiful, but it would seem like nothing here in the dark, so he just squeezed her hair in one hand and moved the other down her flannel shirtsleeve and over her jeans, following her thigh to her calf to her foot, which he found to be callused and warm. He wondered how far into autumn she would go without shoes. When he slid his hands beneath her shirt her breath became audible, like his own, and her muscles tightened and she choked a little. Though everything about the girl had made George move hesitantly over the last few months, he now grabbed her and held her body the way a wild animal might grab its reluctant mate. She twisted away but only enough to tug off her jeans. George couldn't imagine untying his rawhide boot laces, wet from the creek, and so he just dragged his pants down to his knees and rolled on top of her. He felt too naked and too old, but despite that and despite his months of awkward longing, his desire became, for that moment, a simple sexual thing. He wrapped his arms all the way around beneath her and pressed her onto the loose hay, and he couldn't stop himself from coming apart after only a minute. When George relaxed his grip, the girl began to wail, a sound so mournful that his blood slowed in his veins. He tried to pull away from the animal noise, but her arms were locked around his back.

"Damn you," she whispered. "Goddamn you."

He pulled against her grip until she finally let loose of him. "Oh, Rachel," he said. "I am so sorry."

"Shut up," she said, and crawled far enough away that he could no longer make out her face.

"Forgive me."

"Just shut the hell up!" She stood with her clothes in one hand and her rifle in the other, and strode naked out through the open door, leaving George kneeling alone. The duration of their being together had been only a couple of minutes, but George felt like an entirely different person, a bad man, terrible with age, heavy with guilt. He started to pull his pants up, but dropped them and sat on the nearest hay bale and wept into his hands, grateful for the pain of alfalfa stalks poking him.

George began harvesting not long thereafter, and though he said nothing to Mike, who worked with him and hauled wagons to the elevator in Climax Township, he felt sure his soybeans were rotten, and when he looked at each load of beans or corn and saw it was not rotten, he knew it was poisoned. He became afraid of seeing Rachel at the end of each row, her round face bruised or diseased or sad. George had ruined something. He'd broken branches in the fruit trees of Eden, and now he awaited retribution: plagues of insects or weather so fierce and destructive that it would not only signal the end but bring it violently to bear. Every evening afterward, as the sun set, all during the harvest, he thought about driving his tractor or his combine or his truck right down into the river to drown.

9

ON OCTOBER 9, 1999, AS GEORGE THREW THE NINETEENTH bale of hay to David in the old barn to the south, Nicole Hoekstra returned to the kitchen to find her husband had gone off to work. She got the feeling Steve was sneaking away, even though it was normal for him to put in half a day on Saturday. Nicole was never inclined to volunteer for weekend work at the hospital office, but Steve was a born salesman, selling wholeheartedly, unabashedly— even to his own neighbors—with an energy and enthusiasm that Nicole had begun to find irritating. During this second year of their marriage, she had found herself angry with her husband as often as not, and then, a month ago, he'd come home smelling of sex and another woman. She'd felt too confused to confront him that night, and once he showered away the smell, she'd had no evidence. Though she knew the truth, she worried that if she brought up the subject, Steve might trick her into thinking she had been mistaken. Or, worse, it was possible that talking with him about himself and another woman would make it seem natural, even acceptable. Steve had a way of conversing that made you feel, momentarily at least, that everything was okay.

As the twentieth bale of straw got settled into position, Nicole turned on the gas jet beneath the stainless steel kettle in order to make a cup of tea. Steve drank coffee, but Nicole thought coffee tasted dirty and burned. At first the idea of killing Steve had shocked her so much that she'd wept, but she'd gotten used to such thoughts in the last few weeks and even let herself enjoy them. Nicole's desire to kill Steve was never vague or abstract, but always rich in detail. As she waited for the tea water to boil, she thought she might walk behind the recliner she'd bought for his birthday, holding a knife against her right leg. She'd pretend she was just bringing him a bowl of dry roasted nuts. She'd reach around from behind with her left hand, grab his chin and tip it back, then slice his throat. Afterward she'd be in a jail cell with nothing but a toothbrush, a cup, and the memory of Steve's bleeding and gurgling body sprawled across the chair. In her prison-issue blues she'd weep about how much she loved him, and that sort of emotional clarity might be a welcome relief from thinking about him with another woman. The day she killed Steve would be remarkable in a way different from her wedding day, but the two days would be like a pair of bookends around her marriage.

She'd wanted to marry the big, handsome man the moment she met him negotiating window installation at her mother's house. Nicole had marveled at the way he kept saying the right thing—to her, to her mother, to strangers. Nowadays she felt that his saying the right thing was just a salesman's trick to make conversation go smoothly, to cover up the likelihood that things were not fine, that maybe a person was being sold something she didn't really want. Nicole turned up the flame under her kettle to hurry the water and she slid out the chef's knife to study it. The blade was wide enough that she could see in it a crude reflection of herself. She gritted her teeth and the reflection smiled. Nicole gripped the knife in both hands and stabbed downward into empty air with a force that surprised her. Stab, stab, stab. She squeaked out a scream, then looked around, though of course nobody could have heard her.

Nicole wished there were some way to talk about all this with her mother, but she wasn't ready for her mother to think she was crazy, and anyway it was just a fantasy. In reality Nicole was not violent at all; she was a gentle person who liked baby animals and pretty things, who liked to decorate her home tastefully. When they'd moved into this five-year-old house, Nicole had wanted everything to be new for them. For the walls and ceiling, a coat of paint was sufficient, but she'd also wanted new carpeting to make their lives fresh and hopeful. Her marriage plans hadn't included somebody else's carpeting. Maybe having another woman's fibers touching Steve's feet was what made him crave other women.

"The carpet is fine," Steve had said. "They bought this carpet less than a year ago. We have the receipts. Why waste money on new carpeting?"

This morning it had become clear to Nicole that to make things right in their marriage, they needed a new house built exactly to their specifications. In order to make Steve desire only her, they needed two stories, a wraparound porch, and a beautiful view. Only then would Nicole be happy again, as she surely must have been before Steve came home smelling of that other woman. After taking the kettle from the stove, she let the gas flame flicker for a while, gold and blue, before turning it off.

While waiting for her tea to cool, she thumbed further through the new *Beautiful Home* magazine and saw the most charming kitchen curtains in a butterscotch and white gingham. Her own kitchen curtains, which her mother had made for her as a housewarming gift, were looking drab after only six months.

As George Harland handed the twenty-ninth bale to David Retakker, Nicole went into the bathroom to apply her makeup. By the time she returned to her tea, it was too cool to enjoy. She put her lukewarm cup in the microwave, but already she didn't really want the old reheated tea. Already there was something inferior about it. She needed to go to the mall, but she wanted Steve to go with her, and he wouldn't be back until after noon. Such a dull, dreary morning, certainly not the kind of day on which a woman would murder the man she loved.

10

AFTER THE DESPERATE NIGHT WITH RACHEL IN THE BARN
in autumn 1997, George had immersed himself in the business of
self-loathing and tried to leave the girl out of it altogether, but his
efforts only made him think of her more. Pushing thoughts of her
under the surface resulted in roots spreading in all directions: she
sprouted everywhere in his consciousness. Over the course of harvesting, George kept worrying she'd appear in front of his tractor,
perhaps so suddenly that he couldn't avoid crushing her. During his
sleepless nights, he sensed her standing outside the house, cursing
him. During the winter that followed, he walked gingerly through
snow, imagining her lying in hibernation beneath each drift. By
spring he found that the soil under his feet was imbued with her,
and the process of cultivating seemed criminal, as though by disturbing the dirt with his plows, he were tearing her body apart.
George used to see himself as producing nourishment, but now he
feared he was only scarring and depleting the earth.

Though he went over and over it in his mind, Rachel's calling him Johnny made no logical sense. George resembled his brother physically, but there was nothing his missing brother could be to Rachel. Her calling him Johnny did make sense in a more profound way, however, for George felt he had become Johnny. All his life he'd thought himself better than his careless, shiftless brother, and now it was clear he was no better, for surely even Johnny had never done anything as reprehensible as molesting an innocent girl. What made him hate himself most was that he couldn't honestly regret what he'd done, that he'd felt Rachel's rough, warm skin against his, her steady breath on his neck and chest, her muscular limbs twisting around his, her river-smelling hair brushing his face, and the way she'd locked her hands behind his back and held him when he tried to pull away.

He considered going to Rachel and begging forgiveness. He'd offer her anything he had. He'd deed her an Indian grave site if she could find it. He'd help her find it. But night after night he resisted seeking her out, knowing he couldn't trust himself. He became accustomed to not sleeping, to just lying awake each night, trying to imagine her face, wondering if time passed differently for someone so young. He wondered what the girl did all day, whether she hunted alongside her mother, or whether she dug up ground all over Greenland in search of bones. Or would she be in school? (Again he resisted the urge to calculate her age.) What would she and her mother talk about when they sat together on the boat with no comforts, no electricity? Day after day, George worked with or without Mike Retakker and held just enough hope in his heart that he did not once drive his tractor or his truck into the river.

Then, as if in reward for George's steady work and his decision at the end of each day to live to see another one, as though beckoned there by the longevity of his thoughts, Rachel showed up outside George's house one evening in late May, eight months after the incident in the barn. Instead of knocking, she stood by the kitchen door with her arms crossed, her rifle slung over her shoulder. George had no idea how long she'd been there before he saw her after supper. He considered that perhaps she had come to shoot him.

"Come in," he said.

"I want to see your damn garden."

"What garden?"

"You said there was a goddamn Indian garden here."

"Oh, the Indian garden. Let me get my boots on." The shameful memory of his wet boots in the barn all those months ago washed over him. "Please, come in."

She entered reluctantly and stood facing his kitchen cupboards as though she were angry with the dishes there, both the dirty dishes on the left side of the sink and the clean dishes draining on the right; she seemed angry at the store-bought cans of vegetables stacked against the back of the counter beneath the sooty pine cupboard doors.

George had intended to plant sixty more acres before dark that night, and then he would recalculate the planter settings for the sloped field across P Road. Instead of all that, he guided Rachel out the back porch door, into the woods northwest of the house.

"I don't see any goddamn thing," Rachel said. She'd been in or near these woods hundreds of times. She and David had trekked across the edge only a week before to get to some wild onion and wild ginger, which they'd chewed alternately until they'd had enough of both flavors. They hadn't seen anything special.

"Look at the ground," George said, making the motion of waves with his damaged hand. "The way it rises and falls."

For Rachel it was as if the ground rose into sharp relief beneath her feet and rolled like waves. Beneath the trees, bushes, and vines, there were curves. The depressed furrows lay about five feet apart, and between each pair the land rose to about eight inches high, then dipped again toward the next furrow. Rachel reached out and touched the branches of a box elder to steady herself against the sensation of motion. She walked between two of the mounds, and when she felt overwhelmed again, she let herself sink down cross-legged into a shallow trench. Farther out, the curves were less pronounced but still visible once you knew what you were looking for. She said, "I would think this was a big old goddamn graveyard."

"I figure they planted in the mounds and walked in the trenches," George said. "Or maybe they irrigated in them."

"You don't know?"

"I didn't think to ask when my grandfather told me about them," George said. "And I haven't got much experience with vegetable gardens."

Maybe George Harland wasn't a gardener, but Rachel was, and she was thinking that this was the garden for her. She'd assumed all this time that her recurring dream of mounded earth was about dead people. Maybe for the last year and a half since her mother disappeared, she'd actually been dreaming of an Indian garden. She began to feel trickles of relief in her limbs. She remained sitting in a depression between two mounds for a long while, long enough that George sat as well and leaned his back against the same box elder she'd just touched. Rachel lay back into the furrow, and then reached her hands over the mounds beside her and slowly pulled herself up. It made her feel as though she were dragging herself out of her own grave with the strength of her own arms. She had assumed she'd plant her little riverside garden this year, and she liked Milton's big flat garden just fine, but here she got the feeling that a garden might become an extension of a person's body, or maybe it was the other way around, that her body might become part of the garden. If she could get rid of the damn trees, this garden would be even bigger than Milton's. Think of all she could grow! She wondered if Milton had felt this certain when he discovered his god.

Though George had planned to work right up until dark, he knew that if this girl disappeared again, he might never be able to plant another field. If she walked away now, he told himself, he'd just lie down and not get up again, let his body return to the soil, or let the neighborhood dogs drag his sorry dead carcass across the Indian garden. He said, "I think there are drawings of more gardens in the upstairs storeroom. There were hundreds of acres of them at one time, in all different shapes. You want to see?"

"Hell yes." She stood and waited for him to stand, then followed him into the house, up the stairs to the second floor, and to the north end of the hall into a room George had opened only a few times since his grandfather died. They unrolled the maps onto the raw, dusty pine floor, and George strained to remember all he'd been told as a boy. Rachel listened without speaking while he explained that his great-great-great-grandparents had documented all the original garden beds and had saved twenty-some acres, and that his great-great-grandfather, the one who had built the old barn, had continued saving the gardens until the year his pigs made a mess of them rooting for moles. This man finally plowed all but an acre of the garden mounds under and used the land to grow more rye and corn. Rachel continued studying locations and measurements in relation to the river and creek. There were several rectangular plots and one triangular one with more closely spaced beds, and even one site, not far from the *Glutton,* where the garden had resembled a wagon wheel, round with spoke furrows emanating from a central mounded hub. If it were there today, Rachel figured, the creek would run through its center.

George silently thanked his predecessors for documenting those gardens before plowing them under. Thank God he'd had something with which to lure Rachel inside. Though he had never harbored a violent thought against another human, George looked over at the tarnished brass doorknob and considered locking Rachel in this room and keeping her here. Not only did he find this thought reprehensible even as it occurred to him, but he knew a girl like Rachel could get out of a locked room. In order to keep her here with him, he'd have to figure out exactly what she wanted and give it to her.

The sun went down as they were sitting in the attic, and the slanted light through the west window made the air look so thick with dust that George was surprised they were breathing without effort. When it was nearly dark, he asked, "So how's your ma?"

"She's gone." Rachel's shoulders curled away from the wall as she spoke. "I haven't seen her for more than two months." In fact, it had been a year and a half; George was the first person she'd told.

George felt a surge of relief at hearing this, though he knew only a brute could be happy about a girl losing her mother. He moved from the leather trunk and sat beside her on the floor. "So you've been living alone on that boat for two months."

"It's not a big deal."

They sat side by side, leaning against the rough plaster wall as the sun set, as the old dust settled. Rachel sighed and her shoulders sank further, and George imagined her disappearing beneath the floorboards as beneath the surface of a body of water. When she sighed again George negotiated his body between her and the wall so she sat between his legs with her back against his chest. He wrapped his arms and legs around her in a sitting position, so she was contained, buoyed within his limbs. He bent his head so it touched hers, and for hours in the dark he breathed through her hair. Rachel seemed to fall asleep and awaken intermittently throughout the night, stiffening against his arms and legs, then relaxing into them. When either of George's legs fell asleep, he moved as slightly as possible to revive it. He listened for owls, but didn't hear any, and in those hours he decided that from here forward he was all on his own with this girl. There was no manual of protocol that would explain or condone this, no council of elders who could grant approval due to exceptional circumstances. All night Rachel's hands gripped George's arms, but at the first strains of light she stood, disentangling herself from him. She grabbed the doorknob as though making sure she wasn't trapped. She paused and said, "I'll bring my ma's chain saw and we can cut down the goddamn trees."

"Fine. I can use the firewood." George loved the maples, oaks, and hickories northwest of his house; he loved the woods, blossoming now with wild geranium, but Rachel could have it for her garden. She could burn down his house or level it if she wanted. George would gladly live with her in a wigwam if she'd have him. Whatever he'd once felt for his first wife was but a shimmer of what he felt for this person. His long marriage had been one stalk of desire that gradually sagged and then broke beneath the weight and decay of passing seasons. Now he felt acre after acre of this thrilling new crop sprout in a field so vast he couldn't imagine its edges. He already needed Rachel the way he needed the weather, but he didn't get up and follow and didn't say anything to try to stop her from leaving, didn't even mention he had a chain saw she could use.

George went downstairs and made coffee and sat at his round kitchen table while the sun rose. He was unable to focus on any of the jobs that lay before him, and when he heard the buzz of a two-stroke engine outside, the sound of Rachel felling the first small trees, he knew he'd been granted another reprieve. When Mike showed up for work, George sent him to Cassopolis for tractor parts, while he himself stayed and notched trees for Rachel and yanked stumps with the Ford backhoe. When Rachel ran out of chain saw gas, George mixed her more. By sunset, both of them were sweating and exhausted, and they lay together in one of the furrows. Rachel wiggled out of her clothes beside him as though she had never meant to wear clothes at all, but George felt nervous undressing out-of-doors. Thoughts of neighbors and cars passing on the road disappeared, however, when Rachel grabbed him and handled him as though he were a chain saw to be employed, or trees to be felled, some kind of wild land to be tamed. He took his flannel shirt off over his head, though he'd never in his life taken off a button-up shirt without first unbuttoning it. The smell of her sweat woke him again from something he hadn't known was sleep, but instead of grabbing her as he'd done in the barn, he first buried his face in every part of her. Though Rachel's first choking screams of pleasure were so violent that crows returned calls from the trees, her curses gradually softened so that she was swearing in a tone almost tender. When George let himself go, it was with such force that he feared he'd passed his guts into the girl. He knew he'd never be able to put himself back together the same way again.

"Marry me," he said, looking into her dirt-streaked face. Lying on the ground with his chin perched in his hand, he felt as though he were twenty-two again, twenty-two and stupid, happy and afraid. But when he'd actually been twenty-two, nothing had been as rich as this.

He watched her adjust her body in the dirt. She pulled away from him, tipped her head back to rest it against a mound. Her rifle lay within her grasp, and she looked at him with no expression, through close-set, bloodshot eyes. She might reach out to strangle him as easily as to caress him. Her body in twilight was almost too much to look upon; her hipbone, her strange out-poking navel, her breast, the side of her throat were of some other world, and even in that world, where beauty was but the crudest version of whatever power Rachel possessed, there were no words for the fierce line of her jaw or the wing of her cheekbone. He didn't want to think of what they'd just had together as sex. The phrase *making love* seemed like nothing.

"Will you please marry me?" he said.

"Why the hell would I marry you?"

"I'll give you everything I have."

"Your land?"

George was scared but went on. "If you marry me, it's half yours."

"Milton says you're going to sell your land."

"I'm not planning on selling."

"How much land have you got?"

"Almost nine hundred acres, including land I bought from the Parkses." His heart was pounding down in his stomach and his groin, everywhere his guts used to be. "Eight hundred eighty acres."

"So I'll have four hundred forty acres."

"We both own all of it until I die, then it's all yours."

"Fine. When can we get married?" Rachel brushed ants off her shoulder and put her jeans beneath her as a pillow, fidgeting in an effort to stay calm. She had never considered marriage. Marriage was as foreign to her as Milton's god. For the Potawatomi Corn Girl, getting married meant going away and losing everything; for Rachel, marriage would mean staying and getting what she'd always wanted. The thought of owning the land made her dizzy and a little sleepy, as though she had spent a long day hunting and now needed to rest before cooking and eating her kill.

"How old are you?" George asked.

"Fifteen."

"Holy mother of Christ." George looked up at the darkening sky. "Strike me dead, God, if that's what you want. Strike me dead now!"

Rachel studied a deep L-shaped scar on his shoulder, then looked down his long, pale body, to his tender-looking feet. She wondered how a man with such feet had survived here. All men apparently felt free to call on Milton's god whenever it suited them, as if He were up there with nothing better to do than serve, punish, or reward them. Rachel wanted too much in this world to sit around and wait for God to give it to her, and she wasn't about to risk His taking it away.

She dug at the dirt beneath her, mounding more of it up under her head. In the year and a half she'd been alone, she had yearned for this property, but she hadn't considered what she'd do if it were really hers. She supposed she'd want bees to make honey, and Jonathan apple trees, and even more blackcap raspberries. She'd grow tall grass near the river for lightning bugs. She wondered if all those textures of soil—silty muck, sand, blue clay, and dark woods loam—would feel different when she owned them. She considered the low growth beneath wide-spreading oaks on the ridge and the beds of soft needles beneath white pines at the sandy place and the sponginess of heavily rooted soil near the water's edge where ground birds were reluctant to leave nests of speckled eggs. And as for this garden, she would grow more peppers and cucumbers than Milton Taylor. A dozen times a day all summer, she'd bite into ripe tomatoes and let the juice run down her face. She'd produce hundreds of squashes of every color and shape, and there'd be no end of sweetness in her muskmelons and watermelons.

She sank the fingers of her left hand into the torn-up soil of her new Indian garden, which she already loved more deeply than she imagined she would ever love a person, even David Retakker. She rubbed her hip and belly with a handful of cool black dirt. She would lie on Johnny's grave and see how it felt to own his dead body. She wondered how long it took this soil to devour a person completely.

George Harland lay beside her in the dirt, ecstatic and afraid, thinking about how bad a person he had become. He thought he now understood every crooked, immoral man who wanted something he shouldn't have, wanted it badly enough that he'd sell his soul to get it. He sympathized with Johnny, who once went to jail for stabbing a man in a fight over that man's wife. He understood the robbers of banks and liquor stores who needed money for drugs; maybe there was even sense in the cold killing of civilians in times of war if the killing moved the soldiers toward their desired ends. As George lay beside Rachel, the world seemed to him vaster and more complicated than before, and he finally understood the gravity of what his grandfather Harold had tried to tell him all those years ago, that once you had forsaken the simple rules about right and wrong and set out on your own, the universe was a humbling place. In the future as in the past, this farm should be handed along responsibly from one generation to the next, but George would give it away as a love token. His grandmother sharing her land with his grandfather seemed a sober business, but George sharing it with Rachel was like rollicking drunkenness.

If she'd stay, his life would change completely. He'd be chancing jail. He would stop going to township meetings, and he and Rachel couldn't very well go to lunch together in Greenland. George didn't know how April May or Milton would receive the news but he was glad for the first time that his police officer buddy Tom Parks had moved to Texas. (George was able to forget momentarily that Parks had written, saying he would be returning within a few months.) George's life was about to become strange and, to the outside world, sordid. George's mouth watered for that change. He had never liked going to township meetings anyway.

"What would happen if your ma found you here with me?" George asked.

Rachel turned and glanced behind her, but otherwise did not respond. One of her breasts was uncovered, so George leaned into her and pressed his cheek there and inhaled her river smell, for which he would happily forsake all other perfumes. When he opened his eyes, he noticed a bluish welt on her shoulder, and he wondered if she'd been violated in some way, tied up maybe, and it took him awhile to realize it was a disfigurement from carrying that rifle on a sling. He resisted a desire to brush away the dirt from her body. He noticed a starburst of white and red scars near her armpit. Oh, Rachel, he thought, and closed his eyes again in order not to see other wounds. George thought his heart would pound through his ribs with this new emotion, this mixture of love and terror. He tried to breathe evenly so she would think he was asleep. He felt her reach out and touch his forehead. She whispered, "Damn you to hell."

11

ON OCTOBER 9, 1999, SIX WEEKS AFTER GEORGE HARLAND married Rachel Crane (and a year and a half after George had originally proposed in the garden), Officer Tom Parks of the Kalamazoo County Sheriff's Department watched seagulls land and fight over the stale butter-flavored popcorn somebody had tossed out into the cop shop's parking lot. As George Harland threw the thirty-eighth bale of straw to David inside the big barn miles to the east, Tom Parks looked up from the gulls to study the painting he'd recently hung above the window, a depiction of three lean Indian men in buckskin and single-feather headdress. On the way to work this morning, something about the weather had made Tom Parks feel uneasy, depressed even, and a little anxious. Though the grass and farmlands were dry enough to burn, the air felt wet and heavy. This seemed to Parks the kind of day on which a fellow could make a rash decision that would screw up the rest of his life—say, deciding to move to Texas, as Parks had done some years ago. Or agreeing to sell his family's farm or allowing the house to be torn down. On a day like today, a cop might clearly make out a gun in another guy's hand and shoot, only to learn later it had been one of those little telephones or a cable-cutting tool.

Parks unwrapped his carry-out egg, cheese, and sausage sandwich without looking at it. He didn't know why he bought fast food—it didn't fill him up but only piqued his appetite for something finer, less processed. When he was first married, his wife had cooked for him in the mornings, and those breakfasts had filled him, surely. In five bites the sandwich was gone, and Tom Parks searched the wrinkles of the paper wrapper for more, before wadding it into a tight ball, stuffing it in the bag, and throwing the bag into the can under his desk. He knew he'd need something else before lunch.

Out in Greenland Tom Parks rarely saw gulls, but they always showed up in downtown Kalamazoo, in mall parking lots and here at the county cop shop. When the gulls landed on the asphalt, you could see they were big birds, as big as wild ducks. So why was there no gull à l'orange? he wondered. Why no Peking gull? If the gulls had been around when Tom Parks and George Harland were kids, they would've tried eating them. They'd killed and cooked all sorts of creatures from the sky and water—English sparrows, ducks, crayfish, bluegills, even river catfish, which had probably been toxic. Back then neither he nor George had cared that the Harlands owned the creek that flowed into the river, no more than they had cared that the Parkses owned the little pond on the east side of Queer Road from which the creek flowed. Now George owned it all. Parks wondered if the seagulls followed the roads thinking they were streams, if they landed in parking lots thinking they were ponds and lakes. Asphalt probably looked like water from the sky, and once the birds landed, they were too foolish to be disappointed.

Stress always made Parks overeat. He'd overeaten all through his divorce, but his habit had never been so bad as since his return to Greenland last autumn. That business with George and Rachel had been a heck of a thing to come back to. It was bad enough to return from Texas to face two new houses on his old land and the Taylor farm turned into a golf course, but to find his best friend shacked up with a kid was too much. Not only was Rachel a fraction of George's age, but everything about the girl made Tom Parks nervous, starting with her mother's disappearance, and that awful swearing—if any kid of his swore that way, he'd wash her mouth out with soap. Parks hated her dragging that rifle around, though strictly speaking it wasn't illegal on private land. He'd tried to talk George out of marrying Rachel, but George had refused to listen to reason, and Parks hadn't been able to figure out how to encourage a breakup between two people who apparently didn't even talk to each other.

Milton Taylor had been distressed too and for a time had tried to prevent the union, but then Milton changed his mind and committed himself to seeing the two legally joined, figuring it was better than their living in sin. George was Parks's best friend, and so Parks eventually agreed that as soon as Rachel turned seventeen he would testify before the judge that this marriage was reasonable. Because it had been important to George, Parks had even agreed to witness the courthouse ceremony. George had looked neat and clean in a suit jacket, which Parks recognized as the one he'd worn to the funeral of Parks's father years ago, but Rachel looked the way she always did in a pair of George's jeans rolled up over cheap canvas shoes. There was no denying she was a unique-looking girl—even the magistrate, Deborah Vissers, had been visibly shocked by her and looked repeatedly to Parks for acknowledgment of the strangeness of this marriage, when she normally would have been smiling in a congratulatory way at the bride and groom.

"Does the groom have a ring?" Vissers had asked.

George shook his head. Rachel just stared at her. Vissers pronounced them husband and wife without a ring, and despite Parks's reservations, he found himself becoming tearful. Parks had been divorced more than six years, and he doubted any woman would ever again want to marry him or even make love with him.

There'd been some trouble getting Rachel inside the Kalamazoo county courthouse to begin with, because even when she emptied her pockets, she set off the metal detector. She begrudgingly told the guards she had a bullet in the back of her arm from a shooting accident, and she'd rolled her sleeve all the way up to her armpit to expose flesh scarred as though wild animals had clawed at her. The sight had made Tom Parks's skin crawl, had made him feel queasy and confused. George had looked fearful standing on the other side, as if worried the guards would keep Rachel and not give her back. Once outside the building afterward, while waiting for George and Milton, Parks found himself briefly alone with the girl, and he had to ask, "Why'd you want to go and marry such an old guy as George?" Parks couldn't help but compare her to George's first wife, Carla, their old schoolmate, flirtatious and funny; by the end, though, Carla had been bored out of her mind by farm life. She'd headed out to California even before their divorce was final.

"Because I want his damn land," Rachel said. Parks didn't look into her face but down at her hand, which was clutching the marriage license as though it were cash or a blue chip stock certificate— or rather, he told himself, a deed to property. Parks had said good-bye and gone off and sat in his cruiser and stewed. All he could think of was that George had paid for Parks's family land fair and square, while this kid had no right to it. Now, as he sat at his desk in the station, he tried to focus some anger on George for taking up with the girl, but mostly the anger bounced back to himself for selling out, for being such a fool. Way back when Tom and his wife had been on the verge of divorce the first time, when his wife insisted they move to Texas and get a fresh start, Parks had agreed they needed a drastic measure to save their marriage; but if he'd stayed in Michigan, maybe his father wouldn't have died of a heart attack, as he did less than a year after Tom left. If Tom had stayed, he would have found an alternative to selling the family property. And if Tom Parks and his wife had divorced in Michigan, the local courts would never have allowed her to take the kids so far away, but since they'd split up in Texas, Tom had no way to make them move back. Thinking about all this made Parks crave something creamy or chocolate from the vending machine, which stood only about twelve feet from his desk.

When Parks initially asked Rachel what she thought happened to her ma, Rachel had said, "She's probably at the bottom of the damn river." If you could even get Rachel to stand still and answer a question, her words pretty much shot your own words right out of the air. Recently, the girl had changed her story about *when* her mother had disappeared and then tried to take back what she had said; Parks believed the changed story, that her mother had been gone just over three years. Never mind that Milton and George kept saying they were pretty sure it had been less than that. Straighter kids than Rachel had killed less troublesome parents, and Parks had been worried that George might be in danger. Parks had looked into Rachel's past, but found out nothing more than her birth date, the fact that she had no middle name, and that she had attended Greenland schools and had never been in trouble with the law. Dropping out of school at fifteen was illegal, but you couldn't retroactively make a kid go back and take the month of school she'd missed. In the last week, Parks had been coming to a kind of conclusion about Rachel's ma, and he wanted to get out to Greenland to talk to George about it.

Parks was grateful to be assigned to patrol Greenland Township, but watching all the new houses going up on old farms was rough. He couldn't very well take the high ground, though. The real estate agent who bought his family's deteriorating house on a single acre took it down and sold the land as two residential lots.

Elaine Shore and her husband had bought the southern lot, and Parks supposed it was only fitting that he should have to respond to her complaints about bad smells, illegal parking at the farm stand, and George's animals getting loose. Several times Elaine had called about alien spaceships. One night last October, not long after he'd returned to Michigan, Parks had gotten patched through by an amused station operator, and Parks found himself so intrigued by Elaine's description of something in George's field that he got out of bed and drove up Queer Road. From there he saw for himself George's Hollander combine appearing to hover, lit up against the night in a whirring storm of dust and chaff as it worked its way across a field. The sight was so lovely that Parks had leaned against his car and watched for forty-five minutes. When Elaine Shore had called another time describing red and white spaceship lights in the sky, Parks assured her without even bothering to investigate that they were from a small plane making an emergency landing on the dirt strip beside the golf course.

Thinking about Elaine Shore and the rest of Greenland's new development made Parks crave something that would melt in his mouth. As George threw the forty-fourth bale to David inside the oldest barn in Greenland, Parks forced himself to look away from the vending machine's Swiss rolls and cheese puffs and up to the painting that he'd bought at a museum charity function. It was a student-made copy of a museum oil, depicting local Potawatomi men from the 1830s. Decades ago, George's grandpa had told Parks (along with George and any other kid who would listen) all about the local Indians, the Horseshoe Clan, he called them. Parks figured those men—like the ones in his painting—stayed lean and muscular from the hardworking hunting life, where you caught yourself a squirrel and skinned and gutted it and roasted it on a stick over a fire. And maybe you made a complete dinner by adding some wild onions and a few crab apples so astringent they made your saliva glands shoot spit. You weren't tempted to overeat on squirrel and crab apples, now, were you? Without vending machines and fast food restaurants, there had been little opportunity for the Indians to overindulge. Until the settlers brought whiskey, that is. Parks believed what they said about Indians and firewater because that was how Parks himself was with food—he knew when he should stop eating, but sometimes a meal just made him hungry for another meal.

As George threw the forty-fifth bale to David inside the barn, Officer Parks walked to the machine, dropped four coins in the slot, and pushed the button for a peanut butter and chocolate candy bar.

12

ACROSS THE STREET FROM WHERE GEORGE AND DAVID stacked hay, April May licked the suction cup on the back of a glow-in-the-dark blow-up ghost and stuck it to the inside of her new bay window. She noticed a flock of crows circle and land deep within the cornfield beside the barn as though they were children hiding from grown-ups. The old farmers used to complain that crows pulled their seed corn out of the ground as quickly as it sprouted, but April May knew crows preferred meat, most of all roadkill, because it didn't require a lot of chasing down. According to her *Michigan Bird Book*, crows had never been seen in the state before 1864. When loggers cut roads into the woods, however, the crows, like people from New York, realized that Michigan was fertile and accessible, and as quickly as the white pine forests were felled, both the folks and birds arrived in droves. The settlers showed up in wagons packed with seed and tools and dynamite to blast apart the big stumps, while the crows flew overhead with hardly any effort to nest at the edges of woods, forage in meadows, and pick the bones of the unburied dead. The increase in crows coincided with the decline and extinction of the passenger pigeon, which, at the time the first settlers arrived, had a population in the billions. There were records of Greenland Township baseball games canceled due to the sheer number of passenger pigeons flying overhead, darkening the sky and plastering the ball fields and assembled crowds with nutrient-rich guano. Today there remained not a single passenger pigeon in the world.

April May had rediscovered bird-watching in a serious way only about ten years ago, after her third and youngest daughter had moved out, and when April May had begun to think she no longer loved her husband. Outside the dining room window they'd always kept a bird feeder, and April May used to enjoy that view, but while her daughters were growing up, she often forgot to fill it with seed. On the first few evenings of their new life without their daughters, Larry had seemed to her oafish, crude, and passive, as though his years in the GM plant had worn away all that was once lively and sharp in him. He slogged instead of walking; sometimes he grunted instead of speaking. The dread grew in April May for several weeks, until one morning she just stayed in bed until after he left for work. Eventually her foot ached so much she had to get up and walk on it, but she did not go to the greenhouse to transplant seedlings, and did not even bother to call in sick, but stood at the window and stared at nothing, until she began to notice the birds. Larry must have filled the feeder before he left, and he must have tossed some seed on the ground, because there was all kinds of activity out there. Each time a car drove by, the birds flew up from the lawn in a wave, as though they were parts of some larger whole. Around noon she saw a single rose-breasted grosbeak—a Jesus bird, her mother used to call it, because of the blood-red stain on its chest. Just after the mail truck passed, an indigo bunting glimmered like blue metal. As the sun was setting, tiny sparrows with clownish stripes on their heads pecked at the grass under her lilac. When her husband came home that night, though he neither did nor said anything special, she loved him again.

As George threw the forty-sixth bale to David, April May strung pumpkin lights along the top of the window glass and looped the string around six plastic hooks she'd glued to the frame for this purpose. Usually she hung lights only at Christmas, but she hadn't been able to resist this string, with a little plastic pumpkin mounted over each clear bulb. Two black-and-white female downy woodpeckers were feeding at the suet cage, one at each side, perhaps sisters from the same nest, or a mother and daughter, far less territorial in any case than their male kin. Birds were so much less complicated than people, April May thought. They ate and drank as much as they needed, they fought a bit and settled their differences, and they raised their yearly broods and sent them out of the nest right on schedule. Birds didn't plan their lives, and they rolled with changes in weather or their housing situations. If something destroyed its nest, a bird built a new one. Birds took their regular trips without packing or poring over maps. Either they stayed here all year or they followed their instincts south in autumn, and when they died, they toppled from branches or fell out of the sky without a lot of fuss.

In the last few days, April May had noticed the woolly bears crawling across her driveway and beneath the feeders, apparently unconcerned about the birds pecking at seeds near them. April May had heard and repeated the tale that a small orange band on a woolly bear meant a harsh winter, and nobody could argue with that, seeing how every Michigan winter was harsh. She'd also read in her *Audubon* magazine that the width of the orange band more than likely reflected the maturity of the caterpillar, but the first explanation made a prettier story, one that was more fun to tell her grandchildren. She pressed her nose against the glass and let her breath fog the new window. The caterpillars' determined trekking made her yearn to travel herself, maybe not to get anywhere in particular but just to be moving. She also wanted to see a bird eat a woolly bear—it seemed astounding that in her seventy-two years she'd never seen a bird eat one. She wondered if woolly bears tasted bitter.

She looked across at the Harland barn, where George handed David the forty-seventh bale of straw. Though April May's mother had called Harold Harland a bossy old bag of wind, April May had enjoyed listening to his sad stories, especially about the Indians. And when the tornado put that nail through her foot, Harold had made sense of it by telling her that God must have wanted her to take notice of something that day. There were some days like that, Harold said, days that tipped the world on its edge. April May's mother's comment later was, "Harold's off *his* edge, that's for sure." When George was a kid, he had always paid attention to his grandpa Harold, and April May supposed that was why he had deserved to inherit the farm. April May, twenty years George's senior, had worried that all the talk of loss and regret would make George too serious, and George had indeed grown up to be a serious fellow, which made it even harder for folks around here to reconcile his taking up with young Rachel.

When April May next looked at the feeders, they were empty of birds. A chickadee hugged the leafy underside of the burr oak branch just outside the bay window. At the top of a telephone pole perched a red-tailed hawk, turning its head slowly side to side, as though it, too, were wondering what might happen today.

April May had experienced a number of remarkable events since the 1934 tornado swept away her grammar school teacher and also toppled the house across the street from where she would end up spending most of her life. There were the births of her three daughters and the time the Kalamazoo River had peaked six feet above its banks, flooding Greenland and washing Margo Crane's boat onto George's land. There was the day April May had fallen in love with her husband the first time and the day she'd fallen in love again, and there was one bright night three years ago, when April May had stood outside the Harland barn's lower level and watched Rachel dig the grave in which she buried that bastard Johnny Harland. April May knew about Johnny, had learned too late from her adult daughters how Johnny had taken each of the three, as girls, into the hay barn. On that bright night, April May had stood outside the barn watching Rachel dig for so long that she wondered if her feet might have fused to the ground. Her foot had ached with the inactivity, but the planet was tilting so sharply beneath her that she feared the slightest shift of her body weight would send her tumbling downward. She heard, off and on, a great horned owl from the woods, and all the while, April May's only real feeling of regret had been that a girl so young should have to work so hard.

April May was a law-abiding person, but all that following day and then the next she could not bring herself to report the girl's crime or even tell her husband, Larry (who'd slept through the events of the night), and the longer she kept the secret, the more she felt like an accomplice. Perhaps if she had told Larry what her daughters had told her about Johnny, then she could have told him this, but April May had promised she would not tell their father, and then after Rachel buried the body it seemed too late to start telling everything.

At times she felt unsure of what she'd seen, but she never would forget the sound of Rachel's shovel scraping against stones, hour after hour. Mostly what she had felt while Rachel dug was a weird calmness, a satisfaction at seeing that son of a bitch dead. Out there in the cool of night, April May had gotten the sense that eventually things would turn out all right, that if she would be patient, justice would somehow be forged out of this land around her. She'd had no trouble keeping the secret of what she'd seen three years ago, and more recently she'd had no trouble lying to her husband's nephew Tom Parks when he asked her if she knew anything about Margo or Johnny disappearing. "That's so far in the past, Tommy," she'd said. "We all need to be looking toward the future."

As George threw bale number forty-eight to David, April May plugged in the extension cord, then stood back and admired the orange lights and puffy vinyl ghosts. April May knew she wanted some of those new grapefruit-sized pumpkin gourds she'd seen at Rachel's farm stand. As for jack-o'-lanterns, she'd get one pumpkin for her husband and one each for the grandkids. She'd grown most of her own pumpkins in years past, but when Rachel opened up that farm stand last year, April May figured her arthritis was bad enough that gardening was no longer a pleasure, and the decision to give it up had felt like a burden lifted.

Not that she had any intention of giving up on *carving* pumpkins. She always helped the grandchildren carve slowly and carefully, but nowadays she cut her own pumpkins with reckless speed. She'd learned by practice about spacing the features to cover more of the pumpkin, of not skimping on the size of the eye and mouth holes. Nowadays she chose to slash without thinking, and this method, she found, resulted in a scarier face. Her husband seemed shocked at the violence with which she carved and with the wounds she sometimes inflicted upon herself. If the grandkids didn't want the pumpkins—as often they didn't—she gutted and carved more herself. She burned twenty dollars' worth of candles last year just to keep all her pumpkin heads glowing on the porch. Though she hadn't dressed up or gone to a costume party in years, Halloween had become her favorite holiday. Much simpler than Christmas with its endless buying and baking and nice-making.

Before heading out for her Saturday-morning errands, just as David adjusted the forty-ninth bale, April May took a last look at the barn-shaped feeder, set against a backdrop of the barn itself. The doors were properly placed and covered by carpenter's cloth through which the birds plucked seeds. It had been such a success that Larry was in the process of building another feeder, a model of Milton Taylor's Barn Grill, the second oldest barn in the township. On the ground beneath the barn feeder were the first white-bellied snow birds who'd traveled south for the winter from Canada and Michigan's Upper Peninsula. April May hoped they'd be able to hold their own with the English sparrows. When she was young, the Audubon Society had encouraged people to kill English sparrows, an Old World species of finch that stole nesting sites from tree swallows and bluebirds, even pecking the native chicks to death to get those nests. Before the English sparrows came, bluebirds had been the most common species of bird in the eastern United States. Naturalists now called English sparrows "house sparrows" and had since given up on trying to get rid of the conquering species, or maybe the invaders had just settled in so thoroughly that they were no longer even foreign.

13

AS DAVID ACCEPTED BALE NUMBER FIFTY-TWO, HE WAS less than halfway done, but he was already tired; his arms and legs were aching and his chest was beginning to burn. As he dragged that bale and the next and the next up and over and pushed each into place, he felt his muscles swell and thicken. Sometimes a man's muscle didn't show in his arms and legs, David thought, but only in how tall he was, which was how George's muscle showed. Being tall was the best kind of muscle because everybody saw it, even from a distance, even in long sleeves. For the first couple dozen bales, George had stood atop the hay wagon pretty much level with David. From there he tossed bales almost into place so David had only to angle each into position and push it tight against the others with his knees. As the wagon emptied and the stacked bales rose, George eventually was unable to toss a bale all the way up to David, and instead held it above himself and waited for David to reach down and grab the strings. One level of bales ran east-west, and the next north-south, only you didn't just stack one level at a time, you built out, adding a few to each level as you went, so one level tied down the one beneath it. That was the phrase George used, *tied down*. George offered bales in quick succession, and David pushed one after another into place as best he could, grateful for any noise that distracted George from his raspy breathing. Straw rustled, crows squawked, the wagon squeaked. For the next couple dozen bales David slipped into a rhythm and even forgot his exhaustion for a while.

"Did you see Rachel on your way down here?" George said.

"She was yelling at woolly bears."

"Was she?"

"Everybody says she doesn't talk, but she talks to me a lot."

"Maybe it's because you're a good listener."

"She thinks you shouldn't kill woolly bears. I don't know why she cares so much about them when she kills everything else."

"I guess you shouldn't kill anything without a reason."

"Officer Parks doesn't like Rachel, does he?" David exhausted himself with that burst of speaking, and now he hoped George would talk so he could just listen.

"I wouldn't worry about Rachel and Officer Parks," George said. "They'll learn to get along. How many bales you count so far?"

David hadn't been counting. After fifty-two, he'd forgotten to count. He'd put each bale tightly against the others, but he'd been daydreaming about driving tractors and about living with George. David looked around, unable to distinguish the new bales from the old, and for a moment he couldn't breathe at all. He had known something terrible would happen today—everything up until now had been too good to be true.

"I think I counted eighty-three so far," George said.

David sighed and thanked God. George had been counting. And of course George was right. "Sounds right," David said, swearing to himself to keep count from now on. George's nephew might not bother to count bales, but relatives had special privilege and could expect forgiveness even after terrible mistakes. Eighty-four, eighty-four, he repeated to himself as he dragged bale number eighty-four toward the back. His foot slipped into a hole between bales, and his leg went clear down and he was stopped only by his crotch slamming onto the corner of a bale. He saw colors and couldn't exhale until after he'd pulled himself up, but George didn't seem to notice, just continued holding up bale number eighty-five. Eighty-five, David said as he accepted it. David knew how important it was to keep count in order to know how many bales were in this barn at any given time, so that George could sell some and keep as much as he needed for the winter—not that George couldn't probably just look in the barn and give a pretty good estimate. George produced bale number eighty-six.

George, to the contrary, felt unsure about his own count, because counting bales wasn't complex enough or important enough to keep in the front of his head, where he continually performed bigger calculations. Corn was selling for $1.46 a bushel, and soybeans for $4.27. George was expecting a yield of about 110 bushels of corn an acre, so that was going to be about $161 per acre, times 475 acres (including the field he rented next to O Road) so that was $76,475, barring insect infestation or excessive loss to animals. Of soybeans he had 490 acres, and at 36 bushels an acre, he'd end up with $75,323. He owed about $118,000 for seed and fertilizer, which left about $34,000, minus taxes, equipment, and mortgage payments for the Parkses' land, which would eat up more than the rest of it. He'd end up living day to day by selling alfalfa, oats, and oat straw to other local farmers.

George sighed. "David, how is your ma?"

"She's fine." He wished there were something good he could tell George. "She might be getting a job."

"That would be good news," George said. "Where?"

"I don't know."

"Well, your ma's got her troubles," George said. "You're a good worker, anyhow."

Having lied to George about his mom made him feel crummy, made him think of the woolly bears he'd run over and killed on the way here, and he wanted to change the subject. He said, "You know, Rachel says there's somebody buried around here."

"What?" George put down the bale he'd started to lift.

"From more than a hundred fifty years ago," David said. George's reaction made David worry he'd said something wrong, but he continued. "She's Rachel's relative, and she used to talk to the plants, and she killed herself by jumping out of a tree because she didn't want to move away." David usually didn't give his full attention when Rachel told stories about the Corn Girl, but now that he thought about it, he knew just how Corn Girl felt about not wanting to leave.

David saw George was still listening intently. "Or she might have fell," David said. Actually, that Indian girl falling rather than jumping was his own theory, one he hadn't shared with Rachel. He didn't believe people would jump to their deaths on purpose.

George again lifted the bale. Thank God, George thought. Rachel hadn't killed and buried her mother. Of course she hadn't. How could he even think that? George imagined Margo's face as though underwater, pale as in death.

"Rachel calls her Corn Girl," David said.

"That's quite a story." George held the next bale above his head but leaned it against other bales so it felt almost weightless to him. He worked more slowly than he would have with his nephew Todd, but he didn't mind so long as the work was getting done. As George waited for David to grab the bale, he searched the corners of the barn. The swallows had already left their mud nests and flown south, to wherever they lived in winter: Key West or the Bahamas, places his first wife had wanted to go. Rachel, so far, wanted to stay right here, winter and summer. At even such a cursory thought of Rachel, George again felt himself come a little undone. When David took the bale, George said, "Corn Girl, you say? And she's related to Rachel?"

"On her Indian side."

"And she liked to talk to plants, you say?" George repeated the name to himself. *Corn Girl*. Rachel was a mysterious person, all right. George didn't know what had propelled him into each day before she came. Maybe he had always known in his muscles that she'd show up and make life worth living. Reminding himself of his weakness for Rachel made him forgive Sally for not paying rent, made him forgive the Taylors for letting their land become a golf course, and made him even forgive the Higgins kids for wanting to give up their family's dairy operations. He'd been hearing more rumors about an impending sale over the last few months, and George couldn't blame the young Higginses for rejecting a life in which work began at 4 A.M., rain or shine, snowstorm or hangover. He only wished he could afford to buy all their land for Rachel. Of course, Rachel herself would eventually decide that the sun didn't rise and set only on northern Greenland Township. She was bound to figure out that the world was vast and, for a resourceful girl, infinitely rich with experience.

David reached down and grabbed bale number 112 from George, trying not to let on how exhausted he was, that he wanted to collapse and breathe without using a muscle until, as the doctor had explained, the oxygen saturated his blood again. As a rule, David conserved his medicine, only puffing when he really needed to, because his mom didn't get him his new breathers quickly enough. He'd recently started telling her they were gone before they really were, working toward having a full one in reserve. By the time George was standing on the plywood platform of the wagon handing up the last bales, David had to lie on his belly, reach down, and pull up while George pushed. When they'd started, the upper part of the barn had seemed open, but now the bales were filling up the back and the east side, so the walls were closing in, and the ceiling hung more closely overhead. At last, George pushed the final bale toward David, and David accepted it with hands that were raw from the twine. George had offered him gloves from his truck before they started, but George himself didn't wear gloves, and David would just as soon hurry and get his hands as tough and calloused as George's.

"One hundred eighteen," David announced.

"That's it," George said, from below. "Good job."

The words echoed in David's head. He collapsed to his knees onto the silky yellow bales. His head felt light, and he had the sense of floating upward.

"You did a real good job, David." George waited beside the hay wagon for David's legs to appear. "I'm hoping I can bale tomorrow," George called up to him. "If you feel up to it, you can drive the tractor while I stack. You'll just be careful on those turns." George figured that driving a tractor couldn't tax David's breathing much.

David's legs appeared, not in descent, but dangling over the side of the stack, as though he did not intend to climb down anytime soon. George moved around the hay wagon so he could see David's face. "How are you feeling? Do you want to help me tomorrow?"

David nodded yes.

"Meet me at the house at two o'clock?"

David nodded again. The invitation made him feel like cheering but he hadn't even the energy to speak.

"Between you and Rachel, nobody talks to me much around here," George said. "Why don't you come back to the house now for some breakfast? I'll make you eggs and bacon. Or else I got some patty sausage."

David shook his head no vigorously. He wanted breakfast, of course, but then George would see how bad his breathing was, and

David still had the feeling that one wrong move could spoil everything. He was better off not taking a chance. Maybe if all went well
with him and George today, then his ma would hold off a little
longer on moving to California, and a letter would arrive from his
half brother, Jim, saying for her not to come. Maybe then his ma
really would get a job, and they could stay where they were.

George asked, "Are you okay?"

David nodded. He figured he'd get some food from Rachel later.

"You're breathing hard," George said. "But at least you're
smiling."

David shrugged. Despite his burning chest, he couldn't stop
grinning.

"Do you want a ride home?"

David shook his head no.

"I can put your bike in the truck."

David shook his head again.

"You'll be okay on your bike, then?"

David nodded.

"Pull the big door closed when you go, will you?"

It was clear to George that David wanted to be left alone, and
George believed in giving people their own time, kids included.

David watched George leave the barn and listened to his feet on
the gravel outside. Concentrating on George, imagining George
getting into his truck and turning the key and gripping the steering
wheel, helped David regain control of his breathing, and within a
few minutes he was able to climb down. He had done it, had kept
going through the whole wagonload of straw without resting, and
without anything terrible happening.

He walked across the loose straw on the barn floor and went
outside to retrieve his bicycle, which he leaned against the barn
doorway. He sat beside the bike and closed his mouth over his
white plastic breather, inhaled, and counted slowly to ten. The doctor had said he should avoid dust, but David had a different plan.

Just as he was developing calluses on his hands, he wanted to build calluses inside his lungs. He imagined his lungs looking like his wrists and lower arms—red and torn, but getting tougher.

David saw Gray Cat pad around inside the barn, then exit through a place at the bottom edge of the wall where the wood had rotted away. A few months before, in this same barn, David had seen George's nephew Todd whip an orange kitten around on the end of a clothesline. There had been a soft pop, like the air escaping from a can of cola, as though life were a gas when it left the body. Todd hadn't seemed to care any more about the orangie than he would have at busting up a pumpkin, and afterward he'd tossed the kitten, rope and all, out into the ditch alongside the road. David hadn't been able to look at cats the same way since. Nowadays a cat just seemed like a fur-covered collection of body parts from which life could be yanked.

David inhaled his medicine again and held his breath, this time for fifteen seconds. The plain haze of a day like this felt like all the days of a person's life mashed together, but he didn't know what his whole life could add up to if he had to leave everything good behind and go to California. Beyond the door of the barn and the foundation of the old house, the cornstalks stood perfectly still, waiting. If David lived with George, he'd have gotten in the truck and gone home to breakfast as usual, and on the way they would have talked about harvesting plans. If they lived together, George would think of David's breathing as a regular part of David. If he lived with George, he'd get up early every morning and feed the animals. David would go to school if George insisted, but he would make it clear he'd rather stay home and help with farm work. David could use shovels and axes in the daytime, and he wouldn't have to worry about putting them away in the exact positions he'd found them in. He wondered whether, if George had a son, he would let him get a dog.

14

AS GEORGE TURNED NORTH ON QUEER ROAD, GRAY CAT
noted the fluttering of a goldfinch near the barnyard fence. The
goldfinch was pulling at a thistle, and the last of the thistle seed
spilled in a pile onto the ground. Wary of predators, the goldfinch
knew not to stand on the ground for more than a second, so it
landed and alighted, landed and alighted, grabbed several seeds at
each visit, perched again on the thistle stalk or the bedsprings or
the woven wire fence, then went back to the ground. Though it was
wary, this goldfinch was ignorant of the approach of Gray Cat,
who'd been dropped here nearly a year ago, along with the rest of
an unwanted litter. The rest of the kittens—the other gray, the cal-
ico, and the two orangies—were dead. Two had been smashed
under the tires of cars within a week and had their bodies pecked
apart by crows. A third was killed and eaten by a raccoon, and the
fourth was done in by George's nephew.

The surviving gray kitten, however, who had avoided people

from the start, had sped away from the boys who'd grabbed his orange littermate. But Gray Cat had not avoided this barn, which provided mice and shelter, nor had he avoided April May Rathburn's place across the street, where he found that he could steal chunks of dry dog food from a dish in the side yard while the shepherd slept stupidly inside the doghouse to which he was lashed every afternoon. Just once, Gray Cat had eaten cream he'd stolen from a bowl set outside, before April May chased him away. From the other side of the road, he'd watched for a chance to take more, but then one of the woman's cats showed up, licked the cream, and was taken inside. It had been a trap, Gray Cat realized, and he felt clever for having avoided it.

Gray Cat was not considering humans now, for his eyes were set upon a yellow body that flickered down to the ground, then up into the air, and back down, not as bright a creature as earlier in the season, but summer-fattened and no less tasty for being mottled with greenish brown. Gray Cat hugged the ground and approached the bird and thistle so slowly and smoothly that he might have been a serpent slithering or a liquid pouring itself in the direction of the bird. And when he was close enough, he reached out with a paw that stretched farther from his body than any bystander would have expected and pulled the bird to earth. The move was tornado quick but so smooth it could have been a light breeze. The curled claws pulled the bird down with a strength that was greater than seemed possible for a creature that had moments ago licked its paw and neatly brushed its head. When the bird tried to stand, the cat reached out and slammed the feathered body down again.

The bird did not peep or scream but flapped its wings and lifted itself, only to have the cruel paw thrust onto it a third time. Black finch eyes turned toward the sky, toward flight, in the direction the bird meant to travel—up, up—but when it began to lift itself, Gray Cat swatted it to the ground again with a force that broke one of the bird's legs. But legs were nothing compared to wings, and the bird jumped into the air on one leg, never mind the other. Before the bird could launch itself, though, Gray Cat struck hard enough to break the bird's wing. Still, the goldfinch fluttered its one good wing upward, calling to the air where it had lived, to the hazy sky, which tomorrow might be clear. "Sky, pull me up," the bird cried with its almost weightless body, but could only flap its unbroken wing, swishing to no effect. Gray Cat held the bird down, occasionally letting loose in order to circle, stretching out a paw again when the bird began to shift. Eventually the bird did not move, but only stared up at the sky, then into the gray eyes of Gray Cat, then again at the sky, yearning, alighting in its mind the way it had alighted ten thousand times from the ground or from a thistle or fence or from a feeder built to resemble a barn. Never before had the bird known that to desire flight was not the same as to spread wings and rise. The cat sent his claws through feathers, into nerves. The bird's yearning thinned, along with its breath, thinned to something like a whisper of smoke, and the bird was extinguished.

15

HAD THERE BEEN A WAY TO DRIVE WITHOUT RUNNING OVER woolly bears on his way home from the barn on the morning of October 9, George Harland would have done it, but killing some of them was inevitable. He kept his eyes focused farther along Queer Road, so at least he didn't have to see any particular caterpillar before crushing it beneath the worn tires of his four-wheel-drive pickup. He turned in to his driveway but didn't see Rachel. He also didn't see the State of Michigan sign that was usually displayed on two posts in front of his house; George thought probably Rachel had taken it again, to help support her produce table. Somewhere beneath her turban squashes and the bushel of apples would be the green sign, engraved with the message

Michigan Centennial Farm
Owned By The Same Family Over One Hundred Years.

The state historical commission had presented the sign to George because his family had arrived here before Michigan was even a state, purchased their acreage at the land office in Kalamazoo, and built this house. Like other settlers from the civilized east, George's ancestors had quickly learned that property rights were different out here. The Indians felt free to hunt most anywhere, whether a person owned the land or not, and the settlers followed suit. In the beginning, even the relatively well off suffered from periodic scarcity, so folks adopted communal habits and shared with their neighbors: their kettles and churns, their shovels and plows, even their mules. Folks borrowed with humility and loaned with the hope that their tools would be returned in the same condition in which they were borrowed. These folks may not have considered the Potawatomi their brethren, but neither did they deny them sustenance from their modest stores. *"Bukutah"* or *"Bke de"* was a Potawatomi man's way of saying "I'm hungry," and a fellow might make such an announcement before coming into a house. When food was scarce, that utterance filled the woman of the house with dread, but she would then remind herself that it was always an Indian who returned her milk cow when it got loose and wandered into the woods, and it had largely been the strength of Potawatomi arms that had raised the first barns in the township.

Harold Harland was not born into ownership of the farm, but came to it by marrying Henrietta, the only surviving child of an otherwise prosperous farmer. Harold learned the history of the place by listening to his father-in-law and the other old men in the neighborhood. In the next generation, Harold's own son had no interest, so by the time his grandson George was old enough to listen, Harold was nearly desperate to teach the boy all about farming and to tell him what he had learned about the 1830s, when the white settlers first arrived in Greenland. There hadn't been more than a few dozen poor farmers around when Henrietta's great-grandfather started building this house, and Harold said those farmers had disapproved of the man's constructing a little window room up above the southern roof to provide a view south, east, and west. Those neighbors scoffed at the frivolity of the room the way the Potawatomi scoffed at all wooden structures built upon stone foundations, when surely wigwams should have sufficed.

After the Potawatomi were marched away west, and as wealth increased in the region, people gradually stopped depending upon the churns, tools, and mules of others and were expected to take care of their own needs and build their own fences strong enough to contain their cows. Within a single generation of white settlement, the Indians were gone, and the farmers stopped caring about such things as whether or not a neighbor wasted his time building a window room. Within a generation, a white man's stupidity had become his own and was no longer an attribute of the community.

George was ten or eleven when his grandpa started telling him such things, and one summer afternoon Harold proposed the two of them install new glass in the old window room, long boarded up. At the prospect of such a waste of time, George's grandmother Henrietta mumbled a complaint about what sort of fool she'd married. George himself would never have questioned his grandfather's wisdom about the window room or any other thing.

From the second floor landing, George had followed Old Harold up the wall ladder into a six-by-six-foot room and sat beside him on the built-in wooden bench. The first thing his grandfather did was remove a small yellowed photograph from under the edge of the window frame. Harold looked at it a long time before handing it to his grandson. The photo of the young widow at first frightened George, because in her faded form she seemed as much ghost as human. George was squinting to study the photo when Old Harold wrenched loose that first piece of plywood. The light hit the photo so suddenly that the woman seemed to burst into flame. Through the empty window frame, its edges rimmed with glass shards, Harold pointed out the river, and the path alongside, on which, he said, a line of thousands of Potawatomi had walked toward Kalamazoo in 1840. He pointed out the big barn with no house, silo, or shed beside it, and said that right after Mary O'Kearsy was sent away by the school board, the sky had turned green and a twister had spun up across the Taylors' grazing land to Harold's own land, knocking down trees and even rerouting his creek. The tornado tossed dirt into the air with a force that would embed pea-sized stones deep in a fellow's flesh as it did to Enkstra, the man with whom the schoolteacher had the affair. That tornado pushed one way and then another, Harold said, digging trenches across newly planted fields, moving rocks the size of rabbits effortlessly, killing with such a rock a curly-tailed yellow dog with a lame hind leg who'd stood on the ridge barking at the wind as though it were an animal intruder.

As the tornado roared toward the barn, vertical siding boards he had nailed down just the previous day sprang loose. Harold himself lay nearby, facedown in the narrow ditch beside Queer Road with his hands covering his head and his face in poison ivy. Hail peppered his body, growing from the size of corn kernels or blood-engorged ticks to reach the size of husked walnuts. When he looked up from the ditch, he saw a railroad tie pierce the silo, saw the wind blast the tower to bits, flinging glazed blocks out into the field as though they were as light as straw. The tornado seemed about to pass through the barn siding the way the tines of a pitchfork passed through sand, seemed poised to transform the barn to swirling rubble, but then it turned away from the barn and moved toward the unoccupied house and instantly and thoroughly demolished it. The front door ripped itself free and the oval of glass never broke while the door was in the air. The door rose for several long seconds, then spun, parallel to the ground, its window pointing at the sky, like a mirror showing the sky to itself, the oval reflection as calm as a green pond, before spinning toward the earth and, upon impact, splintering.

Harold had sat for a long while in the barn doorway, he told young George, anticipating the onset of poison ivy and contemplating the destruction God had wrought for his betrayal of Mrs. O'Kearsy. God had tolerated all of Harold's other mistakes, but apparently He had taken offense at that one. On that day in 1934, Harold Harland had sat alone until dark, finally concluding that the people in his church were wrong, that God was not the picket-fence spirit they worshiped. Harold's God was the wrathful God of the Old Testament, an awesome God and a vengeful God. Harold knew then, he said, sitting in that barn, that life is both too short to have enough joy and too brutally long for a man who regrets what he has done. Ever since then, Old Harold said, he had tried to refigure the world from scratch. Up in the window room, Harold told George that the tornado changed everything. George didn't understand all of what the old man was talking about, but he knew he'd believe it once he figured it out.

"It's too late for your thickheaded papa, but it's not too late for you," Harold told George. "You may as well know the truth about this place. Only don't tell your grandmother. She's not interested in the truth. She just wants everything to stay the same."

"I won't tell," George whispered.

Harold took the photograph from George's hands and studied it some more.

"Mary O'Kearsy didn't hurt anybody," Harold said. "She stood on her porch and watched for that big dumb fellow Enkstra to come walking along the path. I had no right telling other folks about who she loved."

"You told on her?"

"And don't think that was the only mistake I made. I've made plenty. And the one thing I've learned for certain in this life is that there's no sense in judging people."

"Did the lady become a teacher someplace else?"

"She wanted to stay here," Harold said, "and we should have let her stay."

"Were her students sad about her leaving?"

"Everybody was sad after she left town. And those people knew afterwards that they shouldn't judge a woman so harshly."

In truth, apart from Enkstra, Harold was the only grown-up person who seemed to care about Mary O'Kearsy after she left, but Harold wanted his grandson to think that people could change, that they could learn to be kind. Harold had sighed and looked away from the faded little photo, toward the barn to the south. He said, "That woman was as beautiful as the day is long."

On the morning of October 9, two stories below the window room, George started a pot of coffee, unwrapped pale green butcher paper from a pound of bacon and dropped thick slices into the biggest cast-iron frying pan he'd inherited, along with this house and the rest of the farm, from his grandparents. George was realizing already that he should have insisted David come eat breakfast. That regret would grow larger throughout the day, but for now he satisfied himself by deciding that tomorrow, after they baled straw, he would insist David come to supper with him and Rachel. He couldn't pay the kid much money for helping him, but maybe later today he could give David and Sally some steaks and hamburger he had in the freezer. As the streaks of fat became translucent and then golden, George removed each slice of bacon with tongs and placed it on a paper bag flattened on a Blue Willow plate. With his right hand, George cracked and emptied the shells of two, three, four eggs, letting each slide over his thumb and into the bacon grease. He almost couldn't stand the pleasure the smells of bacon and coffee gave him these days, enough to sustain him eight or ten hours, even in the heat or cold. Breakfast was Rachel's favorite meal too, George was pretty sure.

Sometime in the future, Rachel would undoubtedly tell him whatever she'd told David about the Potawatomi Corn Girl. Probably some day Rachel would talk about her mother, about what it had been like to grow up on a boat with an eccentric woman, and someday Rachel might tell him why she'd called him Johnny in the barn and solve a dozen other mysteries, but George didn't want to rush into conversation. He and Rachel had lived together a year and a half, and they'd been married six weeks, but George still felt shy around her. He figured there was plenty of work to keep him occupied for the next few months, and anyway the dead of winter would be a better time for talking.

George went out the back door and through the porch, which he had screened in at the request of his first wife, and he followed the trail out to Rachel's garden. George used to keep this side yard mowed, but last year Rachel had suggested they stop wasting time and gas, and George hadn't been able to argue with her logic. He'd let the brambles, weeds, and wildflowers grow last year, and then this July the smell of the blackcap raspberries had been like a liquor. It had given him a weird satisfaction, though, the several times he'd seen Rachel out there yanking burdock, ragweed, and garlic mustard.

"Rachel, come eat!" As he waited, he considered that on any sort of day, even today, she might just disappear from his life. Having so much meant a fellow had all that to lose.

Rachel stood up from her garden and looked in his direction. She wore two braids this morning, making her face seemed even rounder than usual.

When he and Rachel got inside the kitchen, she looked down at the table and the two chipped Blue Willow plates and said, "Where the hell's David?"

16

A HALF MILE WEST AS THE CROW FLIES, DAVID'S MOTHER, Sally, was still sitting behind her house in a lawn chair, her feet up on the picnic table. She had remained nearly motionless long enough that birds flying over probably assumed she was something inanimate or dead. Above her, five turkey vultures circled effortlessly, barely shifting their wings to execute turns. They spiraled downward and landed, one at a time, a hundred yards away, where a newly dead possum lay in alfalfa stubble. The birds milled about, their pink heads bald of plumage, their clumsy turkey-sized bodies shifting across the rows scraped clean by the mower, rake, and baler. Sally assumed the birds were just out and about, traveling aimlessly, picking up carrion where they could and digging into it with their hooked beaks. She might have respected the vultures more had she known they were readying to fly south. With the help of winds a thousand feet up, they would be migrating to Central America, fully intending to keep warm this winter. Sally took the last swig of her bourbon-laced coffee. She considered lighting another cigarette from the one in her hand, but instead snubbed it out on the picnic table. A few seconds later, though, when she saw a vulture yank a length of grayish gut from the possum, she fumbled in her robe pocket for the pink lighter. There were four more cigarettes in the pack.

A walnut fell out of a tree onto the barn roof with a clunk that sounded familiar to Sally. Though she had dutifully collected the nuts every autumn of her youth, she would no sooner have shelled one of those walnuts today than she would have peeled her own toe. Without anything else to drink and with only a few smokes left, Sally felt the weight of the gloomy sky. Harsher weather was on its way, as it usually was in Michigan, so unlike California, which would have blue skies, season after season. She mentally rummaged the farmhouse, imagining she might have more liquor. She knew she didn't, and yet she envisioned herself opening closets and unlatching secret wall compartments, pulling out drawers to find false bottoms beneath which farm wives could have long ago hidden flat bottles of alcohol-rich cure-all. Really, those drawers and cupboards contained only mismatched silverware, dishes in all variety of cheap designs, a cereal box with a bit of oat dust in it. In the refrigerator was an old brown heart of a cabbage that Rachel had given David months ago, and some ketchup and mustard. There was no milk and no booze. Fortunately, she wasn't broke—she had twenty-six dollars from the child support, and Mike had just sent her an insurance card for David, so she could get him a puffer, though she'd have to pick up the five-dollar copayment. She'd get another box of cereal and a bottle of milk for David. And bread and peanut butter if she had enough left.

Sally saw the turkey vultures take clumsy flight from the hay field, but from her position behind the house she didn't notice the window salesman's quiet Thunderbird pull into her driveway, and then she didn't see the salesman press the doorbell at the front of the house.

Steve could see the house was badly in need of thermal windows and insulated doors, that it needed minor miracles of hammers, nails, caulk, and paint. He couldn't help it that when he saw a run-down old house like this, he right away imagined the house restored to its full potential, with new windows, doors, and smooth-looking siding. The vision of restoration wasn't a ghostly thing—it was a full-blown, full-color picture overlaying the real house, and he sometimes had difficulty calling back the actual state of things. He pressed the buzzer and waited, but heard no response, no footsteps, no voice shouting *I'll get it*. Perhaps the occupants were sleeping late. When he pressed the buzzer again, he also pressed his ear against the door and realized the buzzer was broken. He knocked and peeked inside at Sally's stairway, on which there was a pair of worn-out boy's sneakers and a few crumpled towels. Steve stepped back on the porch and looked up. Sometimes a woman would be getting out of the shower, and she'd hear his knock and pull aside a curtain and look out a steamy window. He imagined a face showing through mist, but that vision quickly faded. The lower sash of a window to his left was cracked and held together with a length of duct tape. A car was parked on the overgrown lawn at the side of the house, but the front passenger-side wheel was missing and the axle rested on blocks.

Steve retreated from the creaking wooden porch and glanced out over the field of stubble beside the house, imagined it greening and springing forth with a fresh crop, in a scene overlaying the brownish expanse. Such fields just thrust their fertility up at a man, begging him, *Plow me, sow me, reap me*. Steve had gone to school with a few farm kids and had always thought he'd make a good farmer, but his father had been a foreman at a paper mill, and his grandfather had worked for the railroad, as some of his uncles still did. The last farmer in his family, as far as he knew, was his great-grandfather Enkstra, who'd worked on another man's farm until he got his railroad job, but he had died long before Steve was born.

Steve headed toward his car, but then he sensed another presence. He detoured to look behind the house, and halfway between himself and the busted silo, he saw a woman with a coffee cup and a cigarette, her naked, slender legs propped up on the picnic table so that her robe barely concealed her torso. As he approached, he anticipated the smell of her. Steve thought cigarette smoke fit certain women the way fresh-baked cookies fit other women, the way nail polish and potpourri or vanilla-scented candles fit still others. His wife wore perfume that smelled of flowers and babies. Cigarettes and coffee and the sweetness of alcohol were merely the opposite end of the spectrum of womanly smells.

"Morning, ma'am," Steve said to the woman, who did not adjust her robe to cover herself but sat as though her little body were an artifact dropped from the sky to be found and appreciated by a lucky scavenger. She looked up at him through calm, wide-set eyes, raised her eyebrows slightly, but said nothing. He held out a hand to shake hers, and with the other offered a business card. "Steve Hoekstra, ma'am. Harmony Windows. Beautiful October morning, isn't it?"

She moved her head so slightly that Steve couldn't tell if it was a positive or negative gesture. She gave him an uninterested though not limp hand, and she accepted the card but then laid it on the table without a glance, as though inviting the wind to rise up and blow it into the field. Steve took a seat on the bench across from her and looked out over her slender legs, to the north, across the bristle of cornstalks sticking straight up, row after row, acre after acre. He leaned toward her and inhaled her boozy smell. "Have you considered new windows?"

"This isn't my house. Go talk to George Harland."

"George Harland?"

"He's a farmer on Queer Road. Q Road. This house is his."

"I live across the street from him. I didn't realize he owned more than one house."

She looked at him and smiled. "And if you're going that way, maybe you can give me a ride."

"Sure, I can give you a ride, no problem." Steve thought the day was making sense already—he would indeed meet his neighbor Rachel.

"Let me get dressed. It'll just take a minute." She started out walking toward the house, then broke into a jog.

Steve wished he were waiting inside the house, waiting for the woman's breathy arrival, watching the robe slip from her shoulders to reveal the small of her back where he would place his hand. Steve would inhale the light boozy sweat on her skin, taste her neck, lift her little body right off the ground and set her on a dresser and ask her to wrap her legs around him. Steve picked up the business card she'd left on the table and stuck it into the crack between two planks so it wouldn't blow away.

Sally ran up the stairs to her room. She figured George would take her to get cigarettes and a bottle of something. And of course David's puffer and food. This guy's giving her a ride would save her the time walking over there. He seemed helpful, seemed like the kind of guy who would fix things and not get angry and make demands, although you really never knew with men. She'd mention that she had a twelve-year-old son, and she wouldn't mind if he thought her younger than she was. In her bedroom, the dresser drawers hung open and a layer of clothes, some dirty, some less dirty, lay draped over the edges of those drawers and on the floor as though she had surprised them during the execution of a slow crawling escape. There was an old wringer washer in the dirt-floored Michigan basement of the house, but there was no dryer, because the farm women over the years had tirelessly hung their clothes outside to dry. George still hung clothes on lines in winter, said he liked "freeze-drying" them. And that man owned half the township, for crying out loud. Sally selected a pair of jeans from the floor, and she let her robe drop, though the salesman was leaning against his car out front and looking up at her window. She picked a long-sleeved T-shirt off the floor, smelled it, tossed it back down, and found a dark turtleneck instead. Over that, she pulled on a musty but clean-looking wool sweater she found in the bottom drawer. Sally couldn't believe that just this spring she'd had the energy to hand-wash, or maybe Milton had given her this black ribbed sweater from the church box. She looked in the dusty, full-length mirror and decided she looked good enough that this guy might offer to take her to the store if George was out in a field. She'd try to avoid Rachel; talking to that girl was like rubbing up against poison ivy.

17

DAVID RETAKKER DID NOT STEAL AND SMOKE HIS MOTHER'S cigarettes as a result of peer pressure or because he thought smoking was cool; he stole and smoked them in order to scratch and burn his lungs, to toughen his inside skin until, like his hands, it would become leathery brown and strong enough to tolerate any sort of air. And if smoking made his breathing worse now, then it would surely make him stronger later, he told himself, strong enough to conquer his asthma. David envisioned a time when he would be toughened all over, inside and outside, as callused as Rachel's feet and George's hands, so tough he wouldn't even feel hunger or cold. By the time he was grown up, he would be able to walk across a frozen pond barefoot, inhale pure oat dust, and run his hands through flames without flinching. David also hoped to grow tall like George, but he knew that he might not, seeing how neither his father nor his mother was tall, and in that case, he was prepared to be extra strong to make up for it.

From the zippered bag strapped beneath his bicycle seat, David took a green-and-white cigarette pack containing three menthol 100s. He never stole a whole pack, but just took one or two out of his ma's now and again while she was passed out. David moved just outside the doorway of the barn, away from the hay and straw. At precisely the same moment that his mother pulled a sweater over her head and George and Rachel got up from their kitchen chairs, David struck a match and lifted it to the cigarette, with both hands shaking. He needed to figure out a way to steel himself against the shaking caused by his asthma medicine, and of course eventually he wouldn't need the medicine at all. The cigarette tip sizzled and caught, and bits of loose tobacco squirmed like tiny glowworm fireworks, like caterpillar embers inching their way up a small white dead-end road. David inhaled the smoke, stifled his choking, and blew out the match. David had overheard George warning Todd more than once about smoking in the barn, so David knew he had to be careful. He licked the pads of his finger and thumb and pressed them against the match head to extinguish it with a hiss.

Along Queer Road came a police car, white and blue with red lights on top, but rather than drive on by, as David assumed it would, the car slowed. When it turned in to the driveway before him, David jumped inside the barn and peered out between two boards, hoping the cop hadn't seen him. Officer Parks drove up, opened his cruiser door, and planted his wide feet on the dirt drive. David reminded himself that he had a right to be in the barn. He should just sit tight and tell the cop he was helping George, but his instinct was to disappear like a ghost—except of course that ghosts didn't leave their bicycles lying in doorways. He only thought of his bicycle after it was too late to pull it inside without looking suspicious. David moved farther inside and climbed up the bales to the top of the stack, where he lay panting, flat on his stomach, peering down over the edge. He could see from his position that he'd forgotten to zip the vinyl seat bag containing his cigarettes. He then noticed his own hand beside him, as though it was somebody else's, holding a cigarette between two fingers. He could have dropped the cigarette into the straw, he told himself. He could easily have let it slip from his hand while he'd climbed. Thank God he hadn't. He extended his arm and held the cigarette away from himself. Had anyone asked him whether he'd ever bring a cigarette into the barn, he'd have sworn he would not.

Parks, down below, picked up David's bicycle and leaned it against the door frame. He took off his hat and swept his hand over his balding head in a way that made him look tired. The cigarettes were balanced half inside the zippered bag, poised to fall out. Then Parks looked up, pretty much toward where David was hiding.

"I know you're in here. You shouldn't be messing around in this barn."

David held his breath as he shifted and wiggled backward about six feet so that he was even more hidden in the straw. By trying to sneak up on Rachel all those nights, he'd learned to move silently.

"I'll go get George Harland. We'll drag you out of here together." Parks touched the bicycle handlebars and out fell David's cigarette pack. Parks shook his head in disappointment as he bent to pick it up. "Whoever you are, you'd better not be smoking in here," he said.

By a miracle of shadows, Parks wasn't seeing him. David fought a need to cough—he gulped air and stifled himself until his eyes watered—and somehow Parks didn't hear him. When David thought he couldn't hold back his cough another moment, Parks put the cigarettes in his own top pocket, placed his hat back onto his tired-looking head, and walked out. As soon as Officer Parks was out of sight, David coughed onto the shiny bales until he finally stopped from exhaustion. After a few minutes of lying curled, catching up on his breathing, David looked at his hand and saw he was no longer holding the cigarette.

His breathing became fast again. He stood and tried to think clearly, tried to figure out where the cigarette could have tumbled, but it became difficult to concentrate. He might have lost it before or after he slid backward on the straw. He pulled away the bale on which he'd been lying, and he looked into the empty space and saw that something as small as a cigarette might have dropped way down between the bales, especially the loose-packed ones George's nephew Todd had stacked. David jumped down a level and tore some bales away, letting them drop to the barn floor. Some bales from higher above tumbled onto him, sending him crashing down onto the plywood bed of the hay wagon. He twisted as he fell and banged his shin on the metal edge. David lay still, willing the pain to subside, and then three more bales fell around him in a kind of delayed action. After several stunned minutes, he extricated himself and climbed up top again and pulled away more bales. He pushed several down toward the front of the barn and still he saw no smoke. He rubbed his swollen shin and looked around; lying beside a bale of hay beneath him was the cigarette. In the process of jumping down, he turned his ankle slightly. Only after he held that cigarette safely in his hand did he pause to catch his breath. He felt immensely grateful. He would let himself rest before he restacked the bales. Close call. "Thank God," he said aloud, and even just those two words winded him. Through the gap at the back of the barn—where George had stood alone just a few hours before—David could see a white-faced Hereford chewing its cud, gazing off into the corn without any sense of alarm, without an inkling that David could have burned down its home. To calm himself, David focused on that cow's wide, pale face. After his breathing settled, he noticed that two of the fallen bales had snapped their strings and busted open; such bales were impossible to recover and George wouldn't be able to sell them. David drew on his breather, tried to expand his clenched-up chest, and held as much air as he could in his lungs.

Some afternoons when David lay in this barn, cylinders of dusty light shot through the cracks in the wall and landed on the floor like a slow-moving laser show, making the barn feel like a spaceship ready to take off. In today's dull haze, though, the barn was just an old wooden building. David exhaled his medicine. He studied the cigarette in his hand, which showed no evidence of having burned, and he noticed a clump of tobacco was missing from the end. Surely this was the cigarette he'd dropped, but the ash must have separated from the shaft, and he'd foolishly wasted all this time holding the harmless part of the cigarette, when the burning ash had fallen God knew where. And he didn't know when the ash had separated or how far away it could have fallen or bounced. It was possible that the cigarette tip went safely out, just as it was possible that his father would come back from Indiana, and that his mother would decide to stay in Michigan and get a job and stop drinking. It was possible that George would invite David to dinner tomorrow and tell him, "You are always welcome here, no matter what," and Rachel would say, "Hell yes!" and David would grow to six feet tall and become George's hired hand.

David climbed atop the pile again and began kicking bales off onto the floor. He knew it would take him all day to restack these once he found the glowing ember, but it was better than the alternative. If George drove back down here with Officer Parks, David would say the cigarettes were his mother's and that he'd accidentally knocked the bales off, or else he just wouldn't say anything. Two more bales busted open as he tossed them down. There were now about twenty bales in a pile below him, and David decided if there were any ash, it was now probably in one of the bales on the floor. He jumped down onto the pile of straw, slipping on one of the bales, twisting his ankle completely this time, with a crunching sound. He'd sprained that ankle last year, when he slipped in a woodchuck hole, so he knew that it was going to swell and ache. He told himself that the damage would be his punishment for having gone into the barn with a cigarette, and he hoped that the pain would be bad enough to equal his stupidity. He pulled a bale away from the pile on the floor and threw it up onto the wagon and checked it all over for signs of burning. He tore at a second bale and tossed it onto the wagon, but it rolled off the other side. The strings of a third bale snapped open and that bale blossomed into flammable sections, but still no fire arose. He pushed another up onto the wagon and checked all its sides, and then he rested. When he could move again, David lifted a fifth bale, discerning no sign of smoke, fire, or ash.

For a long while, there was nothing, no hint of smoke, no reason to think the lost end of the cigarette had done anything but burn out. There would be no fire, he told himself, and he sat on the hay wagon to rest before starting to replace all the bales he'd knocked down; his twisted ankle and bruised shin would be punishment enough. He would rebuild the stack, one bale at a time, with his bronchial tubes constricting, releasing, and constricting again. Even if it took all night, he was grateful, for he'd been spared this time. David felt like crying in relief. "Thank you, God," he said, though he hesitated to speak louder than a whisper, and he hesitated to move much for fear of losing this second chance he was getting. He would never smoke another cigarette—in order to toughen his lungs he would hang his head over the side of the oat bin and inhale the dust. He sat very still and tried not to cough, because the planet now stood in precarious balance.

David moved into the threshold of the barn for some fresh air and was surprised to see Parks's cruiser still there in the driveway, pointed at April May Rathburn's house, as though waiting for traffic to clear, though there was no traffic. David tucked himself against the wall inside. He slid to the ground with his arms around his knees and closed his eyes.

He couldn't have said how long he was asleep before waking into the smell of smoke. When he first blinked his eyes open, he told himself that the smell was merely a ghost of some memory of smoke, but when his eyes adjusted he saw smoke rising from the edge of the bales stacked above him. Favoring the foot with the twisted ankle, David slowly hoisted himself up, and when he looked into the space between two bales, he thought he saw a red glow at the bottom of a thickening puddle of smoke. The red spot disappeared and smoke rose from the bale the way warm swamp fog rose into winter air over the O Road marsh. David's muscles threatened to freeze, but he moved slowly and was able to pull a few bales down onto the pile alongside the hay wagon. The smoke thinned and then seemed to be coming from several places around him. As he began to drag a smoking bale toward the door, a bale above began to blaze. He ran back and pulled that one down and dragged it outside, then returned to find another was burning one level below, blazing because of the oxygen he'd just fed it. He burned his hands as he pushed it down and then across the floor, where it lit a trail of flame in the loose hay and straw. David pulled apart a triad of burning bales on the floor, two of which burst their strings. The flames grabbed at the loose sections, and the fire flattened and spread out a few yards across the sea of loose hay, toward the front wall of the barn. Gray Cat appeared briefly in the doorway, dangling a headless yellow bird body, then sped away. David dragged another bale to the front of the barn and outside. He planned to wave his arms and call Parks over to help him, but Parks was no longer there—his car was headed north. David couldn't catch his breath and his brain felt muddled. If he could just rest for a second and think, he'd figure out what to do. He pulled at his breather but had to exhale before the medicine could work. Meanwhile, the flames before him sucked up the bales as though they were lighting and smoking giant cigarettes in long, slow draws. In the flames, there appeared to David a ghostly vision of curly-tailed yellow puppies, like one killed on the road this summer and buried in Rachel's garden. Then the flames were orange cats writhing and strangling. David saw a flock of translucent yellow birds hover, then grow as indistinct as puffs of smoke. When he searched the air above him, he saw a hundred more fluttering animal shapes. Already, David thought, he was dead enough to see the dead.

He fought to stay alert, but the brightness of the flames made the corners of the barn seem dark, and he couldn't tell if he was dreaming or awake when he saw a chasm opening beside him like a grave, a hole that reminded him of his mother's mouth as her hand drew a cigarette near, and the mindless stares of his friends as they watched television screens, and the pit of his own hungry belly. He imagined he could see inside his own lungs, with their tiny alveoli gasping for oxygen. Within the crackle of flames, he made out the dull pop he'd heard when Todd swung the kitten, a sound that might be necks breaking or maybe souls being discharged from bodies one by one. David reached into his pocket and grabbed his breather and was surprised when his hand refused to move to his mouth. As he clutched the white tube, he concentrated on George, held on to a pure vision of George leaning against his truck, and his hunger faded and the hole before him shrank and disappeared. David saw, curled on a bale of hay surrounded by fire, a single peaceful orange kitten. If David could have moved, he would have reached his arm through the flames to rescue it.

As David's body slowed and tried to adjust to less oxygen, he watched the fire rise and consume the kitten. David made a last attempt at crawling on his belly toward the barn's open door, and when he looked up, he saw before him a watery vision of a black-haired girl like Rachel. Behind her milled a hundred ghost figures, the spirits, probably, of the people buried on George's land, of the animals killed here by Rachel and her mother and the Indians. David focused instead on the black-haired girl's face. He reached out to her, palm upward in order to be saved, but she only smiled and poured kernels of corn into his hand.

18

WHEN NICOLE HOEKSTRA NOTICED HER HUSBAND'S THUN-
derbird pulling into the driveway across the street, she thought
maybe Steve was going to ask George Harland about buying a piece
of land next to that barn. In her excitement, she got up and put on
her jacket and went out the sliding glass door onto the deck without
even double-checking her hair or makeup. As she followed the
driveway to the road, she was focused so intently on Steve that she
didn't notice a crow descending until it landed right in front of her,
claws downward, on a flattened squirrel carcass. Nicole shrieked at
the bird's sudden blackness, at the sharpness of its beak. Her shriek
was not unlike the caw of a crow, and the crow scrawked in answer
and flapped off, as though relinquishing the roadkill to her. Nicole
looked around, embarrassed, and was glad that no one had heard
her make that noise. A woman in a fifteen-year-old Buick passed
her going north, then made a U-turn and eased off the road beside
the farm stand.

Nicole continued across the road and past the Buick and the vegetables toward Steve, but as she reached the pumpkin wagon, she stopped. A woman was getting out of the passenger seat of Steve's Thunderbird, a small woman with uncombed blond hair wisping around her head. For a few seconds Nicole couldn't breathe. She thought she might burst out crying, for surely this was the woman Steve had been with a month ago. Nicole looked around for a knife, looked for the rifle that Mrs. Harland wore over her shoulder, but the only weapons available were the sword-length Brussels sprout spears standing upright in buckets. Nicole took a deep breath, told herself this might be a different red Thunderbird, except there was the Teddy bear she'd put in Steve's back window. Nicole didn't know whether to turn around and run back home or keep walking toward the car, so she stayed where she was. The tall old woman who'd been driving the Buick appeared beside her. The woman picked up one pumpkin, and another, and a third, studying each in turn, and said, "They have so much personality, don't they?"

This question jarred Nicole from her thoughts of Steve and the blonde. *Who* had personality? The woman seemed to be awaiting a response, so Nicole attempted a "hmm" sound of agreement, but instead she grunted, sounding to herself like a farm animal, somewhere between a cow and a pig.

"The pumpkins," said the woman, who apparently wasn't shocked by Nicole's grunt. "They have personality, don't they?"

Of course, the pumpkins. "You're right," Nicole said, and let slip a laugh of relief that sounded to her like a horse's whinny. Nicole picked up a tall, stretched-out pumpkin and laughed again because it reminded her of her mother's brother. "This one is my uncle," Nicole said, and she was about to go on to describe him, but when the woman didn't look up at her, Nicole stopped herself abruptly. "Bawk," she said, like a chicken.

The tall old woman continued to fondle pumpkin after pumpkin, remaining silent for what must have been minutes before turning to Nicole and saying, "I'll bet you're Steve's wife." The woman looked at Nicole as though she hadn't ignored her earlier. Perhaps she hadn't. "I'm April May Rathburn from down the road. Your husband found me just the right window."

Nicole's heart opened up like a little storm cloud.

Mrs. Harland appeared before them in long black braids, and Mrs. Rathburn said, "Good morning, Rachel." At least three times a week, Nicole bought fruits, vegetables, and flowers at the farm stand, always sliding the exact change into the slot in the honor box, but never while Rachel Harland was actually standing there. Up close, Rachel Harland's young face seemed ghoulish in its round nakedness. Her dark eyes were too close together, and her thin black eyebrows angled nearly straight down into the bridge of her nose. None of the words Nicole had for the looks of women seemed to fit Rachel Harland, and because her face didn't succumb to any other description, Nicole decided that she was ugly. No wonder she'd married such an old man.

"How are you enjoying October?" April May Rathburn asked.

Nicole meant to answer, but at the last second she worried that Mrs. Rathburn was asking the question not of her but of Rachel Harland, and Nicole quacked instead of answering. Nicole wanted to cry out that she didn't usually make these strange sounds. She felt like weeping because she knew she would never explain the noises and because every woman in Greenland Township was happy and content except herself—even old women and ugly women were happy and content. Nicole did not want this to be the day she broke down completely. She looked across the street and saw creepy old Mrs. Shores staring out the window, and for a moment the woman's long face looked sort of inviting.

"The pumpkins this year have so much character," April May Rathburn said, unashamedly repeating to Rachel Harland the words she'd spoken to Nicole. Nicole wished that she herself had spoken to Rachel Harland in an enthusiastic, neighborly way.

Rachel Harland ignored Mrs. Rathburn, but Mrs. Rathburn didn't seem to mind.

"That's all I want to do at this time of year," Mrs. Rathburn said, catching Nicole's eye. "I just want to carve faces in these things with a butcher knife."

Nicole felt her body go rigid. Mrs. Rathburn must have seen her with the knife earlier, stabbing the air of her kitchen as though it were her husband. Or Mrs. Shore must have been watching Nicole, and she must have called Mrs. Rathburn, and now the whole neighborhood knew that Nicole was crazy and violent.

Mrs. Rathburn said, "Oh, I just love to carve pumpkins."

Nicole told herself that the mention of the butcher knife must have been a coincidence. When Nicole relaxed and let herself remember carving a pumpkin as a child, she felt better, and her relief swelled until she concluded that she needed to buy pumpkins. Her mother had bought pumpkins for Nicole the girl, but Nicole had never bought one for herself. Tonight before dinner she and Steve could sit outside and carve together, then set the finished heads in the front window and on the deck to grin at passersby. She'd call her family and tell the people at work they had to drive by in order to see her jack-o'-lanterns. She imagined her house beginning to glow soft orange, becoming like a jack-o'-lantern, with candlelight flickering off the walls, giving the new white paint a creamier tone. That would be a house that was a home; that would be the place that inspired love and a contentment that could last and deepen over a lifetime and would make her forget she'd ever considered disemboweling Steve.

"I'll take six big ones and four of these little gourds," Mrs. Rathburn said to Rachel Harland, and Nicole knew she too wanted six big ones and four little ones, but she thought it would sound dumb to parrot Mrs. Rathburn's request. As Mrs. Rathburn was paying Rachel Harland, Nicole heard a low croaking hum, but she didn't realize it was coming from her own throat until both women turned to look at her. Nicole swallowed. She was fine with her mother and she was fine at her office at the hospital, where she could lean across her desk and shake hands and make small talk before getting down to the business of insurance coverage, but out here in the open with her neighbors she felt awkward, even afraid, because anything could happen in such an unscripted environment. Life should be like a wedding, she thought, so you always knew what to do and say next.

"Let me get some goddamn change," Rachel Harland said, and went off toward the house.

Around the dilapidated farmhouse grew bright mums in orange, yellow, and purple (albeit thinned out from Rachel Harland's cutting and selling them), and it didn't seem fair to Nicole that such a run-down old place should look so cheerful. Nicole knew she had to buy and plant mums. Nicole's mother grew dozens of clusters of mums, and Nicole suddenly didn't know how she had lived without them. No one driving by could possibly know how tastefully she had arranged the inside of the house unless she decorated the outside as well. She'd go into town later and buy mums. They'd be cheap with only a month left to finish blooming. She'd plant flame-colored mums around the front of her deck, to foreground the fire inside her jack-o'-lanterns. She chose her first two pumpkins, the one with her uncle's long face and another that was small and perfectly round with a long stem, before realizing that she didn't have any money on her.

When Steve finally stepped out of the car, he looked not toward Nicole but at the farmhouse, and he seemed to appraise and admire the house as though he wanted to live there, just as he had appraised and admired their own house upon first seeing it and, come to think of it, her mother's house, too. It distressed Nicole to think that her husband might appreciate all houses equally. Steve adjusted the belt holding up his creased khakis and walked toward Rachel Harland, who was now standing by the side door with a bushel basket. Steve's hand was outstretched to shake with her, but when Rachel Harland did not accept his hand, Steve let it fall away, and Nicole felt sorry for her husband.

The blonde beside the car turned enough that Nicole saw her face and realized she was an older woman, as old as Nicole's mother, fifty maybe, and her hair was gray and silver rather than truly blond. Nicole told herself that Steve couldn't have any interest in such an old woman. Everything, then, was fine, for here was Steve giving a woman a ride and stopping at a house along his route in an attempt to sell windows, possibly with the ulterior motive of buying some land for their dream home. Even Nicole could see that the Harland house needed new windows. Nicole could imagine the drafts coming through the old windows, creating a breeze strong enough to extinguish any flames burning inside, whether they were jack-o'-lanterns or romantic dinner candles.

Nicole did not consider that fresh cool air slipping in from outside might actually make flames burn brighter and hotter than they would burn in Nicole's own well-insulated house.

19

BEFORE PULLING ONTO QUEER ROAD, TOM PARKS HAD SAT in the barn driveway and stared across at the Rathburn place, which looked so similar to the house in which he'd grown up: two stories, porch stretching halfway across the front, white-painted clapboards. The new bay window in the dining room seemed like a sensible addition. The Rathburns had always found ways to improve their house, while the Parkses had been so busy farming that they hadn't even kept theirs up. His uncle Larry Rathburn, his mother's brother, was a handy fellow, always fixing or building something. Parks got a kick out of that barn-shaped bird feeder Larry had made and the way the birds fed at the doorways like miniature feathered cattle. Parks's family house used to have a big sugar maple in front that turned orange and red in autumn. Being out here made Tom Parks long for his family—not for his ex-wife and kids in Texas, but for his parents and siblings.

On an autumn day like today, they'd all have been picking the remaining vegetables from the garden or raking leaves, maybe helping the Harlands bring in hay. The Harlands had seemed an opinionated and energetic lot back then, compared to the quiet Parkses, but for some reason it was the Parks family men who died unnatural and unquiet deaths. As a teenager, Tom Parks's older brother had crossed the tracks at Queer Road without looking, and a freight train had dragged his car a quarter mile toward Kalamazoo. One of Tom's uncles had been shot on opening day of deer season. Then Tom's father'd had the heart attack while driving the tractor and crashed into a tree over by the pond. If Tom Parks had been superstitious, he might have suspected his family carried a curse of some kind. He was careful around guns, railroad tracks, and heavy machinery, but he'd chosen a profession in which there were plenty of violent ways to die. Parks knew he had to stop thinking this way, not so much because he feared death, but because the death of a man whom no woman loved seemed wretched.

George ought to keep that barn door closed and locked, Tom told himself. There was no sense tempting kids to damage your property, and an open barn door was an invitation. Had Tom Parks looked over his shoulder one last time, he might have noticed a stream of smoke rising from the doorway, but Parks thought he'd seen enough. Though he still figured there was a kid hiding in that barn, he didn't really want to hassle kids any more than necessary. He believed that kids needed to hide from adults sometimes, which is why they liked barns and tree houses and forts, even unattached garages and old washhouses. Tom Parks had begged his wife to return to Michigan after his father's death, to move into the old family house, to fix it up and save it. The kids would have a better childhood in the country, he'd told her, with wild lands to roam and safe places to hang out, lots of ways to get trouble out of their systems.

As a teenager, Tom Parks had made plenty of trouble, perhaps as a way of rebelling against the mildness of his family. Around

Halloween, he'd soaped windows, strung toilet paper across people's front yards, and once he'd found a veined, milky afterbirth from his sister's horse foaling, and in the middle of the night dragged it onto a neighbor's front porch. Once he and a friend, not George, had even stolen a car, a nearly new Ford coupe, and then left it out on Red Arrow Highway. In fact, Tom Parks had been the one who originally changed the street signs on this road. George's grandfather Harold, and plenty of others besides, had always called Q Road "Queer Road," but young Tom Parks was the one who first doctored the Q RD signs by painting out the D and inserting UEE neatly between, and he had done this at every marked intersection for miles. Others had since kept up the tradition—as recently as two months ago somebody doctored a new sign. That proved kids nowadays weren't all that different than he'd been as a kid. If there'd been drugs when Tom Parks was young, he'd probably have taken them, but fortunately, he'd had only alcohol to screw himself up with. And girls, of course. Once a boy got to be about fourteen, he would always have the option of getting screwed up over girls, whether the girls liked him the way they always seemed to like George Harland, or whether they didn't give a damn about him, the way girls, for the most part, hadn't given a damn about Tom Parks.

Even his wife must have disliked him deep down, or she wouldn't have been able to play such a crummy trick on him, getting him to move to Texas and then, after Tom's father died and the farm was sold, divorcing him there. Tom Parks had done his best in staying out West five more years for his daughter and son, but when his ex-wife remarried, Parks could bear the flatness and the dry heat of Texas no longer. Parks's daughter was fifteen and seemed an exotic, glamorous creature—Parks marveled that something so lovely could have sprung from him. If his boy were a troublemaker, then Parks could show a fatherly understanding, pull strings to keep his son from getting whacked by the full force of the law. Tom Parks would have been happy to drive out to Texas to talk to a cop about cutting his son some slack. But there was no danger of that with the boy's face in the computer screen all the time; the boy hardly even looked up when you were with him. Parks had hoped that his kids might want to move back to Michigan, but neither had even wanted to come visit him this summer. "Maybe I'd come for a week if I had a laptop," his son had said on the phone.

Gray Cat streaked across Queer Road in front of Parks's car and disappeared so quickly that he could have been a ghost. Though Parks might well have looked in the rearview mirror and seen smoke dribbling upward, he instead shifted into drive and turned left, headed north on Queer Road, telling himself that it was foolish to always be looking back and regretting. Like his aunt April May said the other day, it was better to look to the future, at what you could still do to change things for the better. He touched the cigarette pack in his top pocket and told himself again that in the future George should lock his barns. Parks did finally look in his rearview mirror, but he focused only on the flame-colored leaves of the maples that lined the east side of the road, on land his family used to own. The leaves were bright enough to burn a man's eyes.

A half mile north of the barn, Officer Parks slowed as he approached the vegetable stand. He recognized the pretty blond gal near the pumpkins as the occupant of one of the prefabs that had replaced his house. (Unlike Elaine Shore, the young couple hadn't filed any complaints, God love them.) When he saw his aunt April May on the other side of the pumpkins, Parks gave a blip of his siren and light and pulled into the driveway, to park behind George's truck.

20

ELAINE SHORE WAS STRAIGHTENING THE GLASS-STOPPERED bottles in her spice rack for the second time that morning when she heard the blip of the police cruiser, a much-needed reminder of order in this neighborhood. She had already adjusted the condiments in her refrigerator door and lined up all the bottles and tubes in the bathroom. She sat again in her breakfast nook, clad in the quilted nylon bathrobe that had become her uniform in the months since she'd retired from driving the school bus. Across the street at the pumpkin wagon stood the blond wife from next door. Elaine's hair had once been soft and flowing like that, but now even her short strands seemed unmanageable. Elaine had just taken some ibuprofen tablets to fend off a headache she thought might be coming on, but the chaos at the vegetable stand was making her temples throb. First thing in the morning, when the vegetables were arranged in neat rows and the flowers in big glass jars, Elaine admired the colorful rural scene. But when people began getting out of their cars, milling around, turning each squash and melon over in their hands, messing up the piles, Elaine couldn't bear it. Most people parked on the shoulder at angles so that their cars jutted into the road. And if it wasn't illegal parking, it was those animals getting loose.

The first time Elaine had called the police about the Harlands' animals grazing in her lawn this spring, Officer Parks assured her it would be taken care of, and within a half hour that girl tramped over and, without a word to Elaine, grabbed the pony and started walking it home. The other two animals fell in line. When Elaine shouted at the girl and pointed out to her where the pony had done its business, the girl had looked up and said, "Shit makes good fertilizer." Elaine had been startled by the girl's face—just for a moment, Elaine thought that girl was an alien. But alien faces, she had reminded herself, were thin and clean. In fact, that round-faced girl with her rumpled clothing and long, messy hair was the complete opposite of an alien. That girl embodied the problem the aliens were coming to solve.

Once Elaine had composed herself, she'd said, "Maybe it's fertilizer for that garden of yours, but it certainly isn't fertilizer for a decent lawn." Then that girl let go of the pony, walked over, and kicked the pile of manure, sent it spraying all over the lawn so nobody could ever clean it up no matter how long they worked. Elaine was shocked speechless, and it took her a few minutes to regain her composure and march into the house to call the police again. Parks must have talked to the Harlands because the next time the animals got into her lawn Mr. Harland led them away and that girl came over with a shovel and carried the several piles of manure back across the road without a word. Off and on ever since, Elaine had noticed that girl staring over in the most intense way, with her arms crossed over her chest, as though trying to control Elaine's mind. Just seeing that girl made Elaine empty her head of all thoughts in case the girl could read her telepathically.

On October 9, Elaine Shore was grateful to see Officer Parks's uniformed body pop out of the cruiser, which he'd parked in the driveway, where a person ought to park. She would have preferred, of course, that Officer Parks were more neatly pressed, that his uniform was not so tight across his belly, and that it was not loose and wrinkled elsewhere. The police station ought to be more like the military, she told herself, and they ought to line up all the officers every morning and make sure they looked like proper representatives of the law.

On a Saturday like today, Elaine used to enjoy going out to lunch or visiting her daughter and grandchildren on the west side of Kalamazoo, but nowadays the outside world just seemed too complicated to negotiate. First there was the downtown traffic, and then her daughter's house was messy, and her newest grandbaby's face was always smeared with dirt and jelly, and he drooled so much that he seemed to Elaine downright defective. Since she'd moved out here two years ago, Elaine had become distracted by the wide open space, so much so that she was unable to concentrate, even on her romance novels. Of course, she had been mistaken in originally thinking that the open space was empty; after all, the ground was covered with bugs and caterpillars, and on some mornings tumorlike mushrooms bulged obscenely where the night before there had been nothing. Beneath the soil burrowed moles and snakes and possums; the air was filled with pollen, dirt, and more bugs. The farm world was one of chaos, of life growing out of anyone's control. But it was probably that illusion of empty space that made Elaine contemplate the possibility of alien ships every hour of every day. Or maybe she thought so often of space aliens simply because their arrival was imminent and the hour of invasion was nearing. As she watched those women handling pumpkins across the street, she conjured up for herself a vision of identical naked gray figures walking single file, with synchronized steps, down the ramp of a gleaming windowless spaceship that she imagined had landed in that girl's garden. Today could well be day zero, she told herself, the beginning of the new order.

Elaine Shore really hadn't known that living here in the country was going to involve all this disorder, starting with the lawn: in their old place in Milwood the lawn had been all grass, not wild weeds that could grow six inches in one night so you had to beg your husband to mow the lawn practically every day. The most you could hope for out here was that the lawn was short and green. If it was just short and green you were grateful. And how she had loved the neat, fresh rows of farmland corn when she and her husband had driven by in search of a plot of land to purchase. But at this time of year, when you saw the brown stalks drying in the field, you realized that the rows weren't as straight as you'd originally thought and the plants themselves were just plain dirty. And when Harland harvested, the machinery threw dust and reddish chaff into the air. That stuff floated and came to rest on her window ledges, on the sidewalk leading from the driveway to the front door, on cars if they weren't in the garage with the door sealed. It fell in a blizzard on her lawn and on her asphalted and curbed driveway. Afterward, all winter, the fields lay barren in stubble.

She'd driven a school bus for twenty-five years, and in the last five of those years she had been at her wit's end about the way kids refused to sit in their seats, always squirming, tossing objects, snacking despite the sign NO FOOD OR DRINK. There had been a time she'd liked the kids and the driving, just as there had been a time she'd enjoyed her husband, but both interests had expired. Before they moved to Greenland Township, Elaine and her husband hadn't slept in the same bed for years. In the new Greenland house, Elaine had tried to sleep with him again. She had even tried making love with him once, but the result was just too sloppy, and to be honest she felt a little queasy even thinking about the whole business. That was why she slept in the spare room. Love had never measured up to the romance novels, but after moving to Greenland, Elaine knew all that fumbling was over for good.

Which was fine, because it gave her more energy to focus on

talking with her real estate lawyer and with members of the zoning board and other township officials. Elaine was looking toward the future of this neighborhood. Her lawyer said that she should attend every township meeting and file every possible complaint. He said she should consider herself a pioneer, blazing a trail for others who would come here in the future, when the neighborhood would be row upon row of neat houses and paved driveways. The best hope for this neighborhood, the lawyer had told her, was to get enough people moving out here side by side that the property values went up and people like the Whitbys, Higginses, and Harlands couldn't afford to keep paying the taxes. Elaine would be an agent for change, the lawyer said, and Elaine took a certain amount of pride in that designation. When enough folks moved in, city water and sewer and natural gas would be piped out, and then they would begin to get these bugs and weeds under control. Elaine would be responsible for bringing civilization to this untamed place.

Elaine's husband suddenly appeared outside the window, and his physical presence startled her. There he was, walking along the driveway from the mailbox as though everything was fine with the world. He returned to the house by the kitchen door and put a pile of mail in front of Elaine, then calmly filled up his coffee cup again, as though chaos weren't swirling around them. Elaine smoothed her hair back from her face with both hands, but she could still feel it touching her forehead. She straightened the pile of mail in preparation for going through it one piece at a time.

"It's all advertising," her husband said, leaning against the door frame. "Why don't you get outside today, take a walk or something. You haven't even gotten dressed for a week."

Elaine looked back across the street and said, "Do you think they're paying taxes on that money they take in for those vegetables?"

Her husband shook his head and carried his coffee cup back into the TV room. As soon as he was gone, Elaine unfolded a brochure advertising a Florida retirement village and laid it atop the news spread of the alien landing. Of course Elaine was committed to her mission in Greenland Township, but a week ago, without telling her husband, she had called the Pelican Retirement Corporation and requested this information. The glossy picture before her featured white trailers in a row, each with a little attached front porch, and on each porch stood one tidy round table and two or three deck chairs. Each of the homes had a tiny lush lawn containing exactly one miniature palm tree or spiky bush, and the rest of nature was kept at bay. The development looked even better than she had imagined from the display ad in the *Weekly World News*.

Elaine sighed and folded her arms on the table and leaned into them so that her hands rested lightly against her breasts. She told herself that her husband would be singing a different tune come spring, when the wind blew over from the pig farm. Oh, yes. Elaine had discovered that life in the country was not all it was cracked up to be. Out in the country with these selfish farmers, it was apparently too much to ask to sit in your own kitchen with the window open two inches without smelling manure. In this neighborhood, it was considered unreasonable to want livestock to remain inside their fences and out of your lawn. People here didn't care about the difference between legal and illegal parking, and it was foolish to hope that they could have enough self-control to admire the neatly stacked vegetables and pumpkins at the farm stand the way Elaine did and think *how quaint,* and drive on by to the grocery store.

21

RACHEL WATCHED SALLY PETTING THE ANIMALS AT THE fence line. The skinny bitch couldn't be bothered to get food or medicine for David, but she could drive around with neighbor men all day. Rachel wished one of the animals would take a bite out of Sally. Maybe Rachel could teach Martini the pony to bite on command. Then if Sally asked to borrow George's truck, Rachel would tell her to go to hell and give Martini the signal, and he would reach across the barbed wire and chomp her.

"Nice day. The neighborhood is beautiful this time of year," said the man from across the street, as though Rachel gave a damn what he thought of the neighborhood. Rachel meant to ignore him, but he was a big guy, even taller and broader than he had looked from a distance. Rachel wished George could hire a man this size to help him, but this particular man seemed way too clean. He smelled of soap and his skin reflected light—he was probably impossible to tolerate in sunshine. Rachel was only standing there to keep an eye on Sally, she told herself, to prevent her from bothering George. Sally turned away from the animals and approached with an exaggerated swing of her hips.

"Rachel!" Sally said, with fake delighted surprise. Sally could brighten her face and give the illusion of being animated, the way a small, sickly bird puffed out its feathers to look larger and healthier than it was. The layers of Sally's hair fell upon one another in a way that made Rachel think of those stupid white domestic ducks preening on the riverbank. Rachel imagined herself wrenching and twisting Sally's bird body, snapping her in two. Sally picked two pumpkin gourds from the bushel basket Rachel was holding and pressed them onto her breasts so that the stems stuck out like long, curling, alien nipples. The neighbor man laughed hesitantly, as though waiting for Rachel's approval. Upon seeing Sally's big-knuckled hands wrapped around the tiny pumpkins, Rachel smiled and snorted a laugh. She couldn't help noticing Sally's hands looked just like David's. Rachel put down her bushel basket and looked around in hopes of seeing David. She should run out and find him and give him a couple of apples, at least. Wherever he was, he was bound to be really hungry by now. Rachel wiped her hands on her jeans.

Sally put the gourds back in the basket and said, "I need to ask George if he can give me a ride to the store today."

"No fucking way, Sally. He's busy." Rachel watched the animals beside the stock barn and tried to rid herself of having momentarily liked Sally, or Sally's hands anyway. The donkey was chewing on George's ex-wife's llama's neck. Maybe the donkey would be the one she'd train to bite.

George came out of the animal barn and disappeared into his toolshed without Sally spotting him. George apparently hadn't noticed that Tom Parks had pulled into the driveway behind the truck, and was over there fondling pumpkins with April May and the blonde from across the street. Rachel wasn't about to go out of her way to announce his arrival. Even though Parks's concern about Margo's disappearance seemed sincere, Rachel had to hate him for the way he had tried to talk George out of marrying her, right up until the ceremony six weeks ago.

Sally pretended she hadn't heard Rachel's "No fucking way." Sally smiled at Steve before addressing Rachel again. "I'll just ask George if I can borrow his truck. David needs a puffer." Sally tipped her head back and shook her hair and smiled, and in Sally's face, Rachel saw David's widely spaced brown eyes.

"Go to hell, Sally."

"Hey, can I get a pumpkin for David to carve?" Sally said. She didn't seem to notice she'd just been sent to hell.

"Sally, I can take you to the store," offered the salesman.

"Rachel, you must already know Steve," Sally said.

"We're neighbors," the salesman said. "We've been waving to each other for months."

Rachel rolled her eyes, but found herself feeling warm toward the man nonetheless. She said, "Well, I guess you've never called the goddamn police on the livestock."

"I'm an animal lover." The salesman appeared to blush. "Glad to finally meet you."

This time Rachel accepted the big soft hand, and oddly enough, she liked the feel of the damn thing, which made her think of warm, dry sand in her fingers. She hesitated before letting his hand go, grasping it slightly longer and tighter than she had meant to, against the feeling of it slipping away.

Standing so close to the house, Steve could confirm what he'd suspected, that the wood trim was dry, even brittle, and that what had looked like unpainted horizontal boards actually had ancient specks of white paint, which meant that this house was not even stained with a natural finish, but was entirely unprotected from the elements. He couldn't hold back any longer. "You really need some windows and siding. Have you got red squirrels in the walls?"

"How the hell do you know that?"

"Here's my card. I sell insulated windows and vinyl siding. That's one of the biggest problems around here, the red squirrels." He pushed the card toward her.

"We only just got the damn squirrels." Despite an inclination to reach out and accept the card, Rachel stood her ground. "You must have driven them little sons of bitches scurrying out of other people's houses right over here."

"If I did, I certainly didn't mean to." Steve didn't try to defend himself by saying that he'd only been assigned to this part of the county a few months ago. There was nothing to be gained by getting defensive with a customer. He withdrew the card, put it back in his pocket. In truth, Steve rather preferred the cranky women to the nice ones. The nice ones were nice with everybody, so you had no idea where you stood, but once you won over the cranky gals, you were in. From a distance, he'd figured Rachel was about twenty-seven years old, and he'd assumed that the birth date in the *Gazette* marriage license listing had been a typographical error, but up close she indeed looked seventeen. He wouldn't have taken Harland for a cradle robber, but there she was.

"If you sell windows," Rachel said, "then you can get me a piece of glass to replace a broken window pane."

"You may want to replace the whole window."

"It's just a damn pane of glass."

"I can take a look at it," he said. "You guys heat with LP gas?"

"Oil and wood."

Anyone could see the aboveground oil tank behind the house and the pile of firewood outside the back door, but Steve had wanted to make conversation. "You're paying a lot for that oil, and you're probably losing about forty percent of your heat through these windows and window frames. And if we put vinyl siding on, we layer insulation between the wood and the vinyl. Do your windows rattle in the wind?"

"Hell yes, the windows rattle. Windows always rattle."

"If they're rattling, you could be losing even more heat. I'll be able to give you an estimate in twenty minutes."

"We aren't going to buy any damn windows. Any extra money we get we're buying land. Land is all I care about." Rachel didn't understand why she was chattering on to this guy, saying more than she'd said to George all week. It must be something in the air today, she thought.

"Maybe buying windows will save you so much money on oil that you can buy even more land." Steve smiled. "No obligation. I promise not to be a pushy salesman, especially being your neighbor and all." He stared into her face. "I'll check out that broken window for you."

"Go ahead. I don't care." She turned away so he'd stop looking at her.

"I'd like to go in the house to measure the windows, if it's all the same to you."

"Fine, go in the damn house." Rachel didn't know what had made her think she liked this guy. Did everybody have to want something from a person? Could nobody leave another body alone?

Steve, for his part, was surprised that Rachel gave him permission to go into her house alone—he'd figured she'd walk through with him. He wouldn't allow a salesman in his house alone, and the thought of his wife even encountering another salesman made him feel downright itchy. Surely Nicole would send such men away.

Steve opened the side door into the little mudroom, which must not have been swept in ages. Some of the jackets hanging on a dozen wall pegs were connected to each other by a network of spiderwebs. He lifted a stiff nylon shell to confirm that it had hardened into position with the impress from the wall peg sticking out its back. With a tiny metal tape he carried in his pants pocket, Steve measured the windows in either side of this small room and recorded the numbers on a pocket-sized pad of estimate forms. Of course, he'd suggest these windows were the least important; he'd give the Harlands an estimate and then, to knock it down, he'd take these off. Rachel's rifle lay on the windowsill looking black and clean, but Steve resisted his desire to touch it. The next room was the kitchen, where the slate floor made him worry about cold feet on winter mornings. Here he'd suggest replacing the six-pane double-hung job over the sink with a pair of roll-out windows. Women always liked roll-out windows over their sinks, and this Rachel couldn't be so different from other women. Two large double-hung windows on the south wall brightened the table, which was cluttered with papers and books. Steve noticed a hardcover *The Potawatomi* with a library sticker on the binding. He ran his hand across a dog-eared *Wild Plants of Michigan*, which lay open, facedown. He wondered if Nicole would like such a book, if she might take an interest in wildflowers. Or birds, maybe. If he bought Nicole a bird book, he could also buy the binoculars he wanted and say they were for her. At first Steve had liked it that Nicole always read home decorating magazines, but lately it seemed she was holding up those glossy, overdone pages to him as a reproach for their plain house. The top of a small, dusty television in the corner of the Harlands' living room was covered with newspapers. A lower corner pane of glass was busted out of the east-facing six-by-eight-foot window. Glass shards still lay on the windowsill, though somebody had propped an old leather Bible over the empty space to keep out drafts. He'd tell the Harlands that multipane windows were awfully expensive and that they should go with one big window. They could get a snap-on plastic grid to give the illusion of separate panes of glass, and that would be easier to clean. Not that cleaning looked like a priority around here. He and Nicole kept their own place nice and neat. He envisioned the interior of his ranch house across the street, with Nicole glowing slightly golden in the center of the living room, beaming at him as he arrived home. In his vision, the ceilings were slightly higher, and his wife was more solid, her face rounder.

He climbed the stairs to the second story, where he investigated and took measurements in each of the two smaller bedrooms, one of which was solidly packed with boxes and junk. The hall was floored with unfinished pine, same as the bedrooms. If he somehow managed to make love with Rachel, say, while her husband was out of town at a fertilizer convention and while Nicole was at work, he would not walk out onto this floor barefoot for fear of getting splinters—he'd put on shoes just to go to the toilet.

Rachel seemed like a woman who wouldn't need constant reassurance from a man. She wouldn't burst out crying for no reason as Nicole had started doing lately. If Steve moved into this house with Rachel, say if Nicole left him and if George Harland died in a tractor accident, Steve would first replace all the windows, and then he'd sand these floors and apply coat upon coat of high-gloss polyurethane. He imagined his and Rachel's life together in this house when all the woodwork was finished, and immediately the floors began to gleam before him. As Steve measured the two big windows in the bedroom looking out over the driveway, he smelled female sweat rising out of the mussed double bed. Afterward, he sat on the edge of the bed, on what he figured was her side, nearer the windows, and slid one hand between the sheets. He thought of Rachel's muscular, curved body slipping out of the barn jacket and ill-fitting jeans, and climbing naked under the covers. Steve knew he would probably never sleep with her, never have her angry arms wrapped around him, never hear her obscenities whispered into his ears. In houses all over the township, there were so many women Steve would never have sex with. Sitting there on the bed with his hand under the covers, he let himself feel overwhelmed by the sadness of such a world, in which a man was not allowed to love every woman but was bound to only one.

When he looked up to the doorway he saw Sally smiling at him, one small hip thrust out. He yanked his arm out from under Rachel's blankets and stood.

"Lot of windows," he said. "I'll bet this bedroom gets cold."

Sally smiled in a way that told him she knew just how dirty-minded he was and that she didn't care. Steve thought that Sally would be an especially easy woman to please. A few beers and a few packs of cigarettes was all she'd need to keep her going for a day. She might ask a guy to take her to the store, but she'd never want him to stroll with her through the mall. Steve brushed against her as he moved into the hall.

"All these upstairs windows are the same size," Steve said. "That's convenient."

"What about those way up there?" Sally said, pointing to the ceiling. Above where they stood on the landing was some kind of opening into what must be the attic—light showed around two sides of a wooden panel. Sally said, "Let's check it out." Her little body seemed to float upward from the wall rungs, and when she pushed aside the panel, daylight poured down. She said, "Come on."

Steve felt a little uneasy about going up into another man's private space, but light meant windows, surely. He risked the smoothly worn rungs with his 265 pounds and at the top pulled himself through the square entrance, to arrive in a tiny room. He could barely stand with the ceiling as low as it was, so he sat beside Sally on a built-in bench. He was surrounded on three sides by old, rattling multipane windows whose putty had crumbled, whose white paint, probably lead-based, had mostly flaked onto the plank floor. He had noticed this structure in the winter when they first moved in across the street, but he'd forgotten about it since the big sycamore leafed out and covered it from view. From his sitting position, he took approximate measurements, jotted notes, and reminded himself about the tremendous heat loss of keeping such a room. He looked through the branches at his own house, which was nearly identical to Elaine Shore's from above, except for Elaine's protruding corner breakfast nook. He looked beyond the houses, to the cornfields and farther, to the pond that fed the creek, which ran under Queer Road and down into the river. He hadn't realized the source of the creek was so close behind his own house, or maybe it was an illusion. Bushes and small trees lined the creek, and big trees surrounded the pond. His own little half acre had no bushes or trees, and it made his house look lonesome. He'd talk to Nicole about planting a tree or two; he'd tell her he wouldn't mind mowing around them. Trees kept a house cooler in the summer, and they increased resale value.

"Which house is yours?" Sally asked.

"That one, on the left."

Sally leaned against him more than was necessary to look. He reached both arms around her and pulled her light body onto his lap to give her a better view, and she stayed there. Steve ran his hands over the outside of Sally's thighs, but he felt mostly bone. Nicole was small too, but she had firm flesh. Though Sally wiggled and leaned against his chest, Steve could tell the woman didn't desire him one bit. He didn't mind—he was married, after all, and starting such an affair with a neighbor lady would be too risky.

The roof-truss construction of his own house made it impossible to build a room like this at home, but Steve had to figure out how to have some kind of small private place. Nicole had started crying the one time he'd said he'd wanted to sleep the night on the couch in his little office, and he'd given in and gone to bed with her, but he really liked the thought of curling up for the night somewhere small and out of the ordinary, somewhere like this window room. He looked down through the high bleached branches of the sycamore to see that a blue-and-white police car was parked in the driveway. At the roadside, a man Steve didn't recognize closed a hatchback on four bright pumpkins. Steve imagined Nicole still naked under her white bathrobe, sitting at their dining table, thumbing through a magazine depicting tastefully overdone bedrooms while she talked to her mother on the phone.

"Look at this." Steve pulled out a bleached photo from behind a window frame. "It's an old photo. A woman, I think."

Sally took it from his hand and held it up to the light. "I don't see anything."

"Hey, there's *your* house," Steve said, pointing west over cornfields toward a house with a deteriorating, rust-colored silo.

"I need a cigarette," Sally said. "Let's go to the store."

Steve figured Nicole couldn't mind his doing good deeds, say, taking this woman to the store. He'd explain that creating goodwill in the neighborhood would pay off in sales eventually.

To the south, across the street from April May Rathburn's house, Steve saw smoke rising from the doorway and roofline of the old barn. George Harland must be burning that barn, he thought; that must be why Rachel said he couldn't take Sally to the store. Though earlier today Steve had fantasized about putting his office there, he now told himself that the old barn must be unsafe, a hazard for children, and its roof probably leaked, making the building of no use to anyone. Farmers didn't waste anything, so why else would Harland be burning?

"They're burning that barn," Steve said.

"Come on," Sally said, already beginning the descent. "Do you want to stop at the Barn Grill before we go to the store?"

Steve noticed Sally had dropped the little photo on the floor. He picked it up and studied it again. He made out the outline of a woman's head and shoulders. He stuck it back under the window frame before following Sally down the ladder.

22

"GOOD-LOOKING PUMPKINS," TOM PARKS SAID WHEN HE met George in front of the toolshed. George was carrying a greasy shaft eighteen inches long, something from his tractor or combine, but he didn't seem to have gotten any grease on himself. Parks became filthy the minute he opened the hood of his truck to check the oil. Lately he'd been on call so much that he drove the cruiser all the time, which was nice because the county took care of its maintenance.

"Rachel's an awfully good gardener," George said. "Reminds me of my grandmother that way." Only after he said it did George realize what an odd comparison that was: Rachel and Henrietta. Both of them gardeners deep down into their bones, both of them angry and unknowable. Of course George hadn't tried to get to know his stern grandmother—it would have seemed like a betrayal of his grandpa.

"What happened to your front window?"

"A kid tossed a pumpkin into it at three A.M."

"Kids can make trouble, all right," Parks said, but even as he said it, he was thinking that kids just needed some time and space. "You want to file a complaint?"

"Nah. Rachel's keeping the pumpkins on the wagon," George said. "She can pull it into the stock barn at night." George had a way of staring over the horizon while he conversed with a person, as though that person was just one of many rows of a crop over which he was keeping watch.

"I saw a kid messing around in your barn just now. I pulled in and looked inside. His bike was in the doorway, but he was hiding."

"That was David," George said. "Sally's kid. He was helping me stack straw."

"I found these cigarettes on his bike. Sally's brand." He held out the cigarette pack, then felt a little embarrassed to be showing he knew what the woman smoked. Parks figured George must have already noticed he had a soft spot for Sally.

George looked away from the mashed green-and-white pack. "He's a good kid. I don't think he'd smoke in the barn."

"Don't know why he'd hide from me," Parks said, although really he did understand that even a good kid might hide from a cop. Parks put the cigarettes in his top pocket. "I thought you might want to go down and check the situation out, make sure everything's okay." Parks followed George's gaze, turning and looking in the direction of the river, though they couldn't see it from this distance.

George nodded. "I think David's ma's here somewhere."

"I gave her a ride home from the Barn Grill a few nights ago." Parks looked down at his wide black shoe. "Sounds like there's no chance of Mike coming back. How do you think she's doing?"

"She's same as always, far as I can tell."

"You're still letting her live there rent free."

"That's how it turns out." George looked briefly at Parks before letting his gaze sweep over Rachel's garden and through the wind-break of walnut trees separating it from the soybean field beyond. Both Parks and George then looked northeast toward the Whitby pig farm and Higgins's dairy operation, where both men worried to themselves that new subdivisions would appear within a couple years. George had a standing deal with the Higginses, who bought most of his second and third cuttings of alfalfa for their dairy herd. If the rumor was true, if the Higginses were trying to get out of the business, George didn't know who'd buy that much hay from him in the future. Like the Taylors, the Higginses would get a good price from a developer, enough to retire comfortably.

Parks meanwhile was telling himself that if he still owned his land today, he wouldn't sell one square foot no matter what it took to get the money for taxes. He'd sell drugs confiscated from drug busts before he'd sell any of his land. He startled himself with this last thought. Something happened to him when he got out here by his old land; being here made him feel a little like one of those nuts who holed up in an underground root cellar with guns and survival gear.

George nodded and repeated himself. "That's how it turns out, all right. I can't very well stop paying the electric over there, but I did let the phone get disconnected."

Parks imagined he knew why George let Sally live there for free—for the same reason that people fed the birds, because it was a pleasure to watch them land and then fly away at a whim. Espe-cially, it was nice to watch such a carefree, light sort of creature when you felt your own life was toilsome and undignified, and when your own body was growing fat and sluggish.

"So you think I ought to lock that barn?" George said.

"You probably ought to. You said hay was high this year." Parks glanced around for Sally but couldn't locate her, and instead looked over at Elaine Shore's house, where his own house used to be. Elaine Shore was the silliest of the complainers, but at least her alien encounter calls provided some comic relief. The worst folks were a mile or two away in cornfield developments of a few dozen two-story houses side by side, where half the people had motion detector lights that went off all night for every stray cat and raccoon, and the other half were calling the cops complaining about their neighbor's lights. And a lot of them had put in thousand-dollar burglar alarm systems, all hooked up downtown, and on some of those false alarms, fellows had to go out and check, and if another car wasn't able to make it there fast enough, they'd call and wake up Parks at the Greenland Motor Court, where he was still paying the weekly rate after almost a year.

George said, "I should get four dollars a bale for the second and third cuttings of alfalfa, but about a third of that's oat straw."

Parks felt stupid for not having noticed it was straw. He had half a mind to go take another look, to make sure he could still tell the difference. Parks said, "Still, that's worth something, right?"

"I got two-fifty a bale for some straw this week, from a guy who told me he was going to feed it to his fat ponies," George said. "Wind must be picking up. I can smell Whitby's."

Parks sniffed the air but could not smell pigs, probably due to a little allergic trouble he'd been having off and on since returning from Texas. Whitby's didn't have a modern operation over there, just an old-fashioned farm with about three hundred head of Durocs that you saw out rooting for bugs and worms between feedings. Apparently when the Whitbys' neighbors sold those plots for the subdivision, somebody didn't get the word that living downwind of a pig farm was going to be a little fragrant, especially when the farmers in all directions, including Harland, were spreading the manure on their fields. This spring dozens of calls had come in, complicated public nuisance claims that sounded as though they'd been fashioned by lawyers. Folks who spent Saturday and Sunday mornings sitting on their screened porches drinking cappuccino and enjoying the wide expanses were threatening lawsuits, no doubt making their money off pork bellies and corn futures, some of them. Meanwhile the folks growing the corn were working eighteen-hour days and trying to keep the shit off themselves.

"Yessir, you probably ought to lock that barn," Parks said. "How much you got in there?"

"Three hundred–some bales of straw, almost eight hundred of alfalfa."

Both men looked in the direction of the hay barn a half mile down the road, but they couldn't see it because they were standing in front of the toolshed. Out in the open pasture, Martini the pony whinnied.

"No sense taking a chance on losing it, George."

"You're probably right."

"You know, George, I've been meaning to talk to you about something of a serious nature. I'm wondering if you can tell me exactly, or as best you can remember, anyhow, when your brother came up missing three years ago?"

"Oh, I could probably calculate it. It was the last part of September, and it was a full moon. When he got out of jail in August, he came back, and for a couple weeks he helped me some. Then he found out I'd given Margo Crane that sliver of land, and he was so mad he would hardly talk to me for the next few weeks. Last time I saw him was on a Friday evening, third or fourth Friday in September. He asked to borrow my truck, and I said no because he'd been drinking. He took off walking down Queer Road, and I never saw him again."

"And you didn't report him missing?"

"Well, you know Johnny. If he's not in jail, then he's probably hiding out for some reason."

"Last Friday in September, you might be saying?"

"I can tell you it was a bright night, a full harvest moon. Johnny always acted crazy in a full moon."

Parks cleared his throat. "I'm pretty certain that was the same time Margo Crane disappeared." Parks could have said more, but everything was so pleasant out here that he didn't want to disturb the air with what he was thinking, so he only said, "I know you thought she came up missing later, but it was most likely around the same time."

George sighed. "Beans are getting dry enough to harvest. A guy could sure use a brother about now."

Parks nodded in agreement, but it struck him that even when George had bad luck, it seemed to benefit him. If that freeloading Johnny were still here, George would probably feel some kind of obligation to share the farm with him, maybe even give him some land.

"Hope it doesn't rain," Parks said, but he wasn't sure how sincerely he meant it. Parks wanted to be driving his own wagonloads of dry beans and corn to Climax, and he'd be jealous of George driving his. Hard to believe that Parks used to feel put out when he had to help his dad with farm work.

"No rain's forecasted," George said. "But you can't ever be sure, especially when the sky is like this."

23

RACHEL WATCHED HER HUSBAND TALKING TO PARKS OVER at the fence between the stock barn and the toolshed, watched him hold a long piece of metal away from himself until he located a big clean stone on which to rest the end. Rachel caught a few stray words from their conversation: window, pumpkins, alfalfa. Taking George for her husband in that courthouse ceremony meant owning his land, she'd been telling herself for six weeks, and that was all. It was becoming more and more difficult, however, to fight the desire to talk to him, even at the risk of babbling about nothing, even at the risk of spoiling everything with facts George didn't need to know. Watching her husband rest one elbow on the fence post now made her want to go put her hands on him and open him up like an old barn she'd slept in for years, but she didn't want to talk to Tom Parks, especially not since she'd been so damn stupid last week as to tell him when her mother really disappeared. The truth had a way of slipping out without your realizing it, which was clear proof that talking just led to trouble. Rachel turned away so that she could barely see George in her peripheral vision, which somehow made her imagine his body stretched out enough to cover hundreds of acres.

She looked back when she heard George say "David." Parks was holding out a flattened green-and-white cigarette pack. Both George and Parks shook their heads, as though wishing the cigarettes didn't exist. Rachel knew David had been smoking recently—she'd smelled smoke on him and told him he was an idiot. Maybe Parks had something to do with David's not showing up here yet, or maybe that window-busting Todd was responsible. After this rush of business at the produce tables, Rachel would head down to the barn with some apples, and maybe an egg sandwich, to see if he was, by some chance, still there. Because Rachel hadn't noticed Sally entering the house, she was surprised to see her come out in front of the salesman. Sally walked right to Steve's Thunderbird and folded her arms over the top, as though staking a careless claim on the car and the man, maybe even on the land. For months she had already been saying, with her body: I'm just going to live here, even though I don't give a damn about this place. Though Rachel didn't smoke, she considered going over and saying to Sally, "Give me a goddamn cigarette." No, she'd be even more forceful than that. "Sally, give me a cigarette, and then get the hell off my farm."

As Rachel approached the car, the salesman turned and greeted her, plain as day. He still smelled like soap, but he also smelled like an animal captured and subdued. She'd already forgotten how big and soft he was, how different from George, who was wiry and muscled. Something seemed wrong to Rachel, and she didn't know if it was just because the salesman was standing so close to her. The air smelled wrong, burnt maybe, and her body felt as though it might give birth to something small but weighty, the way lead shot was small but weighty. She reached inside her jacket and felt, through her shirt, the bullet lodged near her armpit.

"They make an awful lot of noise at night, don't they?" the salesman said. His eyes were on her hand moving under her jacket.

"Who the hell are you talking about?" She let her hand drop.

"Those red squirrels."

"So?"

"They scratch and scrabble," Steve said. "And they chew wires, too. They can even cause electrical fires."

Rachel looked the salesman square in the face, and though she'd meant to be hostile toward him, she found his face pleasant. "Hell yes," she said, though in truth the squirrels didn't much bother her, because sleeping in this house was quieter than any other place she'd slept.

"You need siding and windows worse than anyone I've seen all year," Steve said. "I'm writing you up an estimate. Seeing how I'm your neighbor, I'll make you a good deal."

Rachel couldn't think of any reason to disagree with the salesman's writing up an estimate. After all, she could start the woodstove with any kind of paper.

"So George is burning today," the salesman said. "I saw the fire from the cupola. That's what you call that little room, right? A cupola?"

"A cupola," she repeated. It sounded like something for chickens. She wanted to go interrupt George and Tom Parks and ask: What is a cupola? And also, she wanted to ask whether George smelled something wrong in the air. But she was in no hurry to leave the salesman; standing there talking to him was like standing beside a big spreading tree. In the months she'd avoided this guy, she'd never considered he might be a good neighbor—not as good as Milton or April May, but good enough.

"The attic room with all the windows up there. And isn't it a little dry to be burning?" Steve said. He was glad Rachel was looking at him. Her eyes were deep and dark, and her lips were red like a tart Michigan apple, inviting him to bite. If they were alone and she kept looking at him that way, he would move toward her until his mouth covered hers, and then he'd slide a hand beneath her jacket.

"It *is* too dry to be burning," Rachel said. "Where's this damn fire?"

"You can't see it from here."

Rachel followed the salesman around the trees to the fence line, and her eyes followed his finger south, across cornfields waiting to be harvested, toward the old barn, where smoke dribbled up from the horizon, a sickening gray inverted waterfall. She stared for another few seconds before shouting, "George!"

George looked up from his conversation with Parks, gave Rachel a contented look that said her scream had not sounded as loud and crazy to him as it had inside her head, or perhaps to him she sounded this crazy all the time, so he was used to it. His look suggested that all was more or less right with the world and the seasons, or as right as it could be with red squirrels in the walls, no hired man, and corn and soy prices lower than they were twenty years ago. George didn't register the panic in Rachel's eyes, perhaps because outdoors he was accustomed to looking across swaths of land to judge the readiness of fields, to know the coming weather from evidence brewing at horizons.

Rachel pointed south, but she felt uncertain about her sense of direction without her gun. George walked around the stock barn and to the fence line.

Parks followed. "Holy shit, George. That's your barn!"

Rachel was grateful to Tom Parks for saying it. Perhaps Parks, too, could someday be a decent neighbor.

George walked quickly to his truck. Because he was still looking at the fire, he didn't notice that the truck was blocked in the driveway by Parks's cruiser behind, the Thunderbird on one side, and eighty-foot-high walnut trees and the pasture fence elsewhere. Parks sat in his cruiser with the door hanging open and his feet, nearly as wide as they were long, planted on the ground. "Come in, this is two-five-five, Parks here." He spoke into his radio. "There's a fire on Queer Road, about twenty-seven hundred north. . . . That's Q Road. Barn belonging to George Harland." He paused. "There's no house." The response that followed over the radio sounded to Rachel like the sputtering of angry crows.

Parks said, "George. There's water down there, right?"

George clutched the door handle of his truck. The other hand still held the greasy tractor part. "There's a well with a hand pump," George said. "Well point might be clogged." George kept staring toward the barn as though gathering more information about the weather between here and there. He opened his truck door.

Martini ran a short distance in the pasture. He stopped abruptly, reared up, and ran back to the fence line. The other animals stamped and snorted.

Rachel knew the well point was fine. She'd rinsed her face in the water just three days ago. All her life she'd drunk from that well, but was there enough water to put out a fire? "And the creek!" Rachel shouted.

Tom Parks nodded and spoke into his radio. Rachel saw him take the cigarette pack out of his pocket and study it as the radio cackled a response. Then he placed the pack on the dashboard.

One after another the people around the vegetable stand either put down or clutched more tightly their melons, pumpkins, and Brussels sprouts as they moved for clearer views of the smoke rising to the south. Nicole Hoekstra, however, continued to stare at her husband.

April May Rathburn was out of range of the men's voices, and she'd left her driving glasses in her car, so as she looked through the trees, she wondered if that smoke could possibly be coming from *her* house.

"George, come on," Parks said. "Let's get down there."

"I've got irrigation hoses out back," George said.

"Hoses won't do you no good. Fire department will be here in five minutes with a lot bigger hoses, and you've got to be there. Leave that thing here."

George placed the greasy metal shaft atop the nearest railroad tie fence post. To Rachel this all seemed to be happening in slow motion, the men speaking, the smoke thickening in the distance, the metal shaft lying forlorn, woolly bears creeping around her feet so slowly that they would never get anywhere, never reach safe places, never in a million years.

Though she had often willed time to slow, she now feared she would be trapped in this hopeless, sluggish moment forever, the worst possible moment, with her still feeling friendly toward the salesman and his talk of vinyl frames and insulating glass. Rachel had never cared about resisting decay before now.

With his back to her, George seemed thin enough that he might disappear. Parks got into his front seat, started the quiet engine, and called out, "Come on, George. We've got to get down there before the trucks."

George looked over at Rachel as though establishing her location, and then turned away and curled his body into the front passenger seat of the county cruiser.

24

NICOLE LOOKED DOWN TO SEE HER HAND STROKING AN acorn squash as though it were a baby animal she'd rescued from abandonment. She caressed the green ribs, admired the way they rose to meet at the top of the squash in a burst of pumpkin orange. When she looked back at Steve, she saw that the old blonde was pressed against him, and both were looking off the way a couple together thirty years might watch the sun setting, without saying a word, because they'd already said all that mattered. They were together inside the Harland house for half an hour, time enough to do just about anything. That woman, a stranger, was having a perfect marriage with Nicole's husband, and Nicole had nothing.

"Look." Mrs. Rathburn elbowed Nicole. "Something's on fire."

Until then, Nicole had been looking so intently at Steve and the blonde that she hadn't thought to wonder what the two of them were actually staring at. When she finally looked south, Nicole saw a plume of smoke rise from what was probably somebody's house on fire. She felt a little ashamed that she didn't remember what house was there. Mrs. Rathburn's? But if it were her house, surely she would be more upset. Nicole looked down at the squash in her hand, greener than the greenest lawn, as dark and cool as the deepest pond. She'd always thought she didn't care for squash, but now she wasn't sure. The flavor was earthy, if she recalled correctly, musky perhaps, and maybe she'd been too young to appreciate it. She had no idea how to cook such a squash, but she could ask her mother.

Nicole looked back toward the rising smoke. She imagined inviting those people to her house—whatever people were losing everything in the fire. Those now homeless people would appreciate the simple but tasteful appointing of her house, the museum prints of flowers and the rolltop desk Steve had given her on their first anniversary. To people without a home, her house would feel like one. They'd admire her things and thank her, and she'd say, oh, it was nothing, that she was glad to help. For the first time in her life, she would devote herself to strangers, who, by continually talking of what they'd lost, would remind her of all she had. When Steve got home from work, she wouldn't have been watching for his car; instead she'd have been busy getting those people situated and fed. And later, when everybody had a cup of tea or a beer or soda, all of them would sit around the kitchen table and listen to the story of how the fire started and within minutes tore their lives apart. Nicole and Steve would look at each other across the table, sharing a sense of how fortunate they were. But would Steve still want another woman?

Nicole understood about a perfect marriage and a tragic divorce, but she didn't know what could occur in between. She stared at the side of Steve's face, at a sideburn that was slightly longer than she remembered it. When Steve finally turned toward her, he looked straight into her face and smiled, but for a moment he didn't seem to recognize her as Nicole, merely smiled and looked at her in the stupidest and friendliest way without recognition, looked at her as he might look at any woman.

He walked toward her, still smiling. When he reached her, he said, "Nice squash."

Nicole looked down at the hard, misshapen green thing and wondered how in the world she had ever considered cooking and eating it.

"We should go down and see what's on fire." Steve picked up a pumpkin from beside Nicole and turned it in his hands. Its roundness gave Steve a vision of his wife bulging in pregnancy and that thought cheered him.

Nicole looked away from Steve's weird grin and saw Mrs. Rathburn standing on tiptoes for a better view. Nicole noticed Mrs. Shore across the street, staring sadly out her window. As weird as the woman might be, Nicole had a feeling that Mrs. Shore would sympathize with her hurt in a way Mrs. Rathburn never would.

"I want some pumpkins," Nicole said.

"We'll get some pumpkins then," Steve said. "First we should go down and see that fire."

"I don't know." Nicole's vision was blurring from tears. She had the idea that Steve would be just as happy with any woman as he was with her. She said, "I just don't know."

"Don't know *what*?" Steve asked Nicole, meanwhile smiling in a friendly way at April May Rathburn.

As soon as April May realized, based on her view through the trees, that her own house might be on fire, she knew that her house being on fire wouldn't bother her. The morning had been so gray and overcast that she relished the possibility of a fire burning away the heaviness of the air, at any cost. As a kid in the 1930s and '40s, she'd been to bonfires behind the high school on the nights of football games. Everybody had been welcome at those bonfires, and she had loved the way people's faces glowed as the night grew dark. "They burn up lumber. They waste good wood," her father complained, which showed the difference that could exist between a German immigrant and his American children.

When April May stretched up on tiptoes as high as she could, anxious to see the blaze that was her house, the pain in her foot suddenly disappeared. Like magic, the pain of sixty-five years was gone, as quickly and completely as a spell being broken.

April May left the window salesman and his wife at the vegetable stand and carried the first two of her six pumpkins to the Buick, walking on the balls of her feet, feeling more buoyant than she had in decades. She liked the salesman, and his self-conscious wife seemed like a sweet girl. April May was also glad to be seeing more of Tommy Parks lately. She had always attended the township meetings, and she wondered if maybe Tommy could talk to George, get him to start coming to those meetings again. The conservative farmers would forgive him eventually for marrying Rachel, and really he shouldn't care if they didn't—the farmers' numbers were dwindling, and they needed him badly enough to overlook his impropriety. Seeing all those people in the same room, even if they were at odds, always made April May think that the farms and new homes could coexist, if houses lined the roads and the farming took place in acreage behind the houses, if new people would be tolerant of the realities of farming, and if the farmers wouldn't automatically resist change. April May saw how they could all fit together as one community, if only everyone would be sensible and tolerant.

Despite this neighborly feeling for her township, April May didn't mind the thought of her home reduced to a burned-out shell. If her house of fifty years were on fire, she thought, she'd stand out there with the neighbors and watch it burn. Well-constructed celebration bonfires were lovely, but it was also good sometimes to be at the mercy of uncontrollable forces. Like the tornado that destroyed a swath of the town when she was seven, disasters brought everybody together and gave them something to remember, put them in a common awe, the way God used to. April May returned to the vegetable stand and retrieved her third and fourth pumpkins. Wherever she had to live now, she'd take her pumpkins with her. How crazy that she wasn't distressed, how incredible that she wasn't in pain. How liberating this lightness!

By the time Larry got home tonight, their house would be in ashes. All his woodworking and her family photos and murder mysteries would be dust. But maybe instead of rebuilding with the insurance money, she and Larry could buy an RV and travel the year round, having their Social Security checks direct-deposited, withdrawing money from machines throughout the Lower Forty-eight, maybe even heading up to Alaska. April May had never used an automatic teller machine, but she could learn how. They'd take it slow in the beginning. On the first night they'd park their RV on a sandy lookout over Lake Michigan, and from there they'd go west. Before they'd even consider coming back east, she would have to see a desert, a mountain, an ocean, northern lights, and a glacier. After she carried her last pumpkins and the gourds to the Buick, she slammed the trunk shut.

April May thought of her little barn bird feeder, imagined it blazing atop its metal pole, and she knew she was kidding herself. She knew this half-mile stretch of road as well as anyone, and even without her driving glasses she knew that her cats and cookware and decades of accumulated knickknacks were fine, because the fire was in the Harland barn. As a way of distracting herself from the disappointment of not losing everything, she thought about having a Halloween bonfire this year. She'd pile twigs and broken limbs into a wigwam-shaped affair and set them ablaze in the dark. April May had been planning to celebrate Halloween with cider and snacks as usual, but maybe this year she would have tricks instead of treats. Or perhaps she'd send Larry to the store, shoo the cats outside, and light her curtains with a jack-o'-lantern. Then she'd step out herself and stand with the kids to watch the fire devour her house. Young ghosts, witches, and costumed superheroes would gather as witnesses. Their eyes would glisten in the dark, and when they realized the house itself was afire, they would scream. And after the destruction of her furniture, keepsakes, and cookbooks, she and Larry would take to the road, roam all over the country to see what they hadn't seen while sitting here in one place. She wouldn't say she'd wasted her life in Greenland—nothing like that—but she had been simmering here on low heat an awfully long time.

Now as she watched George Harland's barn burn in the distance, she could imagine herself running toward the fire, high on the balls of her feet, the way she had chased after the tornado as a child. April May lifted her arms over her head to twirl, but her grown-up body resisted. Throughout the last half century, she had trained herself to walk straight, and it was going to take a while to undo that damage. April May saw Rachel at the fence line and thought she'd like to grab hold of the girl and hug her, transmit through her skin everything Henrietta had taught her about gardening, about bush beans versus pole beans, about using manure in autumn rather than spring. By passing it on, she would free herself from that earthy knowledge. April May looked across the street and saw the long face of Elaine Shore staring out as if yearning to be set free. April May looked in the other direction to see Sally Retakker puffing a cigarette, smiling as though she had a plan. April May smiled back.

Sally saw the smoke rising out of the old barn halfway to the Barn Grill and she wondered once and for all what the hell she was doing here, at this farm, in this town. Maybe like the clothes George and Rachel hung on the line to freeze-dry, Sally would just dehydrate if she stayed through the bitterness of another Michigan winter. Her small body and brittle bones might be crushed beneath the weight of even one more season of lake effect snows. She wanted to be in California, and she didn't care if she was staying with her oldest son or begging outside a liquor store, and she didn't care what she'd have to do to get there, and she didn't even mind if the traveling took a long time, just so she was moving in the right direction. She'd leave now, and not even bother to stop at home. Reminding herself that she didn't care about anything made her feel hopeful. She might as well be aiming a pistol and shooting these people one by one, because shortly hereafter, she told herself, she would turn her back and never see them again. She needed a drink, so she'd stop at the Barn Grill on the way out of town. From the Grill, she'd walk to the highway and hitchhike. Sally didn't care what was burning to the ground, and for a brief, blissful moment, she didn't think of David.

David would be fine, she decided, after the thought of the boy imposed itself. David would be fine without her.

25

OVER THE COURSE OF THE MORNING, ELAINE HAD FELT HER hair growing, and now she would swear it was creeping down from her scalp like a living parasite. Elaine watched across the street as people's heads, one by one, turned and looked south, toward some vision that might change their lives forever. Elaine couldn't look south, because that side of the house was her bathroom and utility room and had no windows. When the Homestead Homes representative first presented the plan to her, Elaine had thought it peculiar to have an entire wall without windows, but the representative had convinced her that this would improve the house's overall insulation value, which would lower heating costs, and Elaine agreed that she'd have plenty of views in the other directions.

Though Elaine no longer read romance novels, she recalled that each story included a special moment in which a meeting of eyes changed everything. A woman noticed a brilliant background glowing behind her lover, and Elaine liked it when the lover became a silhouette as he approached, his feet no longer seeming to touch the ground. Now instead of romances, she had the tabloids. She marveled that a woman saw Elvis in her laundry room, that a cow birthed a three-headed calf, that a baby was born quoting the Bible. Sometimes the revelations were not pleasant, for one could not say that being abducted and taken to a spaceship as the subject of an experiment was pleasant, but at least you became part of something larger than yourself, and you rose above the mess surrounding you down here. At least when the aliens came, they would be clean and organized, and if they hurt you with their dental surgery and probes, at least there would be an order to it all, a master plan into which each needle prick and each moment of agonizing pain fit precisely. Sometimes reading those newspapers made Elaine feel queasy, because reading about the discoveries and salvation of other people was nothing like having those experiences yourself.

In the same way, the sight of all those people looking away at something made her feel shabby. That unknown vision to the south beckoned her from her breakfast nook as a dark-eyed lover might call a virgin girl with alabaster skin from her bedroom on a hot summer night. Though she hadn't even left the house in eight days, Elaine stepped outside through her kitchen door and traveled across the lawn until she could see the distant smoke, gray-white, pouring from what she knew must be an alien crash site. She cupped her right breast in her left hand and held it there warmly, and gradually worked her right hand over her left breast. A siren blared. A pickup rattled along the road, then slowed and pulled next to the farm stand to wait for a wailing fire truck to pass. Elaine knew with the certainty of death that the aliens had failed this time in their attempt to reach the planet safely. The newspaper tomorrow would say that a small plane had crashed or a house or barn had burned, and nobody who hadn't seen it with her own eyes would know otherwise. Though the alien takeover of the planet was going to involve a lot of disruption and pain, Elaine still felt disappointed that the aliens had failed this time.

A four-wheel-drive truck with a portable flashing light above the driver's seat raced past her toward the crash site. The faces of the people standing in Harland's driveway were still turned south, with the exception of the pretty wife from next door, who was looking back across the road at Elaine. Elaine looked down at herself and noticed that her frayed, quilted bathrobe was shorter than the threadbare nightgown she wore beneath it. Her grayish feet looked foreign to her in their worn terry-cloth slippers. She became aware of her own arms crossed over her chest and her two hands, each squeezing a breast, only neither the chapped hands nor the soft, sagging breasts seemed like her own, and she let her arms drop to her sides. The pretty wife waved awkwardly to her from across the street, and Elaine lifted her arm in response, but the arm felt heavy and uncertain, and her hand on the end of it seemed to flail. She knew this was her opportunity to walk over to the farm stand and say hello to her neighbors, to ask what was going on. Or better yet, she could go down there and see the tragic blaze of that spaceship for herself, marvel at the explosion of the volatile fuels, perhaps even glimpse through the flames the remains of an alien. But not like this, not with these people, not today. Instead, she turned and walked a straight line to the kitchen door.

Back in her nook, she opened the Pelican Retirement Corporation folder. She soothed her eyes on the sameness of its metal trailers, on the smallness of its rectangular lawns, on the pleasant neatness of the people seated on decks with cups in front of them. She read the brochure and found that, yes, there was a hair salon on the premises.

26

THAT A MAN'S HANDS BUILT THE BARN MEANT NOTHING. That the man dragged stones from the river and woods, split the stones with a fifteen-pound maul and laid a foundation of them into the side of the hill he'd built up, that he did such work between cuttings of hay and harvests of corn, wheat, and oats, and calving his herd and repairing his mule-drawn machinery, all meant nothing to the fire now blazing. That a man felled the trees which he carved into supports, that for vertical siding he chose from among his own whitewood which he milled into imperfect boards, which he did his best to fit tightly against one another. That he worked every day, in the blistering sun or bitter wind and in all but the heaviest rains and snows, also meant nothing. Nor did it matter that every year folks from his and succeeding generations filled this barn with hay and straw, just as George and David had been doing this morning. None of this mattered to the fire any more than it had mattered to the tornado that destroyed the house beside it. The fire cared no more about this barn than the Federal Land Office cared at the point of sale in 1834 that this site had been the favorite summer camping ground of a group of Potawatomi, who belonged to the Wolf and Bear Clans (and who had no idea why the farmers kept calling them the Horseshoe Clan).

In the eyes of the federal land officials, the ancestor of George Harland who purchased this property did so fair and square. And when such a man had the money and wanted to farm a great stretch of land, he would have been a fool to hesitate, because if he didn't buy the land, at a dollar and a quarter an acre, somebody else would. Decades after the purchase, however, George's great-great-great-grandfather did grow to have an uneasiness that became a kind of tax on his ownership. As he farmed his fields in the years after 1840, he often imagined an endless line of men, women, and children marching single file west along the river. In truth, few of those people crossed his property; rather, the Woods Potawatomi slowly gathered to the west to prepare for their nine-hundred-mile trek. Like all the farmers, George's great-great-great-grandfather had thought he was glad to see the Indians go, and he traveled to Kalamazoo to witness the exodus. For hours he heard the wailing and watched the slow movement of families lugging their sleds and packs and babies. Two decades later, when the farmer's son built a barn on the abandoned Potawatomi campsite, the aging farmer told about those heartbroken people; the vision had been burned so deeply into his mind that he saw them crossing his own land, tramping on his own riverside path. He described that sad departure often enough to his grandchildren that they would pass the story down, along with the maps he had drawn of the Indian gardens. All the years that George's great-great-great-grandfather lived, he saw that barn his son built as a plain, practical wooden memorial to the gone people of a queer, fertile swath of land.

The fire blazing did not care that Harold Harland had learned about the mythical endless line of Potawatomi from his father-in-law or that Harold himself had stood in the barn after the big tornado and thought with regret about a schoolteacher he admired and about losing touch with God. And certainly the blaze did not care that the teacher had made love in the barn with a man who was not her husband. Nor did the fire care that more than a hundred years before the big tornado, a Potawatomi girl who didn't want to go away and marry had wept on this site before she disappeared into the woods. The fire did not give a damn who'd been killed in this barn or buried beneath it, so one could not very well expect such a fire to spare an asthmatic child messing around with a cigarette. On October 9, 1999, with no apparent concern for the life, the livelihood, or the desires of mortals, this fire clung to the hay-strewn floor and also climbed into the rafters of the barn and burned and burned.

The fire ate up the swallows' nests at the ceiling even as it gnashed piles of hay and bales of straw on the barn floor. Fire raged where, for 135 years, boys and girls had played and worked and slept. Flames now writhed across loose hay where some men and women had writhed together—George Harland's parents, for starters, months before they were legally married. And Mike Retakker and Sally got drunk together right here on the night they conceived David, creating the very spark that would thirteen years later set the barn afire. And Margo Crane lay here with a man who'd been raised on a reservation in Oklahoma, a man whose passion for the ferocious white woman seemed to him the only outlet for the bitter and sweet longing he felt toward this place of his ancestors.

Panes of glass, uneven in thickness and slightly distorted, panes of glass that had cracked and grown opaque with cobwebs, now glowed orange as the wood around the panes blackened. The plank floor at the back half of the barn, separating the upper and lower levels, had been cut from maple trees that had sprouted from seeds on this land more than two hundred years ago. Long before white men felled these trees, the Potawatomi had bled them for maple sap, and traded the syrup to the white settlers, who seemed as crazy for the taste of maple sugar as the Potawatomi were for corn liquor.

The swallows of 1999 were already gone from these rafters, headed south for a gentler winter. Though everyone knew the swallows came and went seasonally, nobody had considered that while they were settling in and producing their broods each spring, these birds had been quietly documenting the passage of time. If, instead of lighting that cigarette, David Retakker had climbed into the corners of the barn and crumbled the old swallows' nests in his hands, he might have found some surprising items, such as two ancient silver trinkets: one a disk that said MONTREAL, and the other an inch-long section of a silver chain whose links had been pounded flat. Or a patch of buckskin, gummed to softness, cut away from a shirt Corn Girl's mother might have made for Corn Girl's father, this old skin so fragile that it would probably have crumbled when touched. Or a ragged end from a leather thong, left on the site of a wigwam, now woven together with strands of Mary O'Kearsy's hair. Or velvety fur from a muskrat jowl cut away from a jaw by Margo Crane, or even a bit of foil paper from a candy wrapper that a swallow had added to its nest lining this spring after it fell out of David Retakker's pocket.

There was no reason to think that the fire, or the swallows, for that matter, when they returned to sail through empty air where their homes had been, would give a damn about the flesh and bones of one boy, small for his age, even if that boy could have worked this place for a good part of the next century with the devotion that only love can instill, even if the boy had been the person who, along with George Harland and Rachel Crane, could have kept at bay for another generation the builders and real estate agents who wanted to divide this wide fertile tract into unproductive rectangles and smother it with foundations for homes, concrete driveways, and choking lawns. To suppose that a fire, especially one burning as hotly as this one, would bother to spare rather than devour David would be plain foolishness.

27

TOM PARKS WATCHED GEORGE WATCH THE FIRE. STANDING there so quietly, George seemed thinner and taller than usual, and his face was almost gray. His attention seemed, to Parks, to be focused around the fire rather than on it, as though birds or angels perched at the edges of the flames, delivering the bad news. Parks sympathized with George losing his old barn, but he also couldn't help thinking George was fortunate for having so much to lose. This slice of the planet belonged to George, and if the barn went up in flames, he still owned the charred land beneath. Surely George would find a way to absorb this loss, and Rachel would inherit the farm, with or without this building.

Nobody other than George looked disturbed. Certainly not the firefighters, for they were just doing their jobs, after all. They had known worse disasters than a barn fire and worse ways and places to spend an October day. Four ladder trucks had arrived, one all the way from Kalamazoo, and the firefighters were probably happy to be here and not at some downtown apartment building where a guy with a cigarette in his mouth would screech to a halt in front of the building and run up shouting, "My baby is in there! I only left her alone for a few minutes," and beg one of the firefighters to run through burning doorways, up disintegrating stairs, into a scorched, smoke-filled room where a baby lay asphyxiated. A few minutes ago, George had asked the firefighters about David Retakker, and they said it was unlikely he'd remained in the barn with the door wide open, though by the time they'd gotten there, it had been too late to go inside and check.

"So you figure David got out?" George asked Parks, without turning to look at him.

"A twelve-year-old boy doesn't let himself get burned up in a fire," Parks said. "He's probably hiding somewhere, ashamed of what he's done, and he'll show up full of regret in a few hours."

"You're probably right," George said.

Parks said. "How do you think his ma is going to take this?"

George moved his head slowly side to side. There weren't many of these old barns left, and there was no way a fellow could rebuild one. Recently George had been entertaining the idea that he could get good money selling a one- or two-acre plot beside this barn. Some city person would have paid a premium to build a new house in view of such a monument. The several times he'd mentioned selling property, Rachel had crossed her arms and damned him to hell, said she'd gladly go without food or electricity rather than lose any land. But even she wasn't strong enough to resist the inevitable indefinitely. Today even Rachel would have to see that no matter how tightly you held on to a place, it would eventually slip away. How could it be otherwise, if structures you knew as well as your oldest friends were in reality no more permanent than wigwams? He told himself that they'd had a good run, his family. They'd kept their land as long as anyone, and George'd had a year and a half with Rachel, which was surely more than he deserved.

George lifted his work boot to look at its cracked sole and saw the smashed, furred bodies of two woolly bears. George didn't have any reason not to believe Parks and the firefighters about David, and because anything else was too painful to consider, he believed David got out of the barn. Still, George hated himself for even considering throwing the boy and his mother out of the house on P Road, and he especially regretted not bringing David home for breakfast this morning. Because George still believed in the ultimate justice of the world, he figured the destruction of his barn must be punishment for one of his sins, if not for his considering sending David and Sally away, then for his crime of loving Rachel, for his going into the barn with her the first time, for learning the river smell of her, for feeling her warm muscles against the coolness of loose straw. There were plenty of crimes George might have to pay for around here, but surely none of them merited killing a perfectly decent kid. David was fine, wherever he was. A support beam dropped through the flames and showers of sparks flew up from the back of the barn. Through the doorway, George could almost make out the ancient hay wagon aflame and he thought he smelled rubber tires melting. His thoughts stopped before he completed a picture of David sitting where he had left him, atop the now-flaming stack of hay, for such tragedies did not happen. Except that standing right beside him was Tom Parks, whose brother was killed by a train, whose father died by smashing his tractor against a tree, whose children were a thousand miles away. He had a surge of feeling for Tom Parks, who had lost so much.

George said, "I'm glad you came back from Texas, Tom. It's nice to have you here."

Parks said, "I'm going to miss this barn of yours."

"Me too."

When Rachel appeared on the other side of the nearest fire truck, she looked dark in comparison to the flames, wild-eyed, angry-eyed, so beautiful it made George's own eyes water. At the sight of her standing with her arms crossed, glaring at the fire, George's heart became larger and more liquid, filling more of his chest. Rachel had been more or less pissed off from the day he met her, and today her anger finally made sense.

George watched Rachel uncross her arms and then disappear around the side of the barn. When he saw a bird flit from the building and pursue her, as quick and blue as a barn swallow, he knew it must have been a titmouse or a puff of smoke, for the swallows were long gone and wouldn't return to this place until spring. George would get enough money from the insurance company to construct a pole barn with the same floor area, but by no means with the same capacity for storing hay and straw. It would make no sense to build way out here in isolation anyway, so far from his own house, and wherever he put up a pole barn there wouldn't be cracks between boards or at the roof line, through which the birds could enter and build nests. Next spring, birds would circle above this burned-out foundation with nowhere to land. Such a pathetic creature was the barn swallow, that it required the preservation of a human ruin on the verge of crumbling or bursting into flame. George pitied any creature who relied so heavily on human beings for its survival. Any creature who relied on things to stay the same was hopeless.

28

BEFORE RACHEL LEFT THE HOUSE TO RUN TO THE FIRE, she'd grabbed her rifle from the mudroom and slung it over her shoulder. In her hurried carelessness she kicked the head off a purply ornamental cabbage that had risen out of the ground near the fence line on a spiny alien neck. She bent to slip through the strands of barbed wire and raced south through the pasture, paralleling Queer Road, and before she'd gotten a hundred yards, Martini the pony, the ex-wife's llama, and the donkey were thundering toward her and then slowing to run alongside. The donkey bumped Rachel with his forehead, and she swatted his wobbly ears but kept on going. Martini screamed excitedly and threw his head up. The blaze seemed to gain fury as she and the animals approached the south fence. Rachel climbed through the barbed wire to get out of the pasture and felt a loss at leaving the animals clustered behind her; she felt the cold at her back the way she had upon leaving George the first night they'd spent together in the dusty room with the maps of the Indian gardens. Such stray and ragged feelings nipped at her as she approached the fire, on her path between rows of drying cornstalks, in a field beneath which somebody's dead undoubtedly were buried.

When she reached the end of the cornfield, the fire that appeared before her was huge, hungry, too powerful to believe. She stopped and stared, the way everybody else was staring, but she failed to get any sense of it. She moved around the barn to glimpse the barnyard below, to see the cows milling and snorting restlessly at the creek, as far from the blaze as they could get within the fence she'd repaired with bedsprings. One female jumped on the other, as though the fire had triggered her to go into heat. Rachel sympathized with those dumb animals—she would like to run to George, jump on him, demand to know what the hell had happened, but George was on the other side of the barn, talking to Parks and to a yellow-and-black-clad firefighter. What Rachel knew for certain was that this barn she had always known was disappearing, turning to dust before her eyes, and she wished that she'd paid attention to the way the beams had supported the weight of the structure. She wished that, as she'd lain in the barn all those mornings, she'd noticed how the foundation had settled and shifted. Rachel had watched her mother kill a man in this barn, but she'd never bothered to wonder how the walls resisted blowing apart in high winds, or why the roof had not given way beneath year after year of lake effect snows.

Rachel walked away from the cows, back up the incline. On the other side of the fire, Parks looked solid and ruddy, but standing next to him, George seemed delicate. Until recently Rachel had only rarely looked at George, perhaps because he was so often looking at her, or around her, taking her into his vision along with the weather. Lately, though, she'd felt curious about him, and she'd taken to hiding in her garden at dusk to watch him split wood. As George watched the fire now, she knew he must be thinking about all the work he had to do, figuring that, whatever happened today, he still had to finish the oats and straw and fix his machinery, and he had to be ready by Friday to begin harvesting. Maybe it was because they talked so little that Rachel remembered every single thing George said, even the things she pretended not to hear. Parks kept moving his body as though he was motioning George to look away from the fire, but George would not. The structure began to hiss as though deflating. Rachel closed her eyes and tried to remember how the barn had surrounded her while she slept, but instead she felt weighed down. Maybe the fire was altering local gravity or maybe Johnny's ghost had flown out of the barn and was perched on her shoulders. Johnny had stood behind her that night, and Rachel hadn't known there were better men, and she had ignored the rough-hewn beams supporting the planks above her, the beams covered with chop marks from the adze, each mark in the wood a separate effort expended by some ancestor.

She watched the skeleton of the barn's frame rise out of the disintegrating wooden siding. The fire was translucent and weightless, but more powerful than anything she'd known. The fire trucks were spraying streams of water at the sides of the barn, repeatedly dousing the sugar maples on either end, but the yellow leaves on the larger tree were nonetheless curling and disintegrating against the heat, and Rachel doubted the flesh of the wood could resist much longer. Since her mother left, nobody had tapped those trees for sap, and they must have been ready to burst—perhaps the heat inside those trees had been the source of the fire. Then she noticed, in the doorway, the spokes of a bicycle wheel bathed in flame.

"David!" she shouted, and moved toward the fire, but her voice was drowned by a noise, a whomp, as a vertical post collapsed, dragging the roof of the building down. Sparks flew out, and the bicycle wheel was gone along with the barn's entryway.

"You'll have to move away, miss," a thick fireman shouted above the roar.

"Where is he?" At this range the fire was so loud she could hardly hear herself.

"What did you say, miss?"

"Did anyone see David?" Rachel yelled. "I saw his bicycle."

"Yes, irreplaceable," the fireman shouted, as though in agreement, over the noise of flames and engines. "They don't build this kind of barn, nowadays. You'll have to step away from the fire." He stepped back alongside her, and she could hear him more clearly. "Except the Amish, of course."

"The Amish?" Rachel said. Did the man not want to tell her David was dead?

"The Amish still build these barns," said the firefighter reassuringly. "Down in Indiana."

"What happened to the boy who was here?" Rachel said. "His name is David."

"By the time we got here, it was impossible to go in. Fire marshal seems to think the neighbor boy who set the fire got out."

"David set the fire?" She asked it as a question, but she already knew it in her bones. Had known it the moment she saw the fire.

"According to Officer Parks, the boy was probably smoking."

The firefighter shook his head but he seemed to Rachel as much comforted by the fire as disturbed. She supposed that such men lay at home staring at the ceiling hour after hour, waiting for a fire the way Rachel waited for plants to grow. She supposed such men imagined flames like these while they made love with their wives, while they looked into those wives' cool, watery faces. Of course, the firefighter didn't know anything about David, knew even less than Parks did, about David's asthma and his freakish love for George, a love large enough to keep him in the barn trying to extinguish the fire rather than getting himself to safety. The fireman was looking at her.

"David has asthma," Rachel said. "He probably couldn't breathe in there." She wanted to say David was not the kind of person who would run away from responsibility, that he was likely too weak from hunger to fight his way out. Or maybe that son of a bitch Todd came up here with his friends and locked David inside and set it afire. Except of course that the door had clearly been open. The firefighter was staring wholesale into Rachel's face.

"Stop looking at me!" Rachel said.

"I'm sorry," he said, but he didn't look away.

"That's my barn on fire."

"So that's your dad over there?"

"That's my husband."

The fireman looked away finally. "We did pick something up, near the entrance. Do you want to see it?" Rachel followed him away from the fire, back to a new four-wheel-drive truck with a long bed and good ground clearance, the kind of truck George ought to own. When they stood behind the open truck door, the noise of the fire was muted. The man held out a plastic bag containing a grubby white inhaler. "This was lying on the ground in front. It doesn't look like it was there long."

"It's David's," Rachel said.

Another firefighter, a woman with a walkie-talkie, motioned to the man. Rachel stood back while he replaced the plastic bag and closed the truck door. Could David's asthma inhaler have started the fire? Rachel wondered. It was a stupid thought, she knew, but she wanted to believe that David hadn't started the fire with a damn stupid cigarette. She wanted one reason to think he'd safely escaped, but she knew better than even to hope David was alive.

After the fireman moved away, Rachel did not want to stand there in awe of the fire that had just devoured her best friend. Instead she would get David's inhaler away from the people who had no right to it. Rachel tried the door of the truck but it was locked, as was the passenger-side door, so she climbed into the back of the truck, keeping low, and opened the sliding window to the cab. She reached down to the seat, grabbed the plastic bag, and stuffed the inhaler in her pocket. Rachel would make sure they had no evidence to use against David after he was gone, and that meant she also had to get the cigarettes from Parks. After she slipped out of the truck bed, Rachel moved through the cornstalks, toward the road, to get behind the police cruiser. She crept out of the field on hands and knees, trying to move slowly and invisibly the way her mother had taught her to hunt. Rachel had not mastered the skill well enough to sneak up on an animal, but everyone here was focused on the fire. Parks's driver-side window was open and she pressed herself against that door and kept her head down as she reached inside. She grabbed the cigarettes off the dashboard and put them in her pocket along with the inhaler, then crawled on hands and knees back into the corn. She crept back around to the west side of the barn to study George, who still watched the fire opposite her.

When George had said he'd left David at the barn this morning, Rachel should have run right down here and gotten him, never mind her eggs and bacon growing cold. She was the one who understood David, and she should have been protecting him. George, with his inherited buildings and his machines, his long straight rows of corn, and his never-ending patience, couldn't know what desperation she or David felt about this place, which had in no way been destined for them. David was the only person likely to farm these acres after George was gone, after George burned up like this barn or else deteriorated and crumbled away, two years from now or twenty years or forty. She held on to David's inhaler inside her pocket as if it were the last living part of him.

April May's Buick approached from the direction of George's house, and Rachel watched her negotiate around the parked cars and trucks to pull into the driveway across the street. Gray Cat, who'd been sitting on the porch steps, sped away from April May and the barn bird feeder and back to the fire side of the road, where he slunk into the drainage ditch, making it clear he was nobody's pet. April May got out and leaned against the back end of her Buick to watch another crash send up a wall of fire beside the bigger maple, on which all the remaining leaves dried, curled, and burst into flame. Then walking up the road came the salesman and his little blond wife, hand in hand as though chained together for all eternity. He seemed rosy and ready, eager to reach out and shake with that free hand, while the wife seemed small and hesitant. They approached the fire, and the blonde positioned herself on the far side of the salesman in such a way that Rachel couldn't see her at all.

Milton Taylor didn't keep going along the road as the fireman in the driveway indicated he should. Instead he backed up his old truck and cut into George's field, driving over the drainage ditch, and even when there came a terrible wrenching sound that had to be his exhaust system tearing loose, he just kept coming, his crocheted pink-and-lime crucifix swaying back and forth from the rearview mirror. He mowed down about a hundred cornstalks before stopping near Parks's county cruiser. He got out and walked with his hands in his pockets and stood beside Parks and George. His shirt read LOVE IS JESUS in loopy cursive, with a reddish cartoon heart over his belly. Behind him, running up the road, out of breath, came George's punk nephew Todd and one of the Higgins kids, their eyes and mouths wide open. They stopped alongside Milton and stood awestruck. The kids and grown-ups, and the cows and Gray Cat, formed something like a three-quarters circle around the fire, and Rachel felt those bodies calling out that all of them had lost David, not just her. The heat at the center of this fire, Rachel thought, must be phenomenal, and her desire to speak to these people and hear their voices was a cool place inside her. She resisted moving toward any of them, though, telling herself that nobody had known David the way that she had.

"Fucking fire!" she said, and squatted down so that her rifle clunked the ground behind her. She cooled her hands on the earth, then reached out and touched the fuzz on a woolly bear crawling nearby. She was all the while watching George, thinking she didn't like his looking so thin. She didn't want to feel he needed protection, and she didn't want to think of him dying, even though it would mean the land was hers. Really, she didn't need all the property. She would use the edges, along the road and the river, the windbreaks, the woods, some gardens—that was how the Potawatomi had intended to live with the farmers, she was sure. She was staring at the side of George's face, thinking he should keep tilling his damned flat fields forever, when he turned and looked at her. From this distance she could see what she hadn't seen up close: the ghost of Johnny showed in his face, and the ghost of David, who'd loved George way more than George could have known. Even the ghost of Tom Parks was there, though the living Parks stood right beside him. By staying on his farm, George had taken on the spirits of all the people who had farmed here, his grandfather Harold and grandmother, and Rachel didn't know who else. As she kept looking at him, she saw a reflection of fire there too, flames consuming not just this barn full of straw and hay, but other barns and other houses and acres of crops and woodlands. For the first time she wondered if George might have secrets as terrible as her own.

George was looking back at Rachel as though she were the only thing that could sustain him. Rachel no longer saw or heard anything else, but stared past the fire trucks, into George's eyes, in a way she'd never done before, as if she too needed this liquor, which might have been too strong were there any less distance between them. Rachel felt more solidly planted than ever, as though a complex of roots was connecting her to George under the topsoil. For a year and a half, she'd told herself she meant only to outlive the man and make his land her own, but now he was turning into land before her eyes. When Parks yelled something Rachel couldn't hear, George blinked, and Rachel blinked, and it was over. This was not love as Rachel had imagined it might feel—this was an emotion as complicated as a garden, beneath the surface of which roots stretched in all directions to fill a fertile square mile. This was like the fusing of skin and dirt, the coming together of mineral and muscle, something like eternity sped up so that the decay of bones into calcium-rich grit occurred in fast motion. After George looked away, Rachel felt too full of life, like trees that needed to be tapped, like a cluster of seeds ready to burst out of their shells into the stink and decay of rich soil. She dared not look at George again, or even in his direction. Nobody noticed as she left the fire, except Gray Cat, who followed her for a while at about twenty human paces.

29

OLD HAROLD HARLAND HAD ONCE BURNED A BARN TO THE ground, behind the house George and Rachel now occupied. Harold had not been able to bring himself to look across the flames at his wife, however, so he did not know whether the fire made her appear beautiful. There was no cigarette-pilfering neighbor boy to blame, only himself. Henrietta's family had already farmed here a hundred years, so she had felt within her rights to warn Harold repeatedly against putting damp hay in a barn. When an August rain threatened, however, he could not bear the possibility of losing all that fine hay, and so he had gone ahead and loaded it onto wagons and hauled it to the barn. Even as he and Enkstra pitched the hay into the west end of the loft, Harold heard his wife's voice in his head and chose to ignore it. The great blaze two months later would serve to remind the whole community of the danger of damp hay, for inside the alfalfa and grass grew mold, and that mold swelled the mounds the way yeast swelled bread, though with a good deal more heat. People said the hay deep inside was probably smoldering for weeks, before the pile collapsed and flames erupted.

With everyone in Greenland sharing stories about the barn and calculating the cost of Harold's stupidity, shame hung around him like a weighted collar. If he had been a drinker, he would have turned to drink, but he was a working man, so he just kept on harvesting that fall, and he endured the bitterness of his wife, hoping he would eventually be forgiven. Maybe Harold took a liking to Mary O'Kearsy simply because she showed up in town the following year with no knowledge of the barn fire. She was a young widow, a distant cousin of one of the members of the school board, and everybody liked the idea of having an elementary teacher from back east, as though such a woman were necessarily more capable of providing the rules of multiplication and English grammar than a local person. Her being from the east also meant she had a place to return to should this Michigan town tire of her, as it did less than two years later.

A few days after Henrietta Harland and the other members of the school board told Mary O'Kearsy she was no longer in the town's employ, Harold Harland was working on the barn beside the house she would be vacating. Even though he was glad to be back in his wife's good graces, Harold was feeling uneasy about having reported to Henrietta what he had seen Mrs. O'Kearsy doing with that fellow Enkstra. The woman would be leaving the following morning, though, and Harold told himself that his feelings about her would be easier to bear when he could not see her every day. Surely he would stop thinking of her after she was gone, and then finally he could be at peace with his desires and with God, not to mention with his wife. Harold was grateful that his wife did not ask how he happened to be watching when O'Kearsy met Enkstra in the barn, or how he saw her waiting for the man at the back door. He could never explain that he had felt a surge of confused anger each time he saw Mrs. O'Kearsy with Enkstra and that he had wanted to punish her.

As Harold Harland worked on his oldest remaining barn that morning, he was hoping to get a final glimpse of Mrs. O'Kearsy, so he was not disappointed when she came out and stood on the porch. She continued to watch Harold for a long time, as though he were a great curiosity, such as a puppet show or a parade of interesting automobiles driving along Q Road. She watched him unashamedly, did not peek through a window, the way he had watched her, but stood right out in the open with her hands clasped behind her back. When Harold let himself look up from his work, Mrs. O'Kearsy waved, and so Harold put down his hammer and approached the house, growing more nervous with every step. At her invitation, he sat in one of two chairs on the porch and she took the other. When she sat her skirt rose above her knees.

"I am sorry you have to leave, Mrs. O'Kearsy. I am sorry things did not work out." Harold stared at the porch floorboards.

"Yes, sir, Mr. Harland, everything here was fine." She was squinting because of the sun, but he could see her eyes were red-rimmed and bloodshot as though she had been crying, and it gave her a naked look. She was not wearing a hat or handkerchief, but then, Harold reminded himself, covering one's head was not a hard-and-fast rule anymore. Up close he could see that her hair, which was pulled back and up onto her head, did not lie still, but struggled against its pins and wriggled to loosen itself. Her curls glistened the color of river silt. "I have enjoyed living here very much," she said. "Michigan has been an adventure for me."

"Glad to hear that, ma'am." Harold did not know what she meant by *adventure*.

"They say you are the one who reported seeing me and Mr. Enkstra together."

"Yes, I am." Harold found the discord between O'Kearsy's tear-filled eyes and her cheerful voice unnerving, and it made him speak more honestly than he had intended. "Why Enkstra, ma'am?" His own words surprised him. "Of all the men in Greenland, why that big dumb fellow?"

Mary O'Kearsy laughed. "That is what everybody is wondering, I suppose. What could he and I have to talk about?" When she looked at Harold again, tears were streaming from her eyes, and she made no attempt to conceal them or wipe them away. "Well, I'll just say that any two people can find plenty to talk about if they are able to think for themselves. I like Mr. Enkstra very much."

Harold cleared his throat and made a last attempt to reclaim his indignation. "So you don't deny you were in a sinful way with Mr. Enkstra?"

"Despite all you self-righteous people, I do not want to leave," O'Kearsy said. "It is breaking my heart to leave this place, and I cannot fathom why."

"You could go to Kalamazoo," Harold said. "Maybe you could get a job teaching there, close by." Harold was starting to wonder if not seeing her was going to make his longing for her even greater.

"I do not want to be close by. I am going back home to Boston. Or Salem maybe, to visit my aunt. You know, of course, that Salem is where the witches lived." She smiled.

"I would not want to live in Kalamazoo, either," Harold said. He did not know what she meant about witches. He knew most folks had not considered Mrs. O'Kearsy pretty, because she had a kind of face where the two sides did not quite line up, but Harold had always liked the look of her. Maybe it was just the look of her and nothing more that had made him watch her through the cracks in the barn siding and made him hate that big man Enkstra for entering the house (Harold's house!) without knocking, and maybe the look of her was why his heart ached at the thought of her loving a man other than him. Knowing she was leaving the following morning, Harold could not look enough at her—if it would not have been impolite, he would have stared until he had drunk her in completely.

"Maybe before I go on packing," she said, "I should spend a few minutes with my accuser." Every sentence from her mouth sparkled like a clear stream, faster and brighter than the creek from which the cattle drank behind the barn.

"There were the children to think of." Even as Harold said it, he did not believe it. In truth, he thought the children lucky to have such a teacher, if only for a couple of years. All his own teachers had been unpleasant to look at.

"The children," repeated Mary O'Kearsy, unconvinced.

"Of course, the children all like you," Harold said. "Little April May says you go to Europe every summer."

"Would you like to come in and see a few things I have picked up abroad?"

As a curl of her hair sprang loose, Harold squeezed his chair arms. But it would be silly, he thought, not to accept her offer to go into a house he and his wife owned. As he followed her through the kitchen he snuck a glimpse at her slender, belted fig- ure walking and felt guilty about doing so, but he told himself this would be his last glimpse ever, and so he looked again. She led him to the dining room, where three leather trunks stood full nearly to their brims, lids open. She lifted out some framed postcards: the leaning tower of Pisa and the Parthenon. She showed him a wal- nut-sized chunk of stone, which she said she had taken from Hadrian's Wall. She handed him a small brass model of the Eiffel Tower, which he turned over in his hands and studied. When Harold asked the identity of the man in the small photograph opposite her in the hinged double frame on the windowsill, she said it was her late husband.

"Do you have a picture of, uh, him?"

"Mr. Enkstra, you mean. Where would I get such a thing?"

She placed the gold-framed photos in her trunk beside the Euro- pean souvenirs. When she turned to go back into the kitchen, Harold picked up the frames, slid the small photo of her out from behind the glass and put it in his overalls pocket, then folded closed the frame and replaced it in the trunk.

Of the other objects in the house that morning, Harold would most clearly remember something from the kitchen: the white-glazed ceramic marmalade jars imported from England, lined up on the counter with spices, dried flowers, and odds and ends.

"I have a weakness for marmalade," she said. "It costs too much and I should not buy it."

Harold could tell by the rims that the ceramic jars had been sealed with paraffin and paper for the transatlantic voyage. He wondered how she could have gone about making the decision to buy such a fancy item so many times. He counted fourteen jars.

"You've been a lot of places," Harold said, when they returned to the porch. He sat again, afraid that otherwise she would expect him to leave. The sun had moved behind the barn, so Mary O'Kearsy no longer had to squint. She was a girlish woman, and yet leaning against the wall, she seemed mannish to him, as well, as though he might actually have something to fear from her if, say, they wrestled.

"Since I first came here," she said, "I sensed something peculiar about this place, about this piece of land beneath us, something queer. Secretly, you know, I have always called Q Road 'Queer Road.'"

"Queer Road?" Harold said.

"I had been thinking that maybe I would not go away this June. I thought maybe I would stay and help the families of my students with their summer work."

"Surely you would rather be in Italy or France."

Mary O'Kearsy laughed as she sat in the chair beside him, but when Harold next looked at her face she was crying. At first Harold had wished she would make up her mind to laugh or cry, one or the other, but now he found the confusion making sense.

"Why did you report me to the school board?" she asked.

"How could you love Enkstra that way?" Harold said. "So easily?"

"Easily?" She laughed. "Tell me, how can you love this farm so easily?"

"I don't know how you mean that."

"Having this farm probably feels like the most natural thing to you."

"It was my wife's family's farm." By now Harold was feeling altogether sick in his chest and stomach, and he did not know who he was anymore, or rather he did not know who he had been when he told his wife what he had seen. Harold had made a terrible mistake, and there was nothing he could do to right it. This was worse than burning down the little hay barn; that had merely been innocent stupidity, but this was calculated meanness. Maybe when he burned down the barn, it was the last time he had been himself. Mary O'Kearsy was weeping in earnest now, and Harold felt bad about having sent Enkstra across P Road to plow a field, as far away as possible from this house. Harold wondered how he had let himself become such a mean son of a bitch.

Harold knew he should get up and leave but he could not bring himself to do so. Sitting there with Mary O'Kearsy, his thoughts were clearer than they had been in a long time. He considered the ways he loved his wife, Henrietta. Though he had never felt an inclination to speak the word, he loved her first and foremost for her family's land, which she shared with him. He loved her for her seriousness, and for her knowing so much about fruits and vegetables and about the seasons. While Harold and the hired men worked in fields, she planted and tended the garden, and she cooked, pickled, and canned in the kitchen, with sweat pouring down her temples and into her freckled cleavage. Harold ate jelly or jam with his breakfast every day of his married life, and it never came from the store, except the time that somebody at Christmas gave him some special strawberry preserves, which did not taste as good as his wife's—and he had had the good sense to tell his wife as much.

Sitting there with Mary O'Kearsy, however, he was aware of some of the ways in which he did not love his wife. Henrietta had changed after Harold burned down that barn. She used to be kinder, he was sure, and she had possessed a forgiving nature, and she even used to treat vagabonds with Christian kindness. Henrietta used to admire Harold as a man, had occasionally paused in her labors to watch him work. Since the barn went down, however, she was always looking in other directions, and she had begun sending away vagrants from their door without so much as a Bible verse. Harold had been grateful for his situation, satisfied with the fine hand life had dealt him, but on that sunny afternoon with O'Kearsy, the idea of sitting down to a breakfast with imported marmalade of Seville oranges possessed him. He started thinking of a life beyond this life, where the day would not be only for work, where cleverness and loveliness would be as important as goodness and godliness, and where women were not as hard as his wife, who would later say with certainty in her heart that the tornado had swept away the house because the O'Kearsy woman had been a sinner and a scourge upon their community.

In her hurried late-morning departure the following day, Mrs. O'Kearsy undoubtedly left some things behind, but before anyone had a chance even to go inside and take stock, the tornado ripped the house from its foundation. Harold later tried to clean up the site and bury the rubble of the house and silo, but the comet tail of debris stretched out a quarter mile onto the cultivated earth. Throughout the years making up the rest of his life, Harold noticed those old pieces of painted wood and window glass, and even what could have been bits of the white marmalade jars from England spread out over the same land on which his wife's father had once found flint arrowheads; but instead of collecting the pieces the way his predecessor had collected arrowheads, Harold worked the dumb shards into the earth. Another Christian might have worried about the desire he felt for Mary O'Kearsy, but despite what the church said, Harold told himself the thought was not the deed, and when he reflected on knowing this, he decided that the only time a man really knew God was when he knew God was different than folks said He was. That was when a man really knew something, when he figured it out for himself, and all the better if it disagreed with what was commonly held, for otherwise belief was merely a matter of adopting the community position.

After Mrs. O'Kearsy left for good, that fellow Enkstra just kept working for Harold as though nothing had changed, and nobody said a word against him. The only suggestion of sadness was a slowing in the man's movements, a slightly more exaggerated bend as he tugged on turnips, a lean as he tamped the dirt around fence posts. Enkstra had never been a clever or quick man, any more than the ground beneath them was clever or quick, but Harold found himself at times watching the man as intently as he had once watched O'Kearsy. Harold started calling Q Road "Queer Road." Others soon took up the habit as well, but only Enkstra could have known Harold was renaming the road in honor of Mary O'Kearsy. After a few years, unbeknownst to anyone in Greenland, she married a Boston man whose brother was a railroad executive. Greenland residents knew only that the big fellow Enkstra was suddenly offered a good-paying railroad job working between Detroit and Chicago, and so left the Harlands' employ.

30

RACHEL JOGGED AROUND THE WEST SIDE OF THE BARN, through row after row of brittle cornstalks, until she emerged near the creek. When she felt pebbles cutting her feet inside her canvas shoes, she kicked them off and went barefoot through the cold stream without even trying to balance on rocks. She ran along the creek path, faster than she had in years but almost without effort, without even getting out of breath, as though she were being propelled by the fire toward the water, and she slowed only as she reached the *Glutton*. The houseboat's cabin sagged on its iron foundation, and the deck on the shore side was littered with peeled paint. On the dark, rusting hull someone had spray-painted TODD + JULIE in white. Remnants of a campfire contained broken, burned glass, and on the bank lay a clear, new Jim Beam fifth bottle with its label peeled halfway off. Rachel had not paid attention to this place for months, but this was the first time she'd felt neglectful.

Instead of climbing onto the boat, Rachel went to her old garden at the edge of the woods. It was shaded by an ancient black willow whose branches seemed impossibly dark in comparison to its yellow finger leaves. She lay on the bed of grass and willow switches, and tried but failed to grab hold of David's being dead: when she'd seen him a few hours ago, he'd been more alive than anybody else she knew. Instead, thoughts of Johnny flooded the space she'd opened up for David, and she didn't feel strong enough to resist them. Maybe Johnny hadn't been anybody's favorite person, but, like David, he had been alive one moment and dead the next. It had been more than three years since she disentangled herself from Johnny's limbs and got up and walked slowly to her mother and took away the rifle and leaned it against the barn wall. Rachel hadn't realized right away that she'd been shot herself, that blood was trickling down her right arm and side; she didn't even immediately register the sensation near her armpit as pain.

While Margo stood frozen, Rachel gradually regained her senses. Her mother's final bullet must have entered her as she turned to pull herself out from under Johnny. Rachel picked up her flannel shirt from the dirt floor and proceeded to dress the wound the way her mother had taught her, tearing a wide strip of flannel from the bottom of the shirt and wrapping it around her shoulder and upper arm to stop the bleeding.

As Rachel was slipping back into what was left of her shirt, Margo finally spoke, almost too quietly to hear. "Go get George Harland."

Rachel's shaking hands and the skunk smell made the task of buttoning difficult. "I don't know."

"Just go get him." Margo's voice rose. "Tell him everything. Go!"

Rachel left the barn running but slowed to a walk and fumbled with her buttons as she reached Queer Road. She saw April May Rathburn standing on her porch but did her best to ignore the tall, thin figure. Though Rachel had intended to obey her mother, the half-mile walk gave her the opportunity to think, and by the time she reached George's house, she knew she would not awaken George or anybody else. Rachel would not turn her mother in to the authorities. Margo would no more survive in jail than Rachel would be able to live in a foster home. They had lived together on the edge of this land for fourteen years, and if her mother was unable to help herself, then Rachel would save them both.

To avoid being seen by April May, Rachel returned to the barn through the pasture, lugging the borrowed round-end shovel and mattock, with the pony, llama, and donkey in sleepy pursuit. The skunk smell had grown stronger inside the barn in her absence, but she couldn't see her mother anywhere. Rachel leaned the shovel against the wall and struck repeatedly at the ground with the mattock. When a chunk of soil stuck to the blade, she knocked it against a post to clean it. "We have to do this," she whispered, in case her mother was standing there in the dark somewhere, needing to be convinced. After chopping at the dirt floor for a half hour, Rachel dug with the shovel. She dug without pause until the hole was two feet deep. The skunk smell was disappearing, but she felt some other invisible presence. She stopped and put her ear to Johnny's mouth to hear if he had started breathing again but found him silent and nearly as cool as the dirt floor.

Her armpit had stopped bleeding and her shoveling muscles all seemed to work, which meant she was not likely in danger from her bullet wound. Rachel continued digging through the night, as though this were her life's work, digging and digging, as her hands blistered and then became raw, and all the while she was certain her mother would return to help her finish the job. At the morning's first light, the hole was about as deep as she was tall. Using the sides of the hole to pull herself out was agony, because the rawness of her hands made the dirt feel like shards of glass. Back on the surface, she pushed Johnny over with her foot and rolled him over twice, and he rolled again as he fell to his final resting spot. The sun was beginning to rise, and light shone through the cracks in the walls, lighting most of the way down to where Johnny's pale bloodless body lay naked, awkwardly curled.

However she arranged his body, he would probably lie for all eternity, but Rachel didn't dare climb down and straighten his neck, for fear she might change her mind about burying him altogether. Things were beginning to seem less clear in the morning light, and her mother was offering no guidance. Maybe Rachel had been wrong. Maybe a person couldn't just go burying another person—maybe the earth would spit him out as soon as she covered him. Maybe he would work his way back up the way drowned carcasses floated to the river's surface. Rachel threw Johnny's pants on top of him without checking the pockets. She dropped his cowboy boots in, one then the other, and flinched when the second boot heel thudded on the side of his face. She kicked the bloody straw onto him and tossed in shovelfuls of the blood-soaked dirt, and then the dead chicken. Though Rachel had wanted to slow time the night before, she now wanted time sped up. She hurried to cover the body with dirt, hoping then she could begin to forget. She had not even finished shoveling when the remaining five chickens approached and began pecking at the edges of the grave in search of bugs and worms. Rachel stomped the surface as flat as she could, moved the excess dirt to the corners of the barn, then rearranged the straw to cover the fresh earth, to make it look as though nothing remarkable had happened during the night, as though nobody's life had changed.

And only after all that did Rachel glance at the doorway and see a tall, thin figure just outside, perfectly still, the early light silhouetting her body, so that she had no decipherable face. Rachel didn't know how long April May had been standing there. Rachel glanced over at the rifle against the wall, and she saw April May turn and look too. Rachel tried to speak, but explaining that she hadn't killed Johnny seemed an impossible task, more difficult even than burying him. She could only sigh.

April May didn't move.

Rachel sighed again. She had never felt so tired in her life, and all her work was in vain, for April May would tell the authorities, and both Rachel and her mother would have to leave. She sank down on the grave and hugged her knees and hid her face.

She felt a hand touch her forehead and brush her hair back. "Poor girl," April May said. And for Rachel it seemed as though a long time passed before April May spoke again. "But I don't guess anybody will miss that rotten s.o.b."

After April May's hand left Rachel's head, Rachel didn't dare look up for a long time. When she finally did, the sun was fully risen, and Rachel was alone on the grave. She was so exhausted that she felt almost peaceful. She had done absolutely everything she could, and she could do no more; whatever would happen, would. Rachel dragged her aching body up the wooden ladder and lay down in the soft hay. She passed out as though bludgeoned, and she slept like death until evening.

Three years later, the willow branches beneath which Rachel lay began to shift in a slight wind, and Rachel was reminded that her old riverside garden had never gotten enough sun. Her mother had refused to cut down this old willow. And though her mother had hacked away at the ropes of poison ivy climbing the tree, she'd insisted they leave poison ivy clustered around its base, in order that the hairy roots might prevent the bank from eroding. Her mother had cared that much about the land, anyway. The massive, gnarled trunk might be hundreds of years old, Rachel thought, might even be the same tree Corn Girl jumped out of. If she jumped at all, that was. Killing herself would have been noble—or so Rachel had always thought—but living and finding a way to stay here would have been much better. Her death could have been an accident just as David's was. Her relatives might have made up the suicide story to have something to talk about on their sad march west.

After burying Johnny in the barn, Rachel had never seen her mother again.

Rachel sat up and looked into the woods between her mother's land and the golf course. The leaves on the trees nearest her were orange and yellow like some kind of brilliant harvest. Rachel would have preferred rain or snow for the occasion of remembering that night with Johnny, but all that fell around her were leaves in the colors of pumpkins, blood, and summer squash. Those still on the trees rustled in a wind that had risen out of nowhere. Even as she recalled the pain of her blistered hands and the shock of the bullet entering her, the leaves fell softly and brightly to earth, as though the bit of land George had given her mother was some sort of paradise. Rachel noticed some of her old potato plants still growing among the weeds. She sat up and tugged on the plants and dug with her hands to pull up gritty, wrinkled potatoes the size of crab apples. She tossed them toward the water, but they fell short. Some kind of sniveling was coming out of her own throat, and she wiped her nose with her hand and pressed her fingers near her armpit until she felt her bullet. She'd always thought she wanted to be rid of that piece of metal, but her knowledge of exactly where it was now gave her a tiny, dense measure of comfort. She let the bullet go to reach out a finger and pet a woolly bear. It curled under her touch, its coat the colors of fire and charred remains.

She climbed down the bank to the boat and unfastened the combination padlock. As she entered the *Glutton,* the familiar musty smell calmed her, and she left the door open for light, and so the air could circulate. The shades were drawn and she sat for a while inhaling the cool air, perched on an unsteady chair her mother had made of lumber she'd pulled from river snags. Her mother had claimed that anyone could make furniture. This was the single fruit of her furniture-making labor, though, and it was not sturdy. Her mother was not a builder, she was a killer. Rachel rolled up one deerskin window shade, green with mold, and tied it with the leather strip sewn there. Daylight shone onto sooty iron cooking pots which hung from wall hooks. Grease-coated sugar crystals from maple syrup her mother had boiled down a decade ago still coated the ceiling over the stove. After that experiment her mother decided she shouldn't boil sap inside the *Glutton*. Rachel thought of the way her mother used to crouch perfectly still when she was hunting, so still that she became invisible to her target and even to Rachel. Rachel herself tried to be quiet in her garden, but her mother had been so quiet sometimes that Rachel could look right at her mother's hair curving around her face, and at her pale arm curving alongside the dark, straight rifle, and still not see her mother. It was no wonder that killing Johnny had made her disappear entirely.

Rachel opened the fire door of the cast-iron woodstove, and she placed David's cigarettes on the grate. She went through five kitchen matches whose tips had been softened by humidity before getting one that would light. The plastic on the cigarette pack sizzled and retreated from the flame, then the paper caught fire, blackened, and disappeared. The three cigarettes lay smoldering on the grate.

"Anybody here?" asked a man's voice from outside the boat.

Another person thus startled might have shrieked and stood, but Rachel slid off her chair, squatted, and leveled her rifle at the doorway. A big body appeared there, smelling of soap and musk. "Rachel?" The body stopped abruptly and the arms flew up. "Don't shoot!"

Rachel stood.

"I thought we were friends," the salesman said.

Rachel let the gun hang on her sling and she crossed her arms. She noticed his leather shoes were dry—unlike her, he'd had the patience to walk until he reached the footbridge.

Steve dipped his head to glance inside the open door of the woodstove.

"Don't look at what I'm doing," Rachel said.

"What are you doing?"

"None of your damn business." What a relief to be angry again!

"This is a cute place," the salesman said. "Is it insulated?"

"I don't come into your damn house and nose around."

"You would always be welcome at my house, Rachel. Anyway, I thought you lived with George. You two are married, aren't you?" As Steve moved past her, he touched everything along his way, the primitive cupboards, the old woodstove, the tongue-and-groove pine ceiling, which hung only a few inches above his head. The boat looked small with him in it. How had she and her mother both lived here?

Rachel said, "Just because I own George's land now doesn't mean I don't have land of my own."

"If you're married, then he owns your land the same way you own his."

"What's your fucking point?" What pissed Rachel off especially was that this thought had not occurred to her. George was giving her his land, but in a sense she was giving back the bit he had given her mother. Was it possible George had married her to have his land back?

Steve said, "Did you know that if you use somebody's land for something like seven years, you can make a claim on it. You can own it."

Rachel rolled her eyes.

"Hey, I wouldn't make this up. It happened to a guy down in Climax. Milton and I were talking about it. A guy mowed his neighbor's three acres for ten years, then made a claim on it. Ask Milton."

"Don't go dragging Milton into this." Rachel tilted her head back to loosen a braid from under her sling. She was aware that she wasn't making sense, but she had to cling to her anger until she could be alone to sort everything out.

"I'm only telling you because you said you wanted more land."

"Go to hell."

"Adverse possession, that's it." Steve snapped his finger and pointed at her.

"That's what?"

"That's what it is when somebody gets a piece of land that way."

Rachel gritted her teeth, but she didn't actually feel anger toward the salesman. She was already accustomed to his soap smell, just as every year she got used to the pig shit smell of spring fields. George always smelled of sweat and grain and sometimes alfalfa. She wished he were close to her now. Rachel said, "So where's your damn wife?"

"Nicole wanted to go home," Steve said. "She seemed pretty sad about the fire. She always enjoyed driving past the barn."

Rachel reached into her pocket to assure herself the inhaler was still there. She wouldn't try to burn it in the woodstove; she'd have to sneak back after everybody was gone and toss it onto the barn's coals.

"Sure hope George has insurance on that barn." Steve just kept on smiling pleasantly as though everything were fine, as though Rachel hadn't cursed him and told him to leave, as though David weren't dead. "Man, oh, man," Steve said. "This boat would sure make an excellent hideaway. I'd give it a good scrubbing for starters."

Rachel tried to make the salesman disappear by imagining David's body burned to cinders and spread over where Johnny's skeleton lay curled in its grave. But her mind still wouldn't make room for David's death.

"It's so cozy here." Steve stood between the two narrow bunks and reached up and opened one of the cupboards above Margo's bed. Rachel heard mice paws scrambling. She knew her mother would not like the window salesman, but that was an easy call, seeing as how Margo didn't like anybody—Rachel wasn't even sure her mother had liked *her*. She ought to throw this guy off the boat, but she didn't have the energy. She needed to be out in her garden, among her pumpkins, squash, and Brussels sprouts, those plants that cold hadn't yet killed. She jumped off the deck of the boat and climbed the riverbank and yelled to him from there. "You'd better get the hell off my boat before I come back."

Rachel wished she were already home, watching George from her garden. Around dusk, George often split firewood. He chose from among three kinds of iron wedges, then swung the maul over himself in an arc as though carving a protective circle out of the air. If she sat in plain sight and did not hide, then maybe when he finished he might come into her garden and enfold her in his arms. The desire she was feeling for George was like her body turning inside out, like swallowing herself whole. She didn't know what she was supposed to do with these feelings piling up, blocking out David's death. She picked up the fresh-looking Jim Beam bottle from the riverbank, unscrewed the lid, and sniffed the last drops of whiskey.

"I wouldn't have guessed you for a drinker." Steve grinned at her from the doorway of the boat.

"Fucking idiot." Rachel threw the bottle down hard, but it bounced and did not break on the soft, tangled roots.

31

THE RAILROAD TRACKS RUNNING ALONGSIDE THE KALA-
mazoo River have long been part of the train line between Detroit
and Chicago, and sixty years ago, tramps and hoboes came by the
Greenland farmhouses and asked for food. Those men—and the
odd woman—rode the rails or walked across the land and knew its
shapes instinctively or by memory or anecdote, and didn't care
whose fields they crossed or slept upon but traveled to satisfy a
need, not unlike belly hunger, to feel mile after mile pass beneath
their feet. Perhaps such a traveler stole a chicken or caught a rabbit
to roast over a campfire or else picked a few ears of a farmer's soft
young field corn. George's grandmother Henrietta, as a young
woman, was reservedly sympathetic to these lost creatures of God,
for their not being more firmly planted, but she feared that if she
gave them food they'd have some way of marking the road or the
house to say as much, and so she fed them only after they'd done
some work. In the early summers of her marriage, she kept certain

jobs unfinished in order to have work to offer such men. She might have asked a man to mow her front and back yards with the hand mower, to sweep out a shed, or shovel manure from a barn. Sometimes a man went away angry at the suggestion of work; other times Henrietta had difficulty getting rid of a fellow who said he wanted to stay and become a hired hand. Even back then Henrietta had always made certain her barns were locked on nights when such transients were about, for fear of their carelessly starting fires.

The speed with which the October ninth fire devoured George's oldest barn would not have surprised Henrietta Harland, not after she had watched the barn behind her own house go up like so many cigarette papers. She would, however, have been shocked at the speed with which a home could now be erected atop a poured concrete foundation by the importation, on two trucks from Indiana, of a prefabricated structure, the halves of which were lifted by cranes onto that foundation, bolted in a few hours to the base, and further secured with pneumatic nail guns and caulk tubes of adhesive. A Potawatomi wigwam of sticks and skins could hardly have been constructed more rapidly than one of these modern homes equipped with luxuries such as central air-conditioning, wall-to-wall padded carpeting, and double-pane thermal windows.

In autumn of any year of her adult life, before or after her husband's foolishness cost her family their oldest barn, George's grandmother would have been canning tomatoes and squash. She would have guessed accurately when the first hard freeze was coming, and on that evening she would have gone out into the field and picked well into darkness, perhaps not really even noticing the darkness since her eyes would have adjusted gradually to the dimming light. Using her fine, natural night vision, George's grandmother would have picked even the greenest tomatoes and placed them on the back porch table. During the day the tomatoes would ripen in what sun they could capture, and at night Henrietta laid an old sheet or tablecloth over them to protect against freezing.

Henrietta not only preserved for each winter but planned further ahead, to future generations. Like her mother before her, Henrietta planted walnut trees, several dozen a year at least, as gifts to her descendants. She knew that in hard times a walnut tree could give food, furniture, and, at the very least, excellent firewood. She sprouted them in her garden, and transplanted seedlings to the windbreaks and to the edges of woods and the roadside, wherever the men did not farm. Like all women of her time and situation, she had children, and she expected them to pitch in and help with the work, and she did not often wonder if she had chosen the right life's work for herself. Women such as George's grandmother knew perfectly well that men married them for their farms, and Henrietta had intended to choose for her husband the man who would best care for these acres, but instead she fell for the most foolish man in Greenland, and then she had gotten pregnant one of those several nights with him in the barn and was thus forced to marry the man she loved. For the first decades of her marriage, she tried not to remind Harold too often that she knew a great deal more than he did about a great many things, but after he burned down that barn, she could no longer forgive her own stupidity.

Henrietta had not always been a hard woman, but in the last thirty years of her life she found herself growing hard in response to her husband growing soft. After the barn fire and the school-teacher business, Harold was no longer willing to blame or condemn anybody. Henrietta worried that the man might lose this farm, should he outlive her. A man gone soft would daydream until crops failed and would neglect to prepare for the following year. She knew that a person had to be tough to resist breaking up a place, to resist selling or dispersing land among siblings. Henrietta did not understand how her husband had come to defend everybody against every unkind word, as though he were Jesus Christ himself. While a woman might love Jesus well enough, only a naive girl would want to be married to Him. For had He not advocated love of Himself above all things, especially beyond love of one's property, and had He not demanded His disciples stand ready to abandon their land and riches and follow Him?

Henrietta felt that, despite life's injustices, people needed to accept their places and live with what they had. In her mind, it made no sense to lament not going to college or not taking the train to visit Chicago. Life laid out your work for you like a set of clothing, and you could either put the garments on or go around naked until you found another suit that fit, but you wanted to hurry, because you could not do much while naked, and no one was going to take you seriously. If you did not get to do everything you wanted, say, if your husband died young, then at least you ought to live righteously and not flaunt your freedoms. Mary O'Kearsy should have known that in moments of weakness every woman longed for a big, quiet fellow like Enkstra. But if they had not sent her away, O'Kearsy would have gotten pregnant, and that was no kind of example to be setting as a teacher of children. What if those girls and boys in her charge grew up thinking they should steal together through the fields at night, and into barns? What if they grew to adulthood with no mind for tending crops on the farms their families occupied? What if instead of buying new equipment for planting and harvesting they spent their meager incomes on travel to Europe? What, then, would have been the justification for wrenching this land away from the savages a century ago? Henrietta could have grabbed that little O'Kearsy by the shoulders and shaken sense into her the way her mother must never have done.

There were still hungry transients and homeless people in America on the day David Retakker burned George Harland's barn, but they had become, for the most part, city people. When they felt restless, they did not set off along river trails or into freight yards, but collected returnable bottles and cans; they begged and recycled until they scraped together the money for bus tickets to get to homeless shelters and downtown missions in other cities. Though salesmen in this day and age were comfortable traveling door-to-door offering vinyl siding and vacuum cleaners, homeless folks knew that the people who lived in the country nowadays were suspicious of a traveling man who had nothing to sell. And most of those unsettled folks had themselves grown lazier, too lazy to trek into unpopulated areas. They were unskilled in the skinning and gutting of rabbits, unpracticed in the stealing and plucking of chickens, and they might have lost for good the knowledge and instinct about which parts of an animal were edible, or which unripe crops, or which mushrooms.

32

DAVID RETAKKER LAY ON HIS BELLY IN A DITCH ALONGSIDE
Queer Road, several hundred feet from the fire, as quiet as a corpse
but alive and watching his life dissolve. The only one to notice
David was Gray Cat, who ran across the street from April May
Rathburn's house and slunk into the ditch a few feet away, waking
David from something sounder than sleep. As soon as he awoke,
David began to wish he'd died, because the fire before him was
destroying even the possibility that George could want him around.
David no longer had any right to hope that things between them
would ever be as good as they had been this morning. In one care-
less moment he had negated the whole history of himself and
George.

David didn't know how he'd gotten out of the barn. He'd continued trying to put out the fire, and at one point he was on his
knees, and then he was dragging a bale toward the door through
heat and smoke. He'd stopped to use his breather, and afterward

he'd been unable to move. He had a dim memory of a girl who looked like Rachel offering her hand, and then he'd dreamed he was propelled by something like a gang of bigger boys grabbing his shoulders and tossing him outside the barn, where he lay on the ground. Maybe his body had been possessed by electricity like Frankenstein's monster or the severed limbs of frogs, or maybe the arms of the fire itself had thrown him through the air. As he lay panting outside the barn, he'd yearned to be strong enough to walk back in. Dying within those walls would have been easier than facing the shame he'd now have to face with every hour of every day for the rest of his life. When cars and trucks had approached the fire, David had crawled a few dozen yards farther away and into the ditch.

David now lifted his head out of the ditch and spotted George standing with Officer Parks. David knew he would never again visit the Harland house but would only watch George from a distance like this. The fire had been chewing at the roof for some time, but without warning, the roof collapsed into its center. David had been keeping an eye on the weathervane at the top, holding on to the slim hope that the big hoses could put out the fire, but as the roof collapsed and the weathervane sank, the fire roared like an engine and sent a round of sparks fifty feet from the building. Since the firefighters were watering the flame at the base, the fire grabbed strength at the top. The tar and asphalt burned off as dense black smoke, and the corrugated sheets of tin beneath glowed red and slid inward as though the roof were a ship sinking into a sea of fire.

George looked away from the barn, in David's direction. David ducked but he figured George could sense exactly where he was hiding, the way he'd sensed where the cows were the time they got loose and went down to graze by the *Glutton*. George had known just where to find the nest of woodchucks that were destroying a section of his soybean crop this August—Rachel staked out the area for two weeks and shot five. To avoid being seen, David pushed his face deeper into the ditch. When he opened his eyes, he saw poison ivy. The ditch was carpeted with its flaming red leaves. Because he was extremely allergic to poison ivy, he usually took care to avoid it, especially after the terrible case he'd gotten all over his feet and legs in June. George had given him capsules to take every four hours and Rachel had wiped lotion on him in a way that was so plain and medical, it wasn't even embarrassing. David had stared at her while she was rubbing it onto his ankles, and even after she stopped, he didn't look away from her face. He tried but couldn't. She was only five years older than him, but he'd wished in that moment that she were his mother.

"You're a goddamn jerk for getting in poison ivy again," Rachel had said. "Will you try not to scratch it, at least?"

He'd nodded yes, still unable to look away, as though she needed to utter some magic words in order to release him. But she hadn't seemed to know the words either, and finally she shoved the tube of cream into his hand and picked up her rifle and walked off toward the garden, leaving him sitting on the section of wooden fence beside the stock barn.

Now David stared into the ditch, at the leaves like small poisonous flames. This morning had been so perfect, and tomorrow he and George would have baled more straw, and because driving the tractor didn't get him out of breath, he could have accepted if George invited him to dinner. *Damn!* he whispered. *Goddamn!* But swearing didn't work for him the way it did for Rachel. David longed for his skin to sizzle, longed for a pain worse than any he'd known, a pain that would dwarf the throbbing of his ankle and his shin. Such a pain would be over quickly enough because the fire would steal the last of his oxygen. Then George might know how sorry he was, and that he couldn't bear to live for what he'd done. If David's body had burned, George might at least have known that David had tried with all his strength to stop the fire. If David did somehow die tonight, he hoped that it would be George who came upon his body in the morning, and he hoped George would carry him away in his arms. David grabbed the woody stalks of poison ivy with both hands and tugged upward, squeezing, breaking, and pulling loose the triple red leaves, then crushing them and wiping them on his arms, neck, and face. He would give himself the worst case of poison ivy ever. The combination of itching and pain would be unbearable. He might go blind. He broke off more leaves and rubbed them under his long-sleeved T-shirt, onto his chest, against his ribs and stomach, until he had to rest from the exertion.

On some bright days, David used to imagine that the barn was so full of energy it might take off like a rocket ship, but he had always intended that after flying into space, it would return whole to its place on George's land. A big support beam collapsed with a whoosh of flame, and David felt the fire's heat on his skin, and the air grew thinner.

33

THE TAYLOR COW BARN HAD NEVER BEEN PAINTED SO bright a red or with such virgin white trim as it was now, with BARN GRILL lettered on each side. It was a theme park version of a cow barn, of course, no more useful farmwise than those Rust-Oleum-painted implements displayed on the float stones around the outside, constituting Milton's farm museum. As Steve the salesman approached the Barn Grill, however, he thought he'd never seen a place so old-fashioned and inviting. That was why he'd moved out here to the country, after all, to take comfort in buildings and objects that had histories, and to get in touch with a more traditional life. He'd stayed alone on Rachel's boat for hours enjoying the smallness of the space, fantasizing that Rachel would come back and make love with him. He'd been imagining himself living both at home with his wife and on the boat with the girl, imagining that each time he arrived at either place, the woman there would be glad to see him. As dusk fell, though, he'd grown restless and hungry, and by the time he made his way along the river and under the golf course fences, he was ravenous. A sign tacked to the front door read, BE RIGHT BACK, but all that contemplation of a new polygamous life made Steve feel as though anything were possible. If he no longer had to make love to only one woman, then he shouldn't have to wait for a sandwich, either. When he noticed a side window propped open a few inches, he found an old metal milk crate to stand on and pushed the window the rest of the way up. He tapped at the screen until it came loose and fell out, and then he jumped up and dragged his belly over the sill. He lowered himself, then fell to the plank floor, face first. He recalled such acrobatics being easier years ago, and he swore he smelled animal dung while his face was in the floorboards. He stood up, straightened his pants, and replaced the screen, and only then registered that he'd just committed breaking and entering. Milton should have engaged the safety-lock feature, Steve told himself. Before he could consider going back out the window, though, somebody was unlocking and opening the front door.

"Surprised to see you," Milton said. "Did I lock you in when I left?"

"No," Steve said. "I mean, yes, I was in the bathroom."

"I didn't see you come in. Sally was acting strange so I took her home. I guess she must be all broke up about her kid starting the fire."

"It's quiet for a Saturday," Steve said.

"Oh, everybody else went up to look at the barn—somebody had packages of hot dogs they were going to cook over the fire. What can I get you?"

"A draft would be fine, and I've got to have some kind of a sandwich. I'm starved."

"Ham and cheese coming up. Give me a few minutes."

When Steve looked around the room, he noticed for the first time that the three main vertical supports had been chewed on—

Milton had stained and finished the wooden posts but hadn't sanded out the big animal tooth prints, maybe from horses or cows. Steve got up and and ran his hands over the bite marks. From there he noticed that the dartboard did not have a red bull's-eye at the center, but a locket-sized picture of horned Satan. Steve reached out and touched a plaster relief of Christ's head and pricked his finger on the crown of real thorns. He returned to his seat, and as he dabbed blood on his napkin, Milton placed before him a grilled cheese and ham sandwich, the bread perfectly browned.

"Cooked with butter," Milton said. "I just ate one myself."

"So what's up with that Rachel?" Steve took a long draw of beer and set it down on the bar. "Why won't she even wave hello to a person?"

Milton said, "She's a different kind of girl, all right."

"Does she really own the boat? That camper thing?" Steve bit into the sandwich.

"Yep. The *Glutton* was her ma's boat, but as long as her ma stays gone I guess it's Rachel's."

Steve finished his beer and pushed his empty glass toward Milton. "Think she'd rent that boat out to me?"

"The girl does like money." Milton refilled Steve's glass and took five dollars. "I wish she'd open her heart to Jesus the way she opens it to cash."

"What do you think she'd say to a hundred bucks a month?"

"I'm guessing you'd get her attention."

"That girl's got quite a garden across from my house up there." Steve took another bite and swallowed. "What's with those mounds?"

"You're taking quite an interest today," Milton said.

"I'm just curious." Steve was the kind of guy who could usually trace the lines of a human drama in a few minutes, from a conversation or just the evidence lying around on a kitchen table. Today, though, he'd taken in more than he could make sense of. "Good sandwich," he said.

The bell on the front door jingled as a tired-looking Officer Parks came in and sat on a bar stool, leaving one empty between himself and Steve. He'd changed out of his uniform and was wearing jeans and a quilted flannel shirt. "You guys haven't seen Sally's kid yet, have you? I was so sure he couldn't have been in that barn, but now I'm starting to worry."

"He'll be okay, praise Jesus."

"Amen," Parks said. "Another thing is, I can't figure out what happened with those cigarettes I found in the barn. They were on my dashboard."

"That fire was something," Milton said. "Nothing burns like hay."

"Some of that was straw," Parks said.

"Straw burns even hotter," Milton said.

"Fire marshal told me flames were over a hundred feet high."

"Does that kind of thing happen very often?" Steve asked. "A barn burning, I mean."

Milton said, "One time I saw a barn burn up north but it was empty. Say, Tom, didn't George's grandpa burn down a barn behind his house?"

"That's what my dad told me whenever he was warning me against baling hay too green," Parks said. "Hey, that's a good-looking sandwich you're eating."

"It is good," Steve said, wiping his hands on a napkin. "Nothing like a pan-grilled ham and cheese."

"Maybe I'll have one of those," Parks said. "I haven't eaten anything since breakfast."

Milton said, "That fire makes me think about how George is just resisting the future, holding on to his farm. Of course, Rachel wouldn't go for him selling."

"Speaking of Rachel," Parks said, putting some bills on the bar.

His eyes were on the last corner of Steve's sandwich as he spoke. "You know, Milton, how I been wondering about her ma's disappearance?"

"Yep. You got yourself a real mystery there." Milton drew him a beer and took a buck. "If you don't mind my saying."

"Well, everybody thought Johnny was gone long before Rachel's ma, but I'm thinking Margo and Johnny disappeared at the same time three years ago."

"That's just after my parents moved to Florida," Milton said. "I can't believe Margo is gone as long as all that. Did I ever tell you she threatened to shoot me?"

"Well, I'm thinking pretty seriously they've run off together. Margo and Johnny."

"You tell George that?"

"I didn't have the heart to tell him that his brother run off with his wife's mother. Sounds too much like one of them country-western songs."

Steve said, "That would make George what? Married to his niece?"

"Sounds downright Old Testament–like," Milton said. "You know, I've been thinking of offering to give George a hand in the mornings next couple of weeks, before I open up for lunch. Since he's got nobody helping him."

"What about Rachel?" Steve asked. "She seems like a capable girl."

"She don't even drive," Milton said. "But she might be willing to work down here for a few hours at lunchtime if I'm helping George. She's good with money, and she's an honest girl. I've been trying to save her soul for Christ, but I don't know how well it's working." He stopped and looked at the two beers on the bar. The liquid shone golden by the light through the window. "Sometimes I wonder about this whole idea of serving up the spirit of the Lord alongside these other spirits. I can't say for sure that I've helped save one soul."

"Well, this place sure is an inspiration to me," Steve said, raising his glass. "I've always felt better every time I've come here. Here's to the Lord." He lifted his glass just to show his good humor, but when he took a drink, he felt a little jolt pass through him.

Two guys in John Deere hats came in and ordered beers and asked for the darts, which Milton handed to them in a shoe box. Then two golfing couples came in.

Parks, meanwhile, sitting there on his bar stool next to Steve, felt himself starting to break open. He'd been so full of jealousy toward George that he hadn't considered offering to help. When Milton returned to the bar, Parks said, "That's real nice of you, Milt, to offer to help George. Especially since you don't believe in farms anymore."

"Maybe we have to keep one farm going around here," Milton said. "Helping him is the Christian thing to do, anyhow. We've all got to help each other in this life."

Parks said, "I just couldn't imagine this place without George's farm."

Milton and Steve nodded.

"Well, he says he's starting on the beans on Friday." Parks spoke slowly, though he felt as though he were gushing. "Next few weeks I'm working six in the morning until two, so maybe I could give him a hand in the afternoons. You know, he's still using some of the equipment he bought from my dad's farm."

Steve said, "I always had an urge to farm. That's why I moved into this neighborhood, because I liked being next to farmland." He took another slug of beer and got jolted again, this time with an inspiration about farming. His desire to work the land swelled in him, became as powerful as his desire for any woman ever was.

"So you figure Margo's run off with Johnny," Milton said. "You're saying they disappeared at the same time?"

"Well, I only got Rachel's telling me that other version of her story, but it's about a month after her post box expired and there was a DNR incident report right before that of Margo threatening a conservation officer. Nobody actually remembers seeing her after that September."

"You make it seem like it's no mystery at all. Good thing you come back to Michigan, Tom."

Parks sighed. "Still, I don't know if I'll get used to George and the girl together."

"What do they call that?" Steve said. "A May-December marriage, right?"

Milton said, "Yep, they got a May-December marriage going, all right. God works in mysterious ways."

"A May-December marriage," Parks said. "Well, here's to pinning a name on a thing." He drained his glass.

Milton said to Steve, "If you think Rachel's a different kind of person, you should've met her ma."

"Yeah, Margo was a heck of a woman," Parks said. "Makes Rachel seem downright domestic, I guess."

"Her ma could gut and skin a poached deer in thirty minutes," Milton said.

"And bury the innards," Parks said, "so you didn't know a hole was ever dug."

"She could skin out a skunk without breaking the sac."

"And sometimes you'd find yourself staring at her for a long time without realizing you were even doing it," Parks said, and the clear-flowing memory of Margo's face came to him, as though he'd just seen her. "That woman was as beautiful as the day is long."

"Sounds like a heck of a woman, all right." Every sip of Steve's beer tasted better and better, and as he watched the two men and listened to them talk, Steve realized that Milton was gay. A few minutes later, though, Steve was less sure. He looked up at the muscular carved Jesus. Steve just couldn't assemble the evidence he'd gathered over the course of the day. He didn't really know what was going on beneath the surface of this neighborhood. Maybe that made him a little uneasy, but by the bottom of his glass, he decided he was never one to shy away from a challenge.

"Yep," Milton said, as if that word pulled together the day's events, put it all to rest, at least temporarily. "So you want one of them sandwiches like that, Tom? Ham and cheese?"

"That'd be great, Milt. I can't believe I haven't eaten in more than ten hours."

When Milton returned from the kitchen, he waited on the two golfing couples, then returned and refilled Parks's and Steve's glasses without taking any money.

34

WHILE APRIL MAY WAS WAITING FOR LARRY TO RETURN from visiting his brother in Benton Harbor, she arranged her four biggest pumpkins with some straw out on the porch steps. She supposed it was a good thing she hadn't waited until this afternoon to steal straw from George's barn. Poor George, she thought, as she arranged the pumpkin gourds as a dining room centerpiece. Poor George, she'd continued thinking as she put the two smallest pumpkins over in the bay window with some Indian corn she'd saved from last year. What she was feeling most strongly this evening wasn't sympathy, though—it was elation that the pain in her foot was gone. She hadn't been entirely free of that pain since she was a girl of seven. It was as though all her life she'd been pinned to the ground by that old nail, but she'd finally stood on tiptoes tall enough to free herself.

By the time her husband arrived home, the wild-limbed flames across the street had died down and a house-sized heap of orange coals glowed atop the black earth.

"I don't know if I want to carve the pumpkins this year," April May told Larry during their late supper. "I kind of like them whole."

"You'll have to make at least one into pumpkin pie."

"I make pumpkin pie out of a can," April May said. "I've always made pumpkin pie out of a can. I can't imagine making pumpkin pie out of a pumpkin."

"Well, these little ones here are real cute," Larry said, pointing his fork at the table's centerpiece.

This morning April May might have preferred the smaller, more perfect pumpkins and pumpkin gourds, but over the course of the evening she found herself favoring the big ones, the misshapen, asymmetrical ones with flattened, dirty sides. She was no longer planning to burn down her house, but she was seriously entertaining the idea that on Halloween she'd dress in black and paint her face and jump out from the bushes and scare children who came to the door. She laughed aloud at the thought of it. Maybe she'd skip Christmas altogether this year, keep celebrating Halloween right through to the New Year.

"You seem cheerful," Larry said. "Anything happen today?"

April May couldn't believe that her husband still had not noticed that the barn across the street was gone. He'd pulled in to the driveway, parked his truck, and slogged into the house by the side door, exhausted from spending the day with his brother at the hospital. At first she'd thought it funny that he hadn't even noticed the smell of burned wood, but now she realized she was being cruel. She took Larry's left hand and tugged at him—he stood up automatically—and led him onto the porch. They hadn't sat out there for ages, but now her husband fell into one of the dusty cloth chairs April May had been meaning to get rid of.

"My God, what happened?" Larry still gripped his fork in his right fist.

April May breathed deeply, reluctant to exhale the smoky air.

She'd seen her whole neighborhood sprung open by the wind when she was seven, she'd birthed and raised three children from scratch, and she'd seen a teenage girl bury a man without ceremony. Dozens of bonfires had blazed for her, but never had she seen such a spectacle as the barn. In those flames she'd seen the ferocity she'd wanted in the pumpkin faces she'd carved over the decades. She could never explain all this to Larry. Because Larry did not know what Johnny had done to the girls in that barn, April May could not expect him to appreciate how justice could be beautiful even as it was merciless. The fire may have been started by a boy's careless act, but it had burned with vengeance for her daughters, and for Rachel.

Poor Larry, thought April May, poor Larry had missed the fire, and there was so much he would never know.

"Poor George," Larry said.

"Oh, George will be fine."

Larry continued shaking his head. The sun had already set and the sky was quickly darkening.

"What do you think about buying an RV?" April May said. "And driving to the Pacific Ocean. We can ask Tommy Parks to stay here while we're gone."

Larry said, "That's something to think about."

But April May didn't really hear his response. At the pleasure of even suggesting they drive west she felt a sensation in her chest like birds lifting off the ground.

David Retakker lay deathlike in his ditch all afternoon and then shook himself back to life sometime after dark. Before him, where there had been first a barn and then a blaze, now a pile of coals glowed. David didn't know how long he'd slept, but his breathing was a little easier now, and he was able to stand. He limped to within twenty feet of the coals, as close as he could bear the heat, then circled around slowly. The nearest maple, the bigger, older one, was gone entirely, but the maple on the other side, slightly farther away, smaller and leafless, remained. The cows no longer huddled in fear beside the creek, but simply chewed their cuds under the night sky as they might chew cuds under any sky, fully adjusted to their barnless condition. The old stone foundation of the barn's lower level barely protruded above the coals at the back.

David tried to feel a perverse pride about having caused all this wreckage. Maybe if he lived past tonight, havoc and misery would become his marks. Maybe his life's work would be to ruin things, to tear structures and people apart, to crash and burn through life not caring. But trying to force himself to embrace what he'd done quickly exhausted him, and he let himself sink back into regret.

Maybe he would stop at home now and tell his mother to go ahead, get the heck out of here, leave Michigan and go to California. Before destroying the barn, he might have been able to leave with her, but now he couldn't possibly. If his mother forced him, he'd pretend to give in and follow along, but the moment she got drunk, he'd sneak out and find his way back here, even if it meant hitchhiking the whole country. David would hide in the woods beside the golf course. He might steal food from neighbors but only enough to survive, and people might even leave food out for him as they would for a stray cat or dog they liked. He would try to remember everything Rachel had taught him about trapping and hunting, and for hours each day he'd pick berries at the edge of the woods and collect walnuts and crack them open with a hammer, which he'd return to George's shed as soon as he finished with it. He might grow a few green beans and melons where Rachel used to garden beside the *Glutton*. Maybe he could even live on the boat. And his only goal in his secret new life would be to help George. In the evenings, after George went into the house for dinner, David would continue stacking hay or cleaning a barn or digging a trench, helping George the way elves sometimes helped people. He would never ever again rub poison ivy on himself—he would, in fact, avoid poison ivy with more care than ever, because he needed to be his strongest from now on, needed to be as healthy as possible in order to do the most he could for George.

David imagined his ankle healing thick and twisted, stronger than before but deformed enough to be a reminder of what he'd done. After his skin burned in summer and chapped in winter, after scars covered him, he would be so tough he couldn't even cut himself with a knife. Without his inhalers, David's lungs would reshape themselves so his breath would be permanently ragged and short. Soon enough he would become the monster of this place, living unseen like the ghosts of animals killed here by Rachel and her mother and by the Potawatomi Indians. David was certain that some of Rachel's tribe must have stayed behind, and David would find their hiding places, maybe even find secret bands of Indians with whom he would live while he devoted his life to George. Probably that was what Rachel's Corn Girl had been doing. Probably she'd just been trying to hide and grow her corn, when she took a careless chance and fell. David would no longer take chances in climbing the silo behind the house on P Road or jumping from wagons to haystacks. He held his hands a little farther out in front of him to warm them. The cows murred softly near the creek. Gray Cat stood a few yards away, waving his tail. Since David had last taken a good look at him, Gray Cat had become full-grown, and he looked healthy and whole. David called out, "Here, kitty-kitty."

Gray Cat approached but stopped about ten feet away, when both the cat and the boy heard the porch door of the Rathburn house opening. Gray Cat sped away into the cornfield and David hid beside the bedspring portion of the fence, which had blackened from the heat. From there, squatting down, he watched April May lug an old cloth-covered chair across the street. David knew he should help her, but he wanted to stay hidden, and really she seemed to be doing fine by herself. When April May stopped, David thought she was going to sit in the chair beside the fire, but after a rest she kept dragging the chair closer, so close her skin must have been burning. Then she lifted the chair and heaved it onto the fire. It tipped over onto the hot coals and looked like a defeated throne of hell. David watched it blacken and burst into flame. April May stood with her hands on her lower back for a while, then walked around the fire, as if to see it from other angles.

As she approached his hiding place, April May said aloud, "God, I love a fire."

David assumed she was talking to him, and he almost stood to respond, but when she moved away and said it again, he realized she was talking to herself. Maybe she, too, would need his help sometime in the future. David could help her and everybody else and so become the secret hero of Queer Road. Gray Cat rubbed against his leg, and David ran his hand over the cat's body. Gray Cat purred roughly, made a sound that started, stalled out, and started again. Maybe Gray Cat would become his truest friend in the new life. David didn't notice the car slowing on the road behind him until it turned into the driveway. He stood to see which vehicle it was, and inadvertently showed himself in the headlights before turning and running toward the creek, panting and dragging his bad foot.

"Hey, David!" a man shouted. "Get back here." The voice sounded like George, but when David stopped and turned, he saw the plump outline of Officer Parks silhouetted in the car's lights. David had never noticed how alike the two men sounded. The cop yelled again, but David kept moving, in the direction of the *Glutton,* as fast as his ankle allowed.

When David was out of sight, Parks approached April May.

She asked, "Is that the kid who started the fire?"

"He's not a bad kid," Parks said.

"It's a nice fire."

Parks had to laugh. "Glad to see you're enjoying yourself, Aunt April."

"So when are you going to move out of that crummy motel?" she asked.

"Soon, I hope."

35

THOUGH THE HAZE HAD HUNG IN THE SKY UNTIL AFTER dark, Rachel'd had a feeling about a hard frost, and she'd not only pulled the pumpkins inside the stock barn to protect them from hooligans, but she'd spread a canvas tarp over the top and carefully tied the tarp rings to the corners of the wagon. Pumpkins could generally handle frost, but she didn't want to take a chance tonight. Then she'd sat in her garden for hours, first waiting for George to come out and chop wood, then waiting to shoot a pumpkin-biting possum, all the while waiting for the ghost of David to tell her what had happened, to tell her why in hell he would smoke in the hay barn. Maybe David's ghost would explain that he didn't start the fire, that Todd and the Higgins kid were really to blame, so she could go down to the river where they'd pitched their tents and kick their asses right now. Really, though, she knew David had abandoned her by his own stupidity, and she knew that eventually his death would harden into a stone in her belly to clank against the other indigestible facts of life. In this way, her thoughts circled around David but would not settle. She crept into bed after George had already been there a while.

Rachel did not think that George was asleep, though he lay still beside her and breathed evenly. No man in his right mind could really be sleeping after a boy had burned to death in his barn, not to mention the loss of much of the year's alfalfa and straw and all the work that had gone into it. And the barn itself, a landmark on the land and in the man's brain. Even if George wouldn't yet accept that David had been in the barn, even if he didn't know that his missing brother lay below the wreckage, he had known that barn his whole life, had filled it with hay and straw each summer and fall, and he knew there would be no place for next year's twelve hundred bales. This winter there'd be no hay for Higgins's dairy herd, no place for George's four cows to go for cover. She knew George was too busy to string more barbed wire anytime soon, so maybe she'd try to rig up something for the cows near the house. Or maybe they should just put the cows in with the other livestock and hope they all could get along.

Rachel reached over and almost touched George's shoulder, but stopped herself, because she wasn't ready to comfort or be comforted. David's death and the loss of the barn were not the end of the terrible events. She knew that one night in the future, George would be lying beside her as usual, and then he would stop breathing. She might not notice right away, since she'd be asleep, but his body would gradually grow cool. Everything around here was permeated with death—the soil of this farm, her decaying houseboat, even George himself. Still, the blood pulsed hotly through Rachel's veins and she knew she couldn't stay still much longer. Maybe she'd go back outside and lie in a furrow with her Brussels sprouts towering above her and decide what, if anything, to say to George tomorrow, decide whether to offer to help with the corn and beans. She didn't want to be the kind of farmer George was. In her garden she could know every plant, but in any one acre of his fields there were thousands upon thousands, all alike. Maybe she'd go outside and lie atop one of her mounds and let herself think about Johnny and her mother again, let herself get used to running through the details of that night. Remembering had not made it seem worse, as she'd feared it would. Remembering it all made Rachel feel that, like George, she had a history here.

When David's ghost came to her, she would not let it just fade away without an explanation. She had tried to protect David for the last three years, had tried to nourish him with food, had tried to make him dress warmly. Hadn't that kid realized he had been as important to her as this piece of land? Maybe more important, if that were possible. She pinched at the bullet in her armpit until she could make out its round end. As shallow as it was buried, she thought it might even have passed through Johnny before it found a place in her, maybe putting a drop of his blood inside her, or a tiny piece of his flesh. Well, Rachel didn't want to be the depository of the dead and disappeared anymore. Maybe she'd go outside and scream into the cold air that she was sick to death of death.

There had been several morning frosts, but this was the first really cold night of the year. The Potawatomi women had survived this cold and much worse without houses or houseboats, and according to what she'd read, deer hides were all they had to protect them from the ground and to cover them. As Rachel lay beneath the old goose-down quilt and tightly woven wool blankets, it seemed strange that she could be so rich compared to the people who'd lived here before. In spring, summer, and fall the Potawatomi women gardened and kept their bodies in motion, but in winter they just scraped and sewed hides, and threaded their bone needles, maybe carried buckets of water from the river. They must have suffered from inhaling all that smoke from tent fires, must have ended up breathing the way David did. Those women must have known that their husbands and parents, their sisters and brothers, and even their children could die around them, and it must have been another kind of coldness they just had to bear. And then there must have been one especially bitter day when the men came home smelling of whiskey and told the women about the treaties they'd signed, told the women they would all have to leave this place.

George shifted slightly beside her. His family belonged to the tribe who conquered the Potawatomi, and now that tribe was being wiped out by the new people with manicured lawns, asphalt driveways, and fake vinyl shutters. Rachel didn't know what tribe she belonged to, now that David was gone. Three years ago, David had defeated sure death when the bullet she fired had swerved around him in the raspberries, but that bullet had apparently circled the planet and come back around to ignite the barn with him in it.

When Rachel heard some noise at the back door, she sat up, grateful for an excuse to get out of bed and stop thinking. Maybe this would be the possum who'd been biting her pumpkins. Over her T-shirt, Rachel put on the thick flannel shirt George had been wearing all day. It hung to her knees. She grabbed her rifle from behind the door and stepped barefoot into the hall.

36

IF STEVE HAD A CHOICE, HE TOLD HIMSELF, IF DESIRE WERE
a matter of simply deciding, he would not have thought about
other women as he lay beside his wife. After Steve had returned
from the Barn Grill, Nicole was angry with him, despite his having
lugged two good-sized pumpkins from Milton's garden all the way
home, just for her. He and Nicole then went out together for some
Chinese (he didn't mention he'd already eaten a sandwich) and they
returned home to eat it and watch a movie on TV. Before going to
bed, Steve had not been able to make himself comfortable, not in
his reclining armchair, not on the couch beside Nicole. The
moment he'd put his arm around her, he'd wanted to pull it away,
but he'd made himself sit there with her head in his armpit for ten
minutes before pretending he had to get up and use the toilet. All
evening he'd wished his wife were more than one person, that she
could change day to day and sometimes become a larger woman,
that some days she could embrace him more forcefully, instead of

always being small and focused, like the tender heart of something whose protective body layers had withered away.

He and Nicole would spend Sunday together, possibly going to church with his or her parents, but more likely skipping that and going to the mall to buy clothes and makeup and household knick-knacks. On the way home, he'd suggest they stop and check out the barn to see if it was still burning, and if Nicole didn't want to go, he'd walk there later by himself and then go to the river and check out the boat again. He was already looking forward to Monday, to driving along a country road or a tree-lined street, then stopping at a house that needed fixing up, and meeting a woman in her thirties, forties, or fifties who would offer him coffee or tea, and if she knew what she wanted in the way of home improvement, he would have some thoughts about how well her ideas would work. She might invite him to laugh with her about the parts of her house that were less than perfect, and he would admire the placement of a window or the polished surface of a walnut or oak or pine banister on a stairway leading to bedrooms. He'd pause for a moment in her bathroom to inhale the mingled scents and residual humidity of her morning shower. Compared to the discovery of other women's houses, being alone with his wife was lonesome.

Steve got out of bed and looked up through the window, but he couldn't make out the Harland cupola, which was blocked by the sycamore and the darkness of night. He thought he needed a window room, a houseboat, a barn loft, a tree fort, a hideout of some kind. When he'd first married Nicole, he'd thought she was a small place where he could hide, but he had since learned there was no room for him, for she was surprisingly dense at her center and filled herself entirely. Looking south, Steve could make out a dim glow from where the remnants of the barn burned, the barn in which he might have set up an office and parked his car. He thought of Rachel's face, which then dissolved into the faces of lots of other women.

———

Later that night, while Steve was asleep, Nicole slipped out of bed to pee, but instead of returning, she clicked on the television and adjusted the volume to barely a drone, and, without even flicking through the channels, settled into watching an infomercial for a line of hair care products that would make color-treated hair super shiny. Sunday she would at least get to the mall, and she'd be able to visit her mother. The light glowed in the breakfast nook next door, which meant that Mrs. Shore was sitting at her window like the ghost of future gloom and bitterness. The world was a sad place, Nicole thought, with Mr. Harland losing his barn and with that old woman over there staring out the window day and night, maybe because Mr. Shore had been unfaithful to her long ago, or maybe because life just didn't deliver up what it had promised. When the breakfast nook light finally switched off next door, it made Nicole even more distressed, knowing that sour old Mrs. Shore had found enough peace to sleep when Nicole could not. Nicole wondered if maybe she should bake a cake for the Harlands as a way of acknowledging their loss. God, she hadn't baked a cake since she'd been married.

She'd thought marriage would make her want to do simple things such as bake cakes. She had thought that marriage would make life richer—just the knowledge that the man she loved had committed to her should make every moment sparkle. Surely Steve had promised her that life with him would be warm and fun. But instead it was . . . God, she didn't even have the words to describe what her life felt like. Over the course of several hours of any day, she felt sad, happy, hurt, then vulnerable, then self-confident. Each day she wove the threads of those emotions into a fabric to wrap around herself, but for all that, she thought she might never be able to express another meaningful idea to anyone else ever again. By getting married, she'd put herself on the shelf, and other people now saw her as taken care of, finished off. She'd planned and executed her wedding, and she'd done a fabulous job—everybody said so—but rather than a fresh new start on life, the wedding had turned out to be the beginning of the end. If she didn't do something that made a difference soon, then in thirty years she would be another gloomy old lady staring out of her house at a world that confounded her.

Nicole got up, and in her heart-patterned flannel pajamas, she walked into and out of all the rooms of her little house, including the smaller bedroom, which was Steve's home office, and she ended up in the kitchen, where she stood for a long time before she grabbed the biggest knife from the knife holder and carried it toward Steve. As she crossed the threshold between the living room and the bedroom, she grasped the handle with both hands, and as she approached the bed, she extended her arms straight out in front of her. She studied the big, dumb body of her husband and imagined she could see beads of sweat excreted from his pores. His hair was flattened on the side of his head, and his mouth hung open. His exposed arm looked flabby in sleep. She had hoped that this man could mean everything to her. She was fully aware that she would never be able to explain to her mother or anyone else how murder was the only remedy for her situation. She positioned the knife directly above his chest. She lifted her arms and felt all the forces of the universe collect in her tensed muscles. At the top of her thrust, the clock snapped from 1:52 to 1:53 and she awoke from her trance, a princess of a bride transformed into an aging married woman with bleached hair and a blotchy complexion. She let her arms drop to her sides.

She hurried out of the bedroom, through the living room and kitchen, to the sliding glass door and outside onto the plank deck. She knew that killing Steve was a fantasy, just as her idea of a perfect marriage had been a fantasy, the way her white house with a view of a barn and a bridge over a stream amounted to nothing more than a puff of smoke. On the picnic table before her sat the two pumpkins Steve had brought home earlier. Only now did she consider it was pretty impressive that he'd carried them all that distance from the Barn Grill. She went to the bigger of the two, and without hesitation stabbed it with all the strength in both her arms. With that thrust, she felt something snap in her chest, something like a popcorn kernel popping. It required some force to yank the knife out. She positioned herself over the pumpkin and stabbed it again. When she freed the knife, the pumpkin toppled to the wooden deck. She got down on her knees and stabbed it, again and again, through its ribs, and as she sliced, her white breath fanned from her nose and mouth. The pumpkin rolled over and she stabbed it while it lay on its back. The next attempt missed the pumpkin entirely; she thrust the knife between two boards of the deck. When she looked up, she saw her husband standing in the doorway.

He swallowed audibly. "What are you doing, honey?"

"Carving this pumpkin." She was a little out of breath.

"It looked like you were stabbing it."

"I guess I slipped." She lifted the knife one more time, thrust it into the pumpkin, and left it there.

Steve laughed nervously and shifted his weight to his other bare foot. Beneath his T-shirt, his stomach extended over the waistband of his boxers. When he noticed her looking, he sucked it in. He said, "Aren't you cold?"

Nicole hadn't even noticed that her pajama sleeves had ridden up. Her forearms were goose-bumped and steam seemed to be rising from her skin. Steve tilted his head in a way that signaled he was good-natured, but the gesture seemed forced.

"Tomorrow," he said, and cleared his throat. "Tomorrow I'm going to offer to help George Harland with his farming. Milton at the Barn Grill told me that the guy who worked for him moved to Indiana and left him in a bind. He could lose the whole place."

Nicole was eyeing the knife, wondering if she should pull it out and stab the pumpkin one last time tonight. Or maybe she'd wait until tomorrow, and then do some serious carving.

"If he loses the farm, we might end up living next to a subdivision. I think I'd be good at it, you know," Steve said. "Farming. I'm going to offer to help him however I can. Then I figure when he needs windows he'll come to me."

She said, "Do you think I should bake them a cake or something?"

"You know, cake would sure hit the spot right now."

"Maybe I'll make two cakes, one for us."

Steve said, "Did I ever tell you I took home ec in school? We made cakes, pizzas, cookies, you name it."

"You took home ec?"

"Just the cooking part. I was about the only guy in the class."

Nicole said, "I don't know if we have all the ingredients."

"Flour, baking powder, sugar, milk, butter."

"Eggs. Chocolate, maybe."

They went inside just before Rachel came out from the side door across the street.

37

RACHEL CARRIED HER GUN THROUGH THE KITCHEN AND mudroom. When she opened the side door, cold air rushed her. Standing three steps below her was the spirit she'd conjured up, the ghost of David Retakker. Though the haze had hung on through the day, the night sky above the stock barn and pasture was dark and clear, hungry for its new moon. David Retakker's ghost looked pale and grubby. It was breathing hard, and it scratched its armpit, looked at the ground, and said nothing. For a moment, Rachel herself couldn't breathe, but then she inhaled the cold air too deeply and choked. She didn't look away because she didn't trust this silent apparition not to disappear. It refused to look up at her. She lifted her rifle and looked at the ghost over the sights.

"Damn you, David!" Rachel said. "What the hell were you thinking?" She had no intention of firing, but when she heard the raccoon rustling near the mouth of the stock barn where the pumpkins and apples were, her sighting, shooting, and pulling the trigger were all one motion. Because she hadn't been prepared to fire, the shriek of the bullet made her jump.

"Don't kill me!" David screamed. And in the same moment, the raccoon beyond him squeaked and died. The shot must have missed David by inches. Rachel threw the gun down onto the wet grass.

She descended the cold cement stairs in her bare feet and when she reached David she hauled off and smacked his dirt-smeared face. He was solid. He stumbled and regained his balance and then looked at her as though willing her to smack him again, so she did. As her hand struck his ear he yelped. David's long-sleeved T-shirt was covered with burrs and sticktights. He still wore no jacket, though it was cold enough that breath poured out his nostrils and mouth. Her relief at his being alive threatened to buoy her, but she pushed that aside. She grabbed his shoulders and began to shake him. "Damn you!" She couldn't think of what to say. "And what about the cows?" she said, and with both hands thrust his body to the ground. David lifted himself onto his elbows and looked up at her from the grass and dirt. She kicked him twice in the ribs with her bare foot, and the second kick must have hurt him because it hurt her middle toes. Though he squirmed away from her, he did not fight back. She kicked him again, in the hipbone, and this time hurt the top of her foot enough that she'd have a bruise.

David knew that if he could endure Rachel hitting and kicking him, he could stand anything. He wouldn't defend himself, and he wouldn't complain or cry. Except that he already was crying. He could hardly inhale and his ankle throbbed and so did the lump on his shin. His wrists and armpits had started to itch already from the poison ivy; his chest muscles ached. He hoped Rachel would not pick up her gun and shoot him.

"Stand up!" she yelled. "Stand up, you little son of a bitch!"

When he stood, Rachel slapped his face again, though with little force. "How could you?" She shook his shoulders. "How could you?"

Only when she noticed he was crying did Rachel realize that she was crying too. She stopped shaking him and said, "You ruined everything. You have no idea about that barn." Yet it sounded dumb, what she was saying, because really she'd been thinking that David himself had been in that barn, that *he* was the great loss. Now that he was resurrected from the fire, she could see how the barn had been nothing more than a sorry-ass building, a giant wooden grave marker, a rotting blemish on the otherwise perfect landscape.

"I'm sorry," David said.

"You're sorry." Rachel laughed and looked up at the moonless sky. "You burn down a hundred-and-thirty-year-old barn full of straw and hay and a wagon and nearly kill your goddamn self and you're sorry. You're the sorriest kid I ever knew." She was thinking about the other bedroom on the second floor—not the one with the Indian garden drawings, but the one with less junk. They'd need to put plastic on the windows before winter, because it had been cold in there last year. She and David could do that.

Rachel's bare feet were growing numb from the wet grass. She was thinking that if George died in his sleep, she could walk down the hall and push open the door to the room that would be David's and wake David up and sit on the edge of his bed, and when she told him what they were going to do next, then she would know.

David, for his part, felt exhausted, more exhausted than ever in his life, as if his body no longer had the energy to expand his lungs or to distill the oxygen from the poorly mixed air of this night, and he told himself again that if he could survive tonight, he could survive anything, even living in the woods eating berries and walnuts and wild creatures. When Rachel let go of his shoulders, he braced himself to be punched, but instead Rachel pulled his face into her shoulder and hugged him, and David took comfort in her warmth and in the smell of George that permeated the flannel shirt she was wearing.

Rachel felt stupidly happy with her arms around David's shoulder blades and backbone. She felt happy despite her mother being gone, probably forever, despite the wreckage of the fire, despite knowing that George would die beside her. She just felt glad standing here on the land she loved, hugging this sorry kid brought back to the living.

Rachel said, "Since you destroyed the cows' barn, you'll have to help me make a new cow pen. And we've both got to somehow help George bring in the corn and beans because he can't do it himself." After all, Rachel thought, Corn Girl harvested corn.

"I'm sorry," David repeated, now bawling in earnest, gagging and wheezing, struggling against Rachel's arms to lift his face and breathe. "I'm so sorry."

Rachel loosened her embrace and rested her chin on top of David's head to look behind the house toward her garden mounds, where pumpkin stems lay tangled. She envisioned David's big-knuckled hands reaching down and cutting the stems with the small machete and carrying them up to the wagon one by one, his body straining. She hadn't been all that strong at twelve either, she supposed. This winter David could help her build a new Indian garden in the shape of a wagon wheel. He'd stand in the center, holding the end of a fifty-yard length of twine, while Rachel measured out the spokes of a giant wheel, maybe beside the river, or maybe on the site of the burned-down barn. Rachel imagined David weeding her garden and driving tractors across hay fields, eating dinner with her and George at the round kitchen table, passing the potatoes, busting up the silence of their meals with stupid questions and stupid comments.

She decided to leave the dead raccoon on the ground. She didn't feel like skinning out anything tonight. If it was still there in the morning, she'd bury it in her garden.

"Are you hungry, David?" she asked. "You look pretty damn hungry."

38

_____

GEORGE HAD LEARNED OVER THE YEARS TO RELAX WHEN he couldn't sleep, to lie still and let himself drift, to let his body recover for the next day's work. Tonight he lay quietly and tried not to think about his barn and David. Instead he thought of the day his first wife left him, thought of all those buttons on the yellow dress she wore. There were twenty-two buttons, he remembered, because instead of listening to her he'd counted the tiny black buttons, which he thought made her look like a cluster of black-eyed Susans. Back then he'd assumed that once you got married you stayed married. After Carla left the first time, she did return, but then she just kept on leaving until she was finally too exhausted from all that leaving to come back.

When Rachel got up and left the bed, George kept his eyes closed so he wouldn't see her walk out. There had been one bit of good news coming out of this day: Parks had stopped just shy of pointing out that Margo and Johnny must have run off together.

Despite himself, George had always suspected that Rachel had killed and buried her mother, and his feeling about it grew every time he saw her digging in her garden with a round-end shovel. He could well imagine a scenario in which Rachel's killing her mother would have been justified, but he was relieved that he no longer had to. It made all the sense in the world that Johnny was somehow responsible for Margo's disappearance.

If Rachel were still beside him, he'd stop faking sleep and turn to her, wrap an arm around her and smell her hair, and she would move closer and put one of her strong arms around him. Even if she didn't love him the way he loved her, she seemed at times to desire his body as simply and wholeheartedly as she desired this piece of land beneath them. When Rachel didn't return to bed right away, George figured she'd gone outside. She would have no part of lying still and faking sleep. When she couldn't sleep, she wanted to be fully awake, making love or working or just sitting in her garden waiting for an animal, as she sometimes did all through the night. He never followed her outside on those nights. He felt too much for her already, and if he watched her sitting silently in the dark, his heart might burst.

Just as he raised his arms to adjust his pillow, he heard a rifle crack so close outside that he thought he'd been shot. He lay still until he heard Rachel's voice below the window, then he switched on the bedside lamp and got up slowly so as not to lose his balance, as sometimes happened when he stood quickly. George went around the bed to the window, opened it, and rested on the sill, letting cold air into the room. He continued to hear Rachel's voice but saw only the glimmer of her rifle lying in the wet grass. George pushed up the window screen and stuck his head out in time to see Rachel push David down beside the concrete steps. As the boy lifted himself onto his elbows, she kicked him. At the realization that David was alive, George felt a kind of congestion leave his chest, the way a mouthful of horseradish cleared the sinuses.

George thought David was too good a boy to be treated the way Rachel was treating him. George had never in his life attacked another person, and he would never hit David. But it made sense for somebody to be angry. David had destroyed something irreplaceable. David, at his tender age, had already done something he would always regret.

George thought that a boy who knew regret might listen to the kind of stories Old Harold used to tell, and might even make sense of them in a way George never had been able to. George might try telling David that the people around here had been wrong to send away the Indians a century and a half ago, and that the school board had been fools to send away that widowed teacher, because she might have taught those people something new, might have inspired them to see things differently, the way Rachel had inspired George. George would tell David that if this place was going to survive, the farmers needed a new way of seeing, a new way of farming, maybe a new crop, because clearly with fellows in Iowa getting double his yields, corn and bean farming wasn't long for this region. George wondered if maybe there was a way to combine farming and gardening; he knew some farmers were trying green beans. And there were the oddball crops he'd read about in the farming magazines—organic carrots, hybrid apples, ginseng that grew in the woods. Hadn't he heard something about a special kind of popcorn? Beneath the window, Rachel kicked the boy again.

George had always figured that when corn and beans failed, it would signal the arrival of that monster he'd been watching for at the horizon all these years. He'd always imagined the monster reaching out for him in winter, in the form of bills he couldn't pay, and he'd never considered that he'd do anything other than admit defeat. But maybe he could put up a fight. If he could slay this beast, or if he tried his damnedest, anyhow, then he might survive into the future. Maybe the future would arrive silently and mysteriously, the way Rachel had arrived outside his door on that spring day, full of anger and possibility. Perhaps the future wouldn't knock, but would just stand out there waiting to be noticed, maybe was standing there now. If the future were here, then it could be time to start harvesting those walnut trees his grandmother had planted. How much would they be worth now? A few hundred dollars a piece? A few thousand for the taller, straighter ones? George wasn't surprised when Rachel stopped kicking David, helped him up, and hugged him.

After Rachel and David went inside through the mudroom door, George put on his jeans. He intended to join the two downstairs, but when he reached the landing, he looked up and noticed that the access panel to the window room had been moved. Instead of following the sound of voices, he climbed the wall rungs as he hadn't done in years, shoved the panel aside, and pulled himself up into the dark room. He looked south, to the end of the line of roadside walnut trees, where a pool of orange coals glowed. From here the barn's disappearance was as shocking as the river slithering away downstream, never to return. He looked south and west and assured himself he could make out the length of the dark serpent, but he knew this house was not the same without that barn. Beyond the burning coals glowed the lights of Greenland, which seemed to stretch farther in all directions than he remembered. A string of lights headed west along M-96, toward Kalamazoo. George ran his hand along the bottom of the window frame and found that the picture of the teacher was still stuck where his grandfather had left it decades ago. George didn't bother to look at it in the dark; he remembered the woman well enough.

George considered that he might rebuild that barn after all, just for the hell of it. What was involved in building a barn besides more money and more work? His great-great-grandfather had been a mere mortal. So what if it would take George ten years? So what if they never painted the house or got insulated windows or an electric clothes dryer? So what if the new barn could go up in flames just as quickly as the old one? Tom Parks would undoubtedly get a kick out of George's building a new old-fashioned barn. Milton would help too, so long as he was allowed to see the new barn as a sort of museum. George would tell Milton that Greenland was becoming the town of born-again barns, and surely Milton would appreciate the holy implications of that! If George's grandfather were still alive, he would help. After all, Old Harold was the man who replaced and glazed these windows forty years ago. And for what practical purpose? A 270-degree view of what was gone and what remained? A man like Harold could forgive George for loving Rachel. His grandmother would not forgive him. For his grandmother, George would plant new walnut trees, two or three for each one he harvested to pay for building the new barn.

Of course, an identical new barn wouldn't really be the same as an old one. While the original had been built as a practical affair, George's rebuilding the same would be a defiant act. Frivolous, even, the way that keeping cattle had seemed frivolous to the deer-hunting Potawatomi, the way that building a window room had seemed frivolous to neighbors in 1834. George had always considered himself a practical person, but the practical thing now would be to sell the place for subdivisions. If the future was going to be Rachel and keeping the land, then it was also bedspring fences, crazy Indian gardens, overgrown lawns, experimental crops, and all kinds of disapproval, from neighbors new and old. Now, George thought, if he could find enough of them, he'd build a new cow pasture out of nothing but bedsprings.

39

SHORTLY AFTER SHE WENT TO BED IN THE SPARE ROOM AS
usual, Elaine Shore heard a sharp noise like a gunshot. She got up,
put on her bathrobe, turned on the hall light, and went and sat
again in the breakfast nook. Across the street, in the dim light at
the Harland's side door, she made out the black-haired girl. She
wore a man's shirt that hung almost to her knees, and she was hugging a boy, hugging him as though he were a lost son who'd been
abducted by aliens shortly after birth and who had finally been
allowed to return home. As tightly as she clutched the boy, Elaine
figured that the girl didn't realize she had to be careful with
abductees, for they'd been through a kind of physical trauma the
rest of us could not imagine. It was miraculous that he'd even survived the crash, let alone made his way down the road to the Harland House. In the upstairs window, Mr. Harland was backlit by a
small lamp, looking down on the two below. Elaine felt a spark in
her chest, which expanded into a lightness she had not experienced

in years. Maybe Elaine could help the boy somehow, advise the Harlands how to care for his delicate condition. She watched until the two went into the house and Mr. Harland pulled his head inside and closed the window. Afterward, Elaine could not hold on to her feeling of lightness, and before long she wasn't even sure what she'd felt. She got up and stood before the wooden spice rack over the stove, and her chest swelled with anger toward those glass-stoppered bottles. She never used mace in anything. Not fennel either. Even chili powder seemed suddenly useless. She wanted to throw those bottles down with enough force to break the glass, but instead she carefully placed them all in the garbage receptacle, tied up the quarter-full bag, and walked outside to place the bag in her trash container. As the kitchen light came on at the Harlands', Elaine stepped back into her own house, wiped her terry-cloth slippers on the mat, locked the door behind her, and sat down again. She crossed her arms over her chest to hug herself as she planned her escape from this place. She did not want to be a pioneer; she wanted to be comfortable. She clutched a breast in each hand and gently squeezed.

40

OFFICER PARKS HAD DRIVEN BY THE HARLAND HOUSE, intending to tell George the good news, that he'd seen David, but the lights were out and he didn't want to wake George if he was managing to sleep after all this. When Parks later came across Sally walking up Queer Road from the direction of the Barn Grill, he turned the cruiser around, stopped beside her, and reached across to open the door. She got in automatically, as though she had been expecting him to come by. As she slid onto the seat, her silvery hair flashed in the dome light and she seemed to Parks like some element of nature, like the woolly bears migrating, like birds traveling mindlessly south. When you picked up a spider, it showed no sign of surprise, but just kept walking on your hand and then up your arm if you let it. Sally was an animal that had ended up in Greenland Township the way a woolly bear might get stuck in some kid's science project shoe box. Parks was glad nobody else was on the road, because giving someone a ride was against the rules and, strictly speaking, nobody but another cop should sit in the front seat of the cruiser without prior approval.

Parks said, "Milton told me he took you home."

"I walked back, but Milton wouldn't serve me."

"I saw your son," Parks said.

Sally nodded.

Though Parks didn't generally allow smoking in his car, he didn't object as Sally shook out and lit a menthol cigarette. Sally didn't speak again and neither did Parks, even as he pulled into her driveway, got out of the car, and went around the outside to open her door. He walked into the house with her as though it were the most natural thing.

Later that night, Parks struggled to stay awake, because he had not been beside a woman for years, and despite the gritty sheets and the beery smell of her, lying with Sally felt heavenly. He'd made love with her, but she seemed to have drifted to sleep or at least lost interest after a while, so he'd given up trying to pleasure her. He wrapped his arms around her shoulders, and though she had at first seemed weightless, eventually his arm was being crushed and he had to pull it out from under her. While she snored quietly Parks got up from the bed to open the window and listen for night sounds. As a boy, as George's friend, he'd slept in this house plenty of times, back when Old Harold and Henrietta still lived in the big house on Queer Road. Parks looked in the direction of the barn and thought he could detect the glow of coals and even the smell of ancient wood burning.

As he stared across George's land, Parks thought he might possibly get used to Rachel. After all, if she hadn't killed her mother, then she and George were just another May-December marriage, like the salesman said. He didn't understand why George desired such a girl, but being in Sally's bed forced him to acknowledge the strangeness of desire. Next time Parks saw Rachel, he wouldn't give her time to turn away from him. He'd look into her face without flinching, and as plain as day he'd say, "Lose the gun, Rachel. It scares people." Then he'd move on to some other topic of conversation with George. Rachel was, of course, just a kid, and kids needed time to grow, space to think. And space she had!

David would come home in his own time. God knew, Parks himself had done stupid things as a boy, and even a good kid could screw up. A twelve-year-old would be okay on his own for a few hours, and maybe some regretful nighttime wandering would do him good. Parks liked the thought of his own daughter or son walking through fields and woods, wondering about life, getting away from TV and computers, away from homework and gymnastics practice. Parks thought maybe he would like to live in this house and pay George rent and take care of Sally, and in the middle of the night it didn't sound nearly as crazy an idea as it might have during the day. If Parks could keep his overtime hours down, he could become some kind of part-time partner to George. Maybe eventually Parks could build a new house of his own. Surely George would sell him a piece of land cheap. He'd need enough that if his son or daughter someday wanted to come back and build a house beside his, there'd be room. He needed enough land that if a woman fell in love with him and wanted a horse, Parks could fence a few acres. And being there with Sally made it no longer seem out of the question that a woman might someday want him. When he got ahead moneywise, he'd put up a pole barn or two, and he'd reserve space for a garden in case the woman who eventually fell in love with him was so inclined. Parks left the window cracked two inches and crawled back into the bed beside Sally. Despite his efforts to stay awake, he succumbed to sleep.

Woolly bears continued crawling across the fields separating Sally's and George's houses. As David had suspected, the woolly bears of Greenland numbered in the millions, and while everybody slept, the live caterpillars climbed over the bodies of the dead ones and continued on into the farmlands, yards, and wooded windbreaks between fields. Though the extinction of the passenger pigeon and the disappearance of the wolverine (also called the glutton) from Michigan showed that nature was vulnerable to humans, the woolly bears had proven themselves adaptable, and since few cars passed during the night, a good number of them made it across the road. Autumn woolly bears didn't ask for much, just a little protection from automobiles, tractors, stomping livestock, and spiked golf shoes, so they could survive long enough to freeze, thaw, and build a cocoon of silk and their own bristles, so they could make it to that most remarkable of days in late spring when they would awaken into wings and become invulnerable to the old dangers. Next spring, just like this spring and the one before, a good number of the caterpillars would wake up from under logs, spin cocoons, and emerge as small white moths to dance like pieces of ash above a fire, with only a short time in which to mate before dying.

Across the fields separating the houses, beneath a sky hungry for its new moon, Rachel shaped sausage patties and placed them in the largest cast-iron pan George had inherited from his grandparents. David hadn't been able to decide which he wanted, bacon or sausage, and Rachel couldn't decide either, so she took out a pound of each. When the sausage patties were cooked on one side, she flipped them over and moved them around to make room for the bacon.

David asked, "Do you really think George is coming down?"

"He sure as shit will. He'll smell bacon cooking even in his sleep." Rachel was wondering why he wasn't down already, but she didn't want David to know she was worried. She sat across from him and said, "You don't know how George lost his finger, do you?"

"He got it caught in the baler somehow," David said, scratching both armpits at once. "Baling twine cut it off. Twenty-some years ago, he told me."

"What the hell did they do with the finger?"

"I don't know."

"See, you don't know everything." Rachel went back to the stove. She was sure there was more to the story, and George would tell her if she asked, but the meat was getting cooked through without George coming down the stairs. She crowded the bacon on top of the sausage and cracked the first egg into the grease, then had to pick out pieces of shell. Where was George?

David said, "Why would you care about a dead piece of finger?" He folded his finger back and pressed it down on his thigh, pretending once again it was like George's.

"Why in the hell do you do that?" Rachel said, shaking her head.

David shrugged.

When George entered the kitchen barefoot in jeans and no shirt, Rachel was jolted awake. Her husband was alive and perfect, reborn. She wanted to walk over and press her face to his chest and let his arms fold around her. Instead she turned away and yelled into the frying pan, "David says he's sorry for burning down your fucking barn."

George took three plates out of the dish drainer and put them on the table. Rachel watched him and decided he didn't look anywhere near death. She had seen that gash like a letter L on his left biceps a thousand times and she'd often pressed her finger or her cheek against its ridges. Before today it had been enough to locate and memorize the landmark, but now she wanted to know how that scar and all the others had come to etch him. George got two sets of forks and knives out of the dish drainer, and a third from the drawer. He looked up at Rachel, surprised she was still watching him.

"I'm sorry," David said. "I'm more sorry than I know how to say. I'll make up for it even if it takes me twenty years."

"I'm going to miss that barn." George sat at the table. "That barn could hold twelve hundred bales."

Rachel lifted the bacon strips out and put them on a brown bag she'd flattened onto a Blue Willow plate. "Let's get some damn chickens," she said. "I'm tired of buying eggs."

"I'll feed them," David said. "If you get chickens, I'll feed them and collect the eggs and clean their coop and everything. And I'll feed all the other animals."

Rachel said, "David and I will figure out something for the cows."

"My great-great-grandfather built that barn in 1864," George said.

Rachel fought an urge to scream. Yes, his ancestors built the barn, and yes, his dead brother was buried there, but Johnny and his great-great-grandfather were dead, and just look at the miracle of David being alive. She tipped her head back to hold in what threatened to spill out of her.

George said, "Before the barn was there, it was a campsite for the Horseshoe Clan of Potawatomi Indians."

"Rachel's tribe," David said.

Rachel spooned grease over the eggs to cook their tops and did not turn or shout that her mother had shot Johnny without thinking, that nobody had meant to kill anybody, that her mother was not in her right mind, and that her mother had not always been so bad. Someday she would tell George how sorry her mother must have been.

George said, "There was a beautiful woman, a teacher, who lived in the house that used to be down there. When she left, a tornado destroyed the house."

"Why did she leave?" David asked.

"Barn swallows have nested in that barn for a hundred and thirty-five years," George said. "I don't know where they'll go next year."

Rachel put the rest of the meat on the plate with tongs and scooped up the eggs, and when she turned around, she saw David was crying and wheezing.

"It's time to shut the hell up and eat." Rachel banged the plate of meat and eggs on the table. "David, make toast."

David dragged himself up and put two pieces of bread in the toaster beside the dish drainer and wiped his eyes with his burred shirtsleeve. When George saw how he was limping, he looked to Rachel. She wanted to go stand behind George with his head against her belly and say that David should sleep in the other bedroom, but first she needed to know that George would forgive him. The three of them ate all the sausage, most of the bacon, nine eggs, and half a loaf of bread, plus a quart of homemade tomato juice. As they slowed down and stopped eating, Rachel realized that nobody had spoken at all and David didn't seem to be able to inhale a full breath anymore. His mouth looked swollen and he kept scratching his chest and armpits. What would normally have been tiny pink scratches on his wrists were bright gashes.

"Why are you scratching?" George asked. "Is that from the straw?"

Rachel said, "Did you get in poison ivy again? Let me see."

David displayed his forearms, then lifted his shirt to show his chest, red from scratching and a little swollen. Some loose hay and bits of straw fell to the slate floor around him. His arms dropped to his sides in exhaustion at the effort of lifting them. Rachel noticed his neck was also red.

"Shit! I forgot about your medicine!" Rachel said. She went out to the mudroom and retrieved the inhaler from her jacket pocket and slapped it down beside his plate. "You should be more goddamn careful."

David inhaled the medicine, but was unable to hold it in his lungs. On his next attempt he seemed unable even to breathe through the tube.

"He doesn't look so good," George said. "Maybe we should take him to the emergency room."

———

As Gray Cat slept beside the fire dreaming of summer-yellow birds, and as Parks lay beside Sally dreaming he would be loved, Sally dreamed of California (where she would go at the end of February, without her son) and David, Rachel, and George piled into the Ford truck and headed down Queer Road. David sat in the middle, and both Rachel and George rolled their windows down to let in as much air as possible on the way to the hospital, though George wasn't so sure the cold was good for the boy. As April May dreamed of traveling, as Milton dreamed of Jesus, and as Steve and Nicole began to smell golden butter cake from the oven, George turned onto M-96 and headed west toward Kalamazoo. Rachel let the wind blow on her at about eighty miles an hour, but still David's breathing was shallow. Rachel inhaled deeply and held the breath until David inhaled beside her, and she exhaled and waited for David to follow. Again they breathed together, in and out. And in and out. And again. When they pulled to a stop at a flashing red, Rachel noticed that George was breathing along with her, so she let George take over. She looked through her open window at a road-side rectangle of scrubby weeds beneath a streetlight. The yellow October grass made her think of an animal like a giant coyote that might suddenly roll over or stand and shake itself off. It made Rachel think of her old idea that the south and north sides of the river were animals whose backbones were the two banks of the river. Rachel reached for the familiar hickory stock of her rifle, before remembering she'd left it lying in the grass. The gun had killed Johnny and had nearly killed David twice—maybe she ought to bury it in one of her garden mounds. As Elaine dreamed of aliens transporting her to a spaceship for unspeakable study, as two neighborhood hooligans lay fondling themselves in tents on land they didn't know they loved, as bodies continued to decay in graves beneath the boys, Rachel decided that burying a perfectly good gun would be stupid and wasteful. Whenever they got home, she would clean and oil it.

As George accelerated back up to eighty, as the truck began to shimmy and rattle, Rachel imagined the big animal beneath them shifting and rolling its shoulders, loosening the asphalt, letting them drive over but shaking the broken road off behind their truck. Though she was nearly bursting to speak to George—about chickens and apple trees and bees for honey—Rachel remained silent for David's sake, resting her jaw, allowing her body to fill with *hell*s and *fuck*s and *goddamn*s that she'd expel for the doctors and nurses and all the other strangers they would encounter at Bronson Methodist Hospital. Rachel had the whole of the future to decide what to tell George and what to ask him, but on this night the three of them would need all of her determined cursing as they struggled, bringing David back from the dead, once and for all.

ACKNOWLEDGMENTS

Thank you Heidi Bell and Carla Vissers for your time, talent, and advice—you are the best pals a writer could have; and Jaimy Gordon, you are as generous as you are wise with words. Thank you Amanda Urban and Sarah McGrath for taking a chance on this book and seeing me through to the finish. My fellow writers Rachel Perry, Alicia Conroy, Melissa Fraterrigo, Jamie Blake, Lisa Lenzo, and Rebecca Barnes may notice their fingerprints and lipstick smears on this final version (Peter Brakeman, too, without the lipstick!). Back in the beginning, Kalamazoo Arts Council kindly awarded me a Gilmore Emerging Artist grant. Thanks to my dad, Rick, for the photos, Jim Campbell for his farm stories, Adam Burke for his librarianship, and Loring Janes for help with the rifle. The Kirklin farm in Comstock inspired parts of this story, as did many people and places in my hometown, though every person, place, and event depicted in *Q Road* is fictional. My darling Christopher, thank you for your patience during the writing and rewriting and further rewriting. And, of course, Susanna, having a mother like you makes it all possible.

ABOUT THE AUTHOR

Bonnie Jo Campbell grew up on a small Michigan farm where she learned to castrate pigs, milk cows, and make chocolate candy. When she left home for the University of Chicago, her mother rented out her room. After earning a master's degree in mathematics in 1992 she started writing fiction. Her collection *Women and Other Animals* details the lives of extraordinary females in rural and small-town Michigan. She received her M.F.A. in writing from Western Michigan University.

Q ROAD

DISCUSSION POINTS

1. Campbell begins and ends her book with depictions of woolly bears. What do these orange-and-black caterpillars symbolize? What other symbols or metaphors recur throughout *Q Road*?

2. In addition to the three central personalities (Rachel, George, and David), *Q Road* has quite a few supporting characters. How does the story benefit from Elaine Shore's alien fixation or Johnny Harland's swaggering confidence? What do you learn about Greenland Township through Mary O'Kearsy or Milton Taylor? Why do you suppose the author created such a sprawling cast?

3. In chapter 20, Elaine Shore's lawyer dubs her a "pioneer" for her attempts to bring "civilization" to Q Road. What compels people like Elaine and the Hoekstras to move to rural areas? How do you explain their reaction to the unexpected "disorder" of their rural neighborhood? Analyze the omniscient narrator's tone in chapter 20 and at other points in the novel that address the development of former farmland.

4. Rachel is an unconventional, abrasive young woman. Is it still possible to identify or sympathize with her? Why or why not? How and why has she come to love George Harland's land so much?

5. In chapter 3, Margo says to Rachel, "I thought I could raise a girl to be something on her own, but you act no better than a creature clawing its way up the riverbank to get caught in somebody's trap" (25). How does Margo contribute to what happens that night between Rachel and Johnny? Why does Margo shoot Johnny? What do you think happens to Margo after she kills him?

6. When Margo shoots Johnny in chapter 3, she also shoots a chicken, a detail the author highlights in a darkly comic way. Where else in *Q Road* does Campbell contrast tragedy and comedy? What purpose does such a literary device serve?

7. David feels closer to Rachel and George than he does to his parents. Trace the origin of his feelings. Discuss the ideas of parenthood and family as they are depicted in *Q Road*.

8. What clues in the first half of the novel alert you to the fact that

something disastrous is about to happen? Were you able to predict what the impending disaster would be?

9. Review pages 127 and 128, where David drops his cigarette in the barn, then finds it again. What were you thinking during this scene? At the end of chapter 17, did you think David was dead? What was your reaction when you found he had survived the fire? How do his several near-death experiences fit into the story?

10. Considering the couples in *Q Road*—Rachel and Johnny, Rachel and George, Nicole and Steve, Old Harold and Henrietta, April May and Larry—which seems healthiest? Compare Rachel's and George's reasons for marrying to the other couples' motivations. Are Rachel and George more or less opportunistic, more or less honest than the other characters?

11. Read the passage on page 123 beginning with the description of Sally's bedroom. How does the author's characterization of Sally reinforce and/or confound our cultural stereotypes of the poor? Compare Sally to other poor characters in the novel. How are the poor in *Q Road* similar to or different from the poor in other contemporary fiction? How would you characterize the omniscient narrator's attitude toward poverty?

12. The events of *Q Road* take place on October 9, 1999, but are interspersed with the history of the people who have lived in the vicinity for centuries. What impact does the historical material have on the present action of the novel? Explore the importance of history to selected characters. How do the ancestral stories told by characters such as Old Harold and Margo change as they are handed down to the next generation? Why does Rachel cling to her story of the Potawatomi Corn Girl?

13. Discuss the scene in chapter 36 in which Steve Hoekstra discovers Nicole stabbing a pumpkin on the deck of their prefabricated home. How might Steve and Nicole's life together be different from this point forward?

14. Birds of many species populate *Q Road*—chickens, crows, chickadees, and turkey vultures, to name a few. Compare Officer Parks's seagull observations on page 87 with April May's musings about English sparrows on page 100. How do these passages resonate with the themes of the novel? Why do you suppose Steve Hoekstra drives a Thunderbird? What purpose does chapter 14—the description of Gray Cat hunting—serve within the larger scheme of the novel?

15. On page 117, Old Harold tells George that Mary O'Kearsy "was as beautiful as the day is long." On page 232, Tom Parks uses the same expression to describe Margo Crane. Why do you suppose the author linked the two women (or these two men) in this manner?

16. Many of the characters in *Q Road* imagine that nature avenges human wrongdoing. What is the purpose of personifying nature in this way? Compare Harold's view of the 1934 tornado on pages 200–206 with Henrietta's perspective on pages 219–20. Explain how and why they see the same events so differently.

17. While *Q Road* is a novel about community, it is also about the difficulties of human connection. Consider the causes and effects of loneliness and isolation for Rachel, Margo, George, David, Nicole, and Officer Parks.

18. Read the passage on pages 31–32 that begins "When the cattle had busted down the fence a few days ago, George wasn't around" and ends "The bedsprings were an announcement to the world that farming was no longer a sensible way of making a living . . ." What motivates George and other farmers to continue to farm when they have to struggle so desperately to survive?

19. Why do you think the pain in April May's foot disappears after the barn burns down?

20. Henrietta Harland and Rachel Crane are both gifted gardeners, able to sense the coming of the first hard frost in time to protect their yield. Are Henrietta and Rachel alike in other ways? How are they different?

21. What do you think of Rachel's reaction to David when she finds him standing outside the house after the fire?

22. Tom Parks describes Sally as "an element of nature" on page 263. Does this comparison surprise you? What is fitting about it?

23. April May believes that Greenland farmers and the new residents in the prefab houses can get along "if only everyone would be sensible and tolerant" (174). She muses that a natural disaster like the tornado of 1934 might rally Greenland to a common cause "the way God used to" (175). Does the barn fire have this effect on the residents of *Q Road*? What would you say the future holds for *Q Road*?